Vampire in Charge

Book #10 of Family Blood Ties

Dale Mayer

Book in this series:

VAMPIRE IN CHARGE
Beverly Dale Mayer
Valley Publishing Ltd.

ISBN-13: 978-1-928122-74-6
Print Edition

About This Book

The Family Blood Ties continues to this 10th and final installment of this vampire versus vampire saga.

She thought she had it all solved.

Tessa's had a hell of a time tracking down the blood farm bosses. And it's not over yet. Just when she thinks she has it solved, it unravels all over again.

She should be taking the last of the enemy captive and tying up the final ends. Instead, it appears there's one more secret to uncover – and when she does, it's a doozy.

Cody is desperate to have this mess over with and have Tessa all to himself. But as the secrets start to unravel, the craziness gets worse.

Can they trust anyone? Or does everyone have something to hide?

Watch the stunning conclusion unfold as Tessa, Cody, and the whole gang finally get to the bottom of the blood farms.

Sign up to be notified of all Dale's releases here!
https://geni.us/DaleNews

COMPLIMENTARY DOWNLOAD

DOWNLOAD a **_complimentary_** copy of TUESDAY'S CHILD? Just tell me where to send it!

http://dalemayer.com/starterlibrarytc/

PROLOGUE

***This is the last chapter from Vampire in Control.
Chapter One carries on from here.***

TESSA STRUGGLED TO stay in control. Anger like a wall of red washed through her, taking everything she had to fight Deanna back down. Tessa knew this wasn't a fight she could lose, otherwise, Deanna could take over at any time.

She had to win. But so far, Deanna's fierce anger was taking over Tessa's much softer one. It was incorporating itself into her own anger, building herself up to be stronger and more powerful. Tessa wanted to win. Knew she had to win. But there was an air of desperation about it. Almost a panic. The memories of the last mess were sitting in her peripheral vision, threatening her with the reminder that she failed last time.

That she had been a fool, and Deanna had taken her over by being what Deanna always had been – older, stronger, and so much more devious. Tessa tried to build up the anger to match Deanna, but she didn't have a lifetime of hurts and enemies to draw from. Her short-lived years were merely a blink to Deanna's centuries, who had anger plenty for both of them.

Give me your anger. I'll take it and make it mine, Deanna whispered. *Think of how easily I ruined your life. Think of what I'll do with Cody when I'm you and he's mine. He'll be my lover. Not yours. You'll be stuck inside for the ages while he becomes my man. His young, firm body mine to do with as I please. Feel the anger at my words. Give it to me.*

Tessa wanted to laugh and cry at the same time. There was much terror and fear mixed with the anger. And her words, well, they'd ignited a maelstrom. *Cody is not and never will be yours.*

Her own rage built at the thought of this old crone taking what was Tessa's. Not just her body and her life, but her love. Cody wouldn't be able to free himself. He'd already fought to return to save her. He'd come back to protect Tessa, but there was no way he could fight Deanna.

Then the tiny whisper came, *but he could.*

Hortran?

Yes. You can't let her destroy you.

You helped her to do this. How is it you aren't okay with her actions at this time? Tessa snapped. *You are just as responsible for what she's doing now as she is.*

Yes, but not for the reason you think.

You love her.

Of course. She's my sister. But I'm not blind to her. I helped her because she's right — you are the One. But you've had no training and as Deanna's past has come back to taunt her, you need help. Everything we do in our life has a cause and effect, and right now she's still trying to walk away from her actions. Like she always has.

Tessa's mind was split in different directions. One part on Hortran's words, another desperate to match Deanna's rage that she might win against her, and yet another part aware of the vamp watching the two of them in fascination. He held no weapons, as if content to see who'd win then take out the victor.

You can't match her anger. Her rage. She's done much wrong in her life. She cared not for the repercussions and did as she wanted. But your present has collided with her past, and there won't be a good end to this. She's never faced this — him. She never confronted him. He wanted revenge and had information on her that could destroy her and her husband. He had power over her. Thus, she feared him. Hated him and wanted only to see him die so that he couldn't hurt her anymore. But for all her actions, she is still a mother and knew she'd been in the wrong first. All those memories became a twisted compilation of fear, anger, and guilt.

Tessa was so confused. She got the relationship was complicated. She understood that Deanna had tried to kill her own son, but it had been eons ago. *Hortran, what difference does it make now? She's dead. Her husband is dead. She was trying to extract revenge for his death, but he's dead too. Everyone who mattered to her is dead.*

But her husband was set up to die by another. And that other is the one ultimately responsible.

Who?

Her son…

Tessa's gaze went to Victor, who was still standing at the window. But Hortran was still speaking, his voice low, fading.

…and by Victor's command…her own grandson. And he still lives…still hurts.

Grandson? Oh no. Who is her grandson?

A man raised on poison to hate her and who spent his lifetime creating something that would keep the line pure. To see her die as they all lived — bigger, better, stronger…and not deformed and disfigured like his father.

Shit.

She closed her eyes, caught in a bubble of frozen time, so much going on around her. So much caught up in this moment. Deanna's grandson was the one who'd created the blood farms. He was the one in the background. That shadowy figure that they hadn't been able to identify and had often questioned if he even existed. They'd caught and killed many of his minions…and never him.

He's there. He exists. You know him.

Deanna screamed in the background. *You should have killed him when you had the chance. And you had the chance. Now we'll take out my son first — I was going to let him live — my penance for my wrongs and his penance to live so broken an existence — then we'll go after his son.*

No, Tessa said, struggling for calm. For sanity. For control. *I will make the decision of who I kill — not you.*

And Deanna screamed. It was a rip of rage like Tessa had never heard before.

But it was so like Deanna that Tessa knew it wasn't her own anger. In fact, hers had faded to the background like it always did. She wasn't a hard, cold, angry person. She loved animals and flowers and saved dogs from bad drugs and military men from vampire poison.

Exactly, Hortran said. *You must save yourself.*

How, she said, her mind already looking at her actions, Deanna's actions, and seeing that harsh divide. *She's not me.*

And you are not her.

You are…

She finished the sentence for him. *I am Tessa. And I must be true.*

Together, their voices blended into one as they said at the same time…*to me.*

Exactly. She felt Hortran's smile rather than saw it. *Wor-*

ry not about Deanna when her anger blows out as she'll have nothing left – her life force has been used up in the conflagration. She'll sink back in here with me and spend the rest of her life realizing the life choices she made and how she could have chosen to be more like…you.

And his voice faded away.

Cody whispered, *I just heard all that.*

You're different now, too. She smiled. *Because you spoke with Hortran, he can now speak to you.*

And did he help? Do you know what to do?

I do. She smiled and tilted her head back. *I have to be me. While I'm doing that, I need you to keep this guy away from me.*

I can do that, but what do you mean about being you? he asked cautiously.

I'm a healer, not a hater. And that means I have to heal myself, and therefore Deanna. I can't win this battle with anger. Or fear. I can only win it with…love. As I have always done to help those in need. Being me means operating from goodness. Not darkness. Deanna crossed over a long time ago. Whether she wanted to return or not, I think once that choice is made…it's almost impossible to return.

In the background, Deanna raged. Now all Tessa needed to do was to show her the love inside her pain. Somehow.

Cody. I love you. I just wanted to say that. And she closed her eyes and said, *Let this war rage. I will win. But it might take a little bit.*

And she dove into the red wall of rage.

WAIT, CODY CRIED. But it was too late. She was gone.

He didn't understand what he was seeing, but it's as if

there was a red haze in his mind.

There had to be something he could do to help her besides protect her from this bastard. He studied Victor, seeing the pain in his features, the shiver to his frame against the window as he leaned back and watched Tessa. There was also a deep satisfaction permeating his features.

"How is it you want this young girl to suffer for your hurts?" Cody asked him bitterly. "Tessa did nothing to you."

"And I've done nothing to her...yet."

Cody studied the older man, realizing he was already dying. His disability was taking its toll on his body that didn't heal well. He had not long to live. And like his mother, he wanted to see justice done before he was gone. "You're quite a pair," Cody growled. "A chip off the old block."

Victor glared at him. "I am nothing like my mother. She's a cold, heartless bitch."

"And you think you're so much better?" Cody snorted with disgust. "I think not. You helped your son create this monstrosity of a blood farm, hurting thousands of humans, and for what?"

"A better life. A simpler life. An old-fashioned life. One of clean lines, with no more of this mixed breeding. Enough abominations. We are a pure race. We should be living to our noble standards."

"And yet your mother was an ancient. One of the strongest and purest of lines." Maybe mental instability was part of the disability because none of this made any sense.

"And she bred with another ancient, her uncle. And I was the result. They bred like animals when they wanted and where they wanted. Did you ever think about the ancients of old – how few of them there actually were? How did they procreate? Inbreeding causes birth defects like the one I suffer from. Nan, the woman who raised me, had the same fate as I. But someone helped her, so she in turn helped me."

"And yet you procreated." Cody didn't get that. If he was so against random genetic breeding, why would he risk perpetrating the same genetic faults he carried?

"Only after much testing. My DNA was only compatible with one female out of hundreds we tested. And I managed to produce a small, healthy and whole offspring with her." The older vamp shuffled forward. "The child was perfect. He was what I should have been."

"And the mother?"

The vamp waved his hand. "She is dead. When I realized she couldn't breed a second child, then it was important she not be allowed to breed again. Her genetics couldn't go to another line." He shrugged. "So of course I killed her."

Cody swallowed. Victor had killed the mother of his child because she couldn't provide him with more children. Yet he didn't see the similarity to his own mother? And they thought humans were a terrible species. He wondered if vamps should be allowed to live at all. Look at this animal and what he'd created.

"And your son. Has he founded a dynasty for you?"

The old vamp grinned. "He has indeed."

Only there was something off in his voice. As if Cody wouldn't like what he meant. But as he went to ask him, he realized the air had thickened, like tiny sparks flying with every breath.

Beast whined deep in the back of his throat.

Tessa and Deanna. The air swirled around Cody, tension filled him so tight he felt he would snap if he moved even the slightest bit.

Fascinated and horrified, he watched, catching tiny glimpses of life on the other planes. Planes he'd touched and felt himself. There were bits and pieces, but the explosions were small and red, like micro-fireworks going off. As if Deanna was losing control and in her frustration, blasting at the only person she could reach – Tessa.

And yet, he could sense Tessa in there this time. Strong. Stalwart. Calmly standing on the side of right.

Where she always stood.

That was one of the many things he admired about her. She knew the difference between right and wrong. She knew her own morality and ethics and held herself accountable. She wasn't crying, hiding, or cheating. She knew what she had to do and she was doing it.

Her way.

He smiled.

"You can't help her," Victor cried. "They are both going to die today. I didn't plan it. But that's going to be the outcome."

"No," Cody smiled at him. "You don't understand Tessa. She is so much more than Deanna."

"No," the vamp cried, hobbling closer. "She can't win. It's not possible. She can't be allowed to live on in Tessa."

Cody stepped in front of him. He'd been through this once with Bart, and he wasn't going to let that happen again.

No one was going to hurt Tessa.

"When Tessa defeats Deanna, your mother will be relegated to the archives where she belongs. Along with your uncle."

The crippled vamp shuddered to a halt. "Uncle? I have an uncle?" He bent over as if from a blow. "Not possible."

"Well, you do, but he's a Ghost. Well, he *was* a Ghost,"

Cody amended. "Tessa carries him as well. She's trying to keep them as part of a living, historical archive."

"Hortran? The Ghost?" Victor asked in a daze. "He's my uncle?"

Cody could sympathize. It was a lot to understand all at once.

"I thought Hortran was her lover," Victor whispered.

"No," Cody snapped. At least, he hoped not because that was just plain wrong. "He was her brother."

"Then I carry his DNA as well." the old vamp brightened. "We thought the Ghosts were gone, and yet here I was carrying that genetic marker all this time."

"You might be, but maybe not," Cody knew nothing about DNA and genetic markers. "And besides, so what if you do?"

"Then we can reproduce it in the lab," he cried. "Don't you see? I thought he was her lover, and I was angry at her because I could have been whole and have that genetic marker as well if she'd chosen a better father for her child." He waved his arm, adding, "Instead, this entire time I had it already."

"*Maybe* you have it," Cody snapped. "And maybe not."

But Victor beamed with the possibility. "Maybe not, but there were markers in my DNA that I didn't know, didn't understand. And now I do. I have to go to the blood farm. I have to start the testing. We have been after the Ghost DNA since the beginning," he cried, taking a step toward Cody. Beast howled. Victor paused.

Suddenly the air, as if the calm after a storm, cleared.

Tessa spoke up – a smiling, wholesome-looking Tessa. Although weak and tired, she looked…normal. "And what good would that do you," she asked Victor in a low voice.

"We can create the perfect race." Victor laughed. "All births will be controlled. There will be no more abominations like myself." His eyes turned black. "No more like you…" and he ran toward her in as fast a gait as his crippled leg would allow him.

Beast sent out a chilling warning again.

Cody stepped in front of Tessa. "You will not hurt her."

"She can't be allowed to live," he whispered. "Surely you see that. She's not perfect."

"You're wrong," Cody snapped. "She is perfect."

Victor shook his head. "Then you are damaged, too." He glared down at Beast beside Tessa. "And that thing is an abomination."

Beast, his hackles rising as if he understood, growled.

Behind him, Cody turned to see Tessa staring at Victor with distaste. "You will not touch my pet," she snapped. "Or else…"

"Tessa? Are you…okay?"

She released a heavy sigh and straightened, letting her shoulders slump as if released from tension inside. "I'm fine. Deanna burned through her anger faster than I thought. The more love I poured over her, the more pissed off she became. She lost control quickly – now she's only bits and pieces of what she used to be. Like her brother." She smiled at the crippled vamp. "In fact, I'm more than fine. And now I can see everything."

Waving an arm at Victor, she said, "Don't worry about Hortran. You don't carry his genetics. The Ghost DNA is lost to you."

"No, that can't be."

"It is," she said. "Ghosts were trained. Not born. You don't have what it takes."

Victor, anger flashing on his face, rushed across the short distance between them, but Tessa, in a move reminiscent of Hortran, waved her hand, bringing him to his knees. Beast lunged forward.

Eye level to the dog, Victor glared at the animal. "He needs killing."

"Tessa?" Cody wasn't sure what he was to do with this. "Does Beast get him?"

"No," Victor cried, pulling out a UV light weapon from his pocket. "Do you really think I'd be here without protection of my own?" Holding it up for them to see, he turned it on.

Only it wouldn't turn on.

Tessa laughed. "Did you really think I'd let you have a working model of one of those? I saw the battery on it a few minutes ago."

She turned to Beast and said, "Are you sure you want him?" She shook her head. "He's going to make you really sick. But not just yet."

Beast, as if understanding, growled in eagerness.

She grinned at him, then turned to Cody and added, "I know how now."

"How what?" he asked, struggling to keep up with the switches in the conversation. "What do you know how to do?"

Tessa gave Victor a fat smile. "You know, don't you?"

Still on his knees, his legs too weak to help him get back up, he shook his head. "No, you can't hurt him."

"Hurt who?"

"My son. You can't hurt him," the cripple cried.

"This son of yours is the one running everything," Tessa said. "And I will have to kill him. He's someone we all know.

Someone on the Council. Someone who helped us – is even now helping us to 'win' this war. All the while he's laughing inside."

Victor pulled out a different weapon, this one tipped in silver.

Beast lunged at the crippled vamp.

"No!" Victor, using the large silver knife, stabbed himself in the throat and blew to ash in front of them.

Cody stared. "Damn it. We needed information from him."

Beast whined and lay down beside the ash.

"No, we didn't." Tessa pulled out another granola bar and offered it to Beast with a big grin.

"But we don't even know who the son is," Cody cried. "We can't kill him if we don't know."

"Except for one thing," Tessa said, with a bright happy smile of the Tessa he'd fallen in love with, making his own heart smile. More than just smile…his heart recognized the color, the tone, the feel of her energy. It was his Tessa. He could recognize her for who she really was now.

Thank heavens.

She linked her arm with him, reaching up as if to kiss him. She whispered, "I do know who he is. And now…I know how to win this war."

And sealed her promise with a kiss.

Chapter 1

T ESSA LED THE way back downstairs, her footsteps as quiet as she could make them. Beast raced in front and Cody followed behind them. They needed to find the rest of the group and figure out what had happened. Then they could put plans in motion.

"When were you going to tell me?" Cody asked from behind her, his tone lighthearted but also peeved.

She laughed. "I still don't have any proof," she said. "But I *think* I have this figured out."

"Who is behind this?" Cody asked. "And is he – are they – here at the Hall?"

"I'm scared to say anything in case I'm wrong," Tessa said in low tones. "I don't want to influence you one way or have you treat the others any different. It would put you in grave danger." She corrected herself, "At least until I know for sure. We need to get all of these assholes, not just the top man."

"And I don't want to walk into a fight with one of them and let him walk away because I didn't know who he was," Cody said in a hard tone. "There's got to be a middle ground here, Tessa. Don't treat me like the others."

She spun and looked up at him at shock. "Never."

Still, Cody had a point. Yet she was hesitant to tell him. And why was that? She trusted him. She knew him better than she knew herself. So why did she not want to tell him who she thought was behind this?

Because it didn't make any sense, and she was afraid he wouldn't believe her.

At the bottom of the stairs Beast came to a stop, his hackles up, a snarl rising deep from inside his chest, Tessa flattened against the wall. Cody grabbed her hand and held a finger to his lips as he slipped past her to stand beside Beast. He peered around the corner until he could see into the big open hall.

Is there anything there? she murmured into his mind.

I don't know. Maybe this guy you won't tell me about, he countered in irritation, shooting her a sideways look.

What if I tell you and then you focus on him while someone else is the real killer and attacks you from behind?

And what if this asshole attacks me in the front and I consider him a friend and am unprepared?

She understood he was pissed at her, but she had to weigh the facts. *Okay,* she said, *but you need to keep in mind I could be very wrong.*

As if you have been yet, he scoffed, twisting to look behind at her. He reached out and snagged her, tugging her up to his chest. She went to hug him when his gaze widened and he stepped back hurriedly. "Sir?"

Tessa spun to stare at Councilman Adamson glaring at the two of them in irritation.

"We've been looking for you," he snapped. "It's bad enough we have attacks going on in all corners of the city, but you two are enjoying time alone with…" He motioned at Beast. "That thing."

"This is Beast," Tessa said defensively, hating the guilty look on Cody's face and even her own retreat from his arms.

This blood farm crap had to stop so she and Cody could have a decent start to the relationship. Once this was over…"Whatever it is," Adamson said in distaste. "Now let's get you back to where the Council is meeting. We need to regroup and start fresh."

He stalked off, irritation stiffening his spine. Tessa fell into line behind him and she motioned at Cody with a finger to her lips, but Councilman Adamson spun and saw her. "Enough games," he barked. "We have enough problems to deal with."

She nodded an apology and fell slightly back, keeping Beast with her and out of Adamson's sight.

It was too important to make sure they caught everybody involved this time. They needed to know who ran all the foreign dignitary groups as well. The blood farm mess had spread so far now. That's why she needed to know who the spider was at the center of the web and all that he might have spawned. They'd removed the aging leader, but what about his son? She needed proof of his identity.

Before he went underground for centuries and everyone would forget until he rose up again with a whole new infrastructure in place and massive blood farms running again.

CODY STAYED WITH the small group. It was hard to trust anyone anymore. Still, he was no fool. There were only so many people left on the Council. Almost all of them men. He pondered that slowly as they walked behind Adamson.

Why were there not as many women as there were men on the Council? Even Gloria had not been on the Council, and she had been Adamson's right-hand woman. More like an associate. Was that going to be an issue? He knew eight Councilmen that had survived, including his father, Tessa's mother and father, as well as Councilman Adamson and Sian. Then there were Jameson, Baker, and Roberts. The latter were recovering from drugs they'd been injected with.

Had anyone else survived?

Deanna was now gone, so her place was up for grabs. Although she hadn't attended in many decades, her place was always there for her. It wasn't easy to join the Council. The people that were there were very long-lived and lasted hundreds of years. Only those that had attained a certain level of maturity could be appointed, and even then it was based on experience and skills and power. Vampires were always about power.

Tessa slipped her hand into his. He grasped it firmly, so happy to have her at his side even after all of this. It never would have occurred to him that he could meet someone so powerful and yet so full of heart as Tessa was.

Would she gain a place on the Council? She was beyond young. Most of the Council members wouldn't even see her as being an adult, yet she carried both Deanna and Hortran. Did that make a difference? And was it appropriate? Not likely.

"Where is everyone meeting?" Cody asked. "There's been so much destruction already, it's hard to imagine there is a safe place left anymore."

"There are offices in the lower levels that few know about," Adamson said. "We're going to those sets of rooms."

"Is my father okay?" Tessa asked. "I haven't heard an update in a long time."

Cody heard the worry underlying her words. He hoped they all survived this mess, but the odds of that happening had been against them from the beginning. He could only hope they could maintain at the same level they'd been operating at so far. And still stay safe. Tessa deserved to have her family.

He only had his father left, and he would do anything he could to keep Goran alive.

He also knew that Goran would do anything to keep him alive.

Tessa felt the same way about her family.

They'd been incredibly lucky so far.

Ahead of them, Adamson led the way to the double stairwell at the back of the building. He pushed open the doors and jumped lightly to the next landing and then to the next, reminding Cody that not only was Adamson a flyer, but that he was also very skilled in many other ways. Adamson himself could be at the head of this mess. Although he doubted it. He'd barely survived the attack by his longtime partner, Gloria. In fact, she'd tried to kill him twice.

"We're going to the third floor," Adamson said. "They are waiting for us."

Cody studied the area as they walked along the empty hallway. Very little of the destruction above had filtered down to this area. Tessa still hung onto his hand, tension vibrating through her.

He'd always been aware of her, but now there was a heightened sense as he could feel energy split off from her system as she pondered and puzzled over this turn of events. He didn't understand what worried her but trusted that she knew more than he did when it came to sensing energy. *Trap?* he asked quietly.

She shook her head. In an equally soft voice, she answered. *No, I don't think so.*

Councilman Adamson opened the door and disappeared from sight, then he popped his head back out, looked at them, and said, "Hurry up."

They picked up their pace and raced after him, Beast loping at their side. As they went to go in the door, Tessa froze and backed up. Cody, already halfway inside the doorway, immediately threw himself backward so he wasn't trapped in the room. They stood in the hallway as he watched and waited for her to decide what was wrong.

Tessa looked at him and then shrugged. "I can't tell what's wrong," she said. "It feels…off."

"Are you coming?" Adamson called from inside the darker room, his voice impatient. Cody listened hard, but he couldn't hear any deception in his tone. So far Adamson had been a straight shooter. Really hoping he wasn't about to make a major mistake, Cody walked inside.

The door closed behind him, leaving Tessa still on the other side.

"Wait," he cried. "Tessa is still out there."

"And that's where she's going to stay for the moment."

RHIA HAD NEVER been this tired in her life. Sweat dripped off her back. And rage like she'd never felt before poured through her body. She'd fired up her vampire genes – who knew that was even a thing to do – and still she was wearing down. These bastards just never quit.

Seth was unconscious on the floor beside her, Wendy and Jared huddled over him, both still suffering the after-shocks of what they'd been through. Ian was at her side, doing his darnedest to give as good as he was getting.

And failing.

This shouldn't be possible. But even if they could get past this seemingly endless wall of enhanced vampires, she had the four blood farm staff still to get through. Assholes.

All of them.

And suddenly, the wall of vampires crumpled as she sliced and diced her way through the last ones. She crashed to her knees, gasping for breath.

"Ian, you okay?" she asked when she could, her gaze locked on the four medical staff in front of her now. She couldn't trust them. But if they were going to attack, it would be now when she was at her weakest.

Only they were staring at her like she'd grown three heads.

Or maybe like she'd shown them what she was made of.

"He's not going to be happy when he wakes up," the closest one to her said. "Seth wanted this."

She shook her head. "He doesn't know what he wants. You've created a monster who thinks he's willingly walking in the direction you're pointing him in. But he's not."

"And if he is, what are you going to do then?" the doctor who'd been prepped to do the surgery asked. His gown was bloodstained, likely from his previous patient. "He's going to hate you."

"And likely destroy you," one of the others said. "Are you ready for that?"

Rhia staggered to her feet. "If that's the case," she said. "I'll kill him myself."

She walked over to where Seth lay on the ground, unconscious. "What else did you do to him?"

"Nothing." The doctor stared at her. "He was one of the best specimens we've had who was untouched in here."

Rhia jerked in shock at the doctor's reference to her son as a specimen. It was all she could do to stay quiet, and she needed to preserve her energy at this point. Not rail at him over an insult.

"Drugs?" Ian said. "We know he was given some of those."

"A few." The doctor nodded. "Only because he hated to see his friends receive the enhancements that he wanted. But we kept it to a minimum, and nothing experimental or dangerous. He was one of the chosen."

"Chosen?" Rhia asked. "Chosen for what?"

"He was in line to be part of the boss's inner circle." The doctor shrugged. "At this point in time, there are not many of the chosen left."

One of the other members of the team snapped, "There are not many of any of us left."

At her words, the others nodded. "We've taken a huge hit on our numbers."

"We cannot survive this," the one woman added. "The blood farm will shut down now. You've destroyed everything."

Ian laughed. "It's already shut down," he said. "In case you hadn't noticed."

"We thought we could get the old blood farms up and working in time to keep the supply line running, but there was too much damage everywhere. Blood is spoiling in the canisters. We have no new donors. So many of our old donors have died." She glared at Ian and Rhia. "Who do you think you are to destroy us and all we have worked for like this?"

Rhia, feeling the power surging through her body once again, stood tall and stared at them. "We are vampires who believe in the sanctity of human and vampire life."

The doctor stared at her in disgust. "No wonder your son wanted to join us. You are one of those that prefers the lives of animals over the lives of your people."

Rhia shook her head. "No," she said. "But neither do I believe in keeping people as livestock, sucking their blood while they have no choice but to hang on until the last drop drips from their veins." Her gaze narrowed. "There are so many other options for us."

The doctor drew a spike from his pocket. It was short, only inches beyond his fingertips, and he said, "No, your options just ran out."

And he attacked.

JARED WAS DAMN near helpless against these people. With glazed eyes, his body wracked with shivers, he watched Rhia fight like a crazed Amazon woman. Was her son worth this?

They were likely all going to die because of him.

He studied the unconscious man on the floor. Was he good or bad? Willing or unwilling? How did one tell? He hadn't seen anything that redeemed him, but who knew. Maybe he was an innocent victim in all of this. But he found it hard to believe. If nothing else, he was guilty of the same idealism that hung Jared in the blood farm.

Seth had seemed like a nice guy when Jared had met him. He'd delivered Jared to the blood farm and hadn't hung him up. Nor had he attacked Taz, who'd been there working. Then again, that was getting his hands dirty type of work, and he didn't see Seth or his arrogant friends doing that.

The doctor sprang past him, his arm out, ready to attack

Rhia. Jared stuck out his foot, sending the man tripping to the floor. Rhia was on him in seconds.

There was an ugly cloud of nasty-smelling ash. Jared coughed and coughed as his lungs filled, crouching on his heels as he tried to clear his lungs of that nasty shit. "Oh, he smelled bad," he managed when he could.

"Worse than bad," Ian muttered, his arm over his mouth and nose, glaring at the three remaining vamps.

Jared struggled back to his feet and studied the three vamps in front of him. "Don't kill them just yet," he said, watching as the three cowered back. "They know where Clarissa is."

Wendy, her voice weak and wavering, spoke up. "Do you? Do you know where the latest humans have been taken to?"

The older male sneered. "So what if we do? We need people to start a fresh blood farm."

"You won't be starting fresh with her," Jared snarled, finding some strength from somewhere. "She didn't do anything to you."

"Why do you think that matters?" the vamp laughed. "We've been picking up lost sheep humans for centuries, but we actively hunt out the meddling ones. Like you. Jared." He snorted. "We've always had a hook with your name on it."

"Really? Don't mind if I refuse your offer," Jared growled. "Besides, you never did explain my mixed blood to me."

"What's to explain? I don't know your history myself, but it's no surprise if you did have it. One of our ancestors likely raped one of yours. There have been other abominations in the past. It's one of the reasons we like to hunt those like you down. We test to see if your blood is acceptable and if it is, great. If not, then you either go into an experimental group or we kill you. But either way, you aren't free to reproduce and further bastardize our bloodline."

"I was supposed to go into an experimental group," Jared snapped. "But escaped first."

"And was caught again…and again…" smirked the other man. "That's okay. Like I said, we do like your blood. It's a great way to test these new drugs. It gives us early results. With you, we can watch how the drugs affect your vampire heritage." He shrugged. "And if we're not doing experiments with vampire blood, we can use your human side to test new drugs for humans."

Jared felt sick to his soul. "Is that what you're doing with Clarissa right now?"

"The new batch hasn't been fully processed yet," he said comfortably. "But she'll be hanging soon with all the other kids we have now. We have quite a few of them after emptying out the high school. Their blood is so much sweeter."

And he smiled. He pulled out another spike and waved it at them.

"I wouldn't do that if I were you," Ian snarled. "That hasn't worked out so well for your friends."

The man launched himself at Ian. Ian laughed and took him out with one clean stroke of silver. He went down in a puff of smoke.

This time Jared managed to stay on his feet. He stared at the pile of ash billowing to the floor. "He did that on purpose, didn't he?"

"Yes," Rhia said. "He's got no future and if he was taking drugs, they aren't going to be available any longer to him so he was dying anyways."

Jared turned ever so slightly so he could see the last two of the medical staff. Enough of this garbage. He had to find Clarissa and the others and fast. "So what's it going to be? Take yourselves out, or shall we do it for you? Tell us where the humans are being kept."

HOLDING DOWN THE Hall had seemed like a reasonable job. But that was easy before the blasts rocked out one corner of the hallway. Sian had the bulk of the building secured and even though they knew there would be another wave of assholes coming, she was trying to assess the damage and see any weaknesses the enemy had opened up. The Council was in an emergency meeting down below. Most of the men wanted to focus on defensive measures, but that chafed at her. She wanted to go on the offensive and take these assholes out. Their numbers were declining, but so were hers. She'd sent out a call for help to other clans but was getting the same answer back – they were all facing the same takeover bids that her people were.

She'd heard from Serus that he was alive and well and that the team he'd led had taken out the enemy on two sides of the building. Now with everyone having gone to ground, this was a respite she desperately needed. She wasn't just fighting for herself, she was fighting for her daughter's future. Not just her daughter's...at this point, it was everyone's future.

Now if only they could find the head of this blood farm and take him out fast.

GORAN SLIPPED TO the back of the wall as the last of the

men ran past.

The double doors slammed shut.

His heart pounded as he realized the enormity of the trap laid in front of them. He hadn't glimpsed many men on the catwalk around the top of the room, but they'd still managed to get the humans inside the pen easily without using much muscle.

They were working smarter.

And he was stuck working with humans – and they were getting dumber. Damn it.

His mind cast back over what he'd seen, looking for options. The doors were locked, but he'd get through if he tried hard enough. Speed was the biggest issue.

But he was alone, and that was another issue, though not one he was willing to admit to Serus.

Neither was he willing to go down in history as the man that led the soldiers into a trap. Like hell that was going to be his legacy. He spun back to face the double doors. He had one shot.

He had to make it good. *Serus old buddy. This could be it. I sure as hell hope not but just in case…see ya.*

Just as he sprang head down, shoulders in towards the door, the damn things opened just before he hit them.

He tripped and almost fell but managed to open his wings, pull hard, and soar high above the men.

And that's when he saw the vamps with gas masks on.

Oh shit.

SERUS RACED TO the mountain that started it all. The same entrance he'd used at Moltere's original homestead was in bad shape, with the bulk of the mountain having collapsed.

He had to get in another way. He needed to reach Goran. His heart still pounded in panic at Goran's last words. Always in the past, his friend had gone down joking.

This time, he sounded…different.

That difference had lit a fire on his feet and air to his glides. Thank God it was a dark night. He'd been moving steadily, but he was still twenty minutes away. And that was too damn long. He wove through the trees, silent as the other predators of the night.

He was the more dangerous one.

The birds watched him with unblinking yellow eyes glowing in the dark as he raced from tree to tree and then down to the ground. He didn't dare start back where Goran had started. That would take too long. Tessa had told him about the empty village she'd seen on the other side of the mountain and the several mine entrances there. He figured if he could come in from a different angle, then he'd be able to take these assholes by surprise.

Goran, hang on old buddy. I'm on the way.

No answer.

There were a lot of reasons for that – he wasn't going to panic yet. As long as he could feel Goran, then he was alive. Besides, he'd be at the mine entrance in minutes.

Less if he could make it faster.

Closing his eyes and feeling stupid but willing to try anything, he called on his vampire genes and ordered them to full power.

Holy crap. He almost cried out as his glides powered up and he doubled the distance covered.

With a feral grin, he leaned into the next glide and moved even further. Wait until he raced Goran next time. Serus would leave him in the dust.

"JEWEL, HAVE YOU heard from anyone?" David asked, worried about his family. This was crunch time. There was only so much anyone could do right now, and the waiting was killing them. The group that had gone out looking for the cause behind the blast that had rocked the south wall of the Hall had yet to return. They'd checked in, so that wasn't the worry. But what was taking them so long?

David knew Jewel was sick of this. She wanted it all to go away. Hell, so did he.

"No," she said, turning to look at Sian buried in data on the computer. From where she stood, she could see scrolling code interspersed with the odd text. "Not since Sian heard from Cody. Although they should be coming up soon."

"Good.' David studied the fields and grounds outside the Hall on a map. Knowing an attack was imminent and hearing the blast outside, but not being able to see what was going on – yeah, that was going to drive him nuts.

He wanted to speak with Cody himself, as he'd just checked in with Sian that he was okay. However, he was at the Council chambers and wouldn't be able to check back in again anytime soon. Ah well.

As long as they were alive, he was good.

In Cody's case, he wasn't as worried. Tessa seemed to be able to move mountains to keep Cody alive. He wondered if he'd ever get the full story of what happened with those two.

The door opened suddenly and Motre walked in.

They jumped on him in joy.

He laughed and said, "Look at you guys. Sitting here and having a party. And didn't even know that bastard who lived on the top floor was behind so much of this mess."

"What?" Sian cried. "Are you serious?

David listened in shock as Motre brought them up to date.

"Monster vampire cats?" he asked cautiously. "Beast is an enhanced vampire…what?"

Jewel wrapped her arms around her chest and made an odd sound. He tugged her close and wrapped his arms around her. "It's going to be okay."

She leaned back to shoot him a look. "I know we were warned about them earlier, but good Lord, I don't want to see them myself."

"Or fight them," Motre said. "Now I have to tell you about that damn blast."

It took time and with lots of cries of shock from the women, Motre managed to get the story out. David stayed silent until Motre was done. Even then, David didn't have a clue what to say. To think that Tessa had brought Cody back…

Holy shit.

And that they were linked deeper than ever…who knew such a thing was possible?

"He really died?" David asked, his gaze hard and intent on Motre's face.

Motre nodded. "He did. I've never seen anything like it." He hesitated then added unwillingly, "As I understand, Hortran managed to speak to both of them at the same time. More pathways, or maybe doors is a better word, were forged, allowing Cody to make a decision as to whether he wanted to return or not."

"It was a choice," Sian asked in shock. "How is that possible?"

Motre nodded. "Because of Tessa – it was a choice." He shrugged. "She's done some pretty wild shit, but I'd never seen anything like that. But she was bawling and knew she couldn't do more for him then somehow…" He opened his arms. "She did more."

Sian sat down heavily. "She's become so much, learned so much, more than any of us thought possible."

"She's kept us alive so we can win this war," David snapped. "But this has to end. At one point, she's going to fail. I can't imagine how that's going to affect her then."

"We have to make sure that doesn't happen," Sian said. "Failure is not an option." She stroked her belly and added in a hard voice, "For any of us."

CHAPTER 2

TESSA GLARED AT the closed door. If it didn't open soon, she was going to tear it down and be damned with the consequences. Cody was inside and Council members or not, she was going in after him.

Beast growled at her side.

"I hear you, boy," she said in low tones. "They've got ten seconds until I take down the doorframe and serve that damn door to them as a platter."

He sat down, his heavily muscled haunches rippling in readiness.

She understood. "It's almost time." Then started a countdown. "Five. Four. Three," she said, her voice hardening. "Two…" She backed up, prepared to batter the door down. "And…"

The door opened. Cody stood there, a grin on his face. "I tried to get it open as fast as I could, but they don't like to be defied."

"I'll defy them," she snapped as she walked inside, relief at having worried needlessly angering her even more.

Easy. They are only silly fools who don't understand what's been going on out there. They are the retired Councilmen — the elders. When the problems started, they were roused from sleep and moved down here. They don't get it.

She spun to send him an open-mouth look. They *what?*

You heard me.

Unbelievable. But her anger did abate with his words. She studied the old men that she'd only seen glimpses of until now, sitting at a large circular table with more empty seats than full ones.

"Tessa, please come in," Councilman Adamson said. "I'm sorry for the rudeness in the way this was handled, but the Council needed to speak to Cody first. He is an apprentice on the board."

"Right." She had forgotten that. Secret societies with secret rules for secret men.

She felt Cody's sidelong look and realized she was still pissed at them, and it was showing. "As he is safe and alive at my side, I'm very glad to hear that it was not yet another attempt on his life." And she smiled, her fangs showed slightly, the remnant of her temper.

"Not likely." The closest man stood up. "He tells us that the situation is worse than we knew."

"It is." Tessa gave a clipped nod. "And the crunch is happening right now."

"Hence being sequestered down here," the same man said. "Not our choice, I assure you."

"And why is that?" Cody asked in a deferential tone.

"Several of us were asleep, retired, you might say. Like Deanna, we were waiting for our replacements to be brought in and were no longer active in our positions. We have only been brought back to active status due to the heavy losses the Council has sustained. Not being on active duty also meant we were oblivious to all the goings on here."

She raised her eyebrows. "You were friends of Deanna's?"

"She didn't have friends," the standing vamp said drily.

"But we knew her, yes. Given the current circumstances and the diluted numbers on the Council, we can no longer relax at the sidelines. Neither can the younger generation run the Council. It is not an easy system to understand."

She could believe that. But it wasn't going to be easy for them to step back in to power again either. "And what is your first move now that you are looking to lead the Council again?" she asked, her voice cool. There was still something very off in this room, but she couldn't place what it was.

"First, we are attempting to gather facts so that we understand the situation," a wizened old geezer of a vampire said in a voice as dry as dust. "And that means finding and connecting with the remaining Council members to get a clearer picture of how bad things really are." He studied her then added, "At least those that are still alive."

Cody said, "Both Councilmen Goran and Serus are alive but are currently waging war on the blood farm."

"Have you seen them?" Jameson asked. "Do you know where they are now so that we can get ahold of them?"

Another man at the table shook his head. "Do either of you two know?"

Cody opened his mouth to answer when Tessa shook her head. "No idea," she said cheerfully. "Underground in the mine somewhere."

Silence.

"It would be more beneficial to have them here where they belong than out there in the trenches," the dust dude said. "Anyone can fight in the trenches."

"Not anyone can lead the army," Tessa said quietly. "Both of those men are uniquely skilled to do so."

"We have only located two other Councilmen still alive. They are recovering from being drugged. If what we have heard of the drugs is true, then it's possible they might not recover fully enough to be of assistance anytime soon."

She frowned. "I don't recall seeing any of our Councilmen. Foreign ones, yes. If there are several ill or dealing with drug issues, let me know where they are and I'll do what I can."

The men frowned, stared at each other, but stayed quiet. Then again, they had no idea what she'd learned to do these last few weeks. And Tessa doubted they'd believe it either. There were also several people they hadn't mentioned, and that oversight made her very wary. "What about Sian and Rhia."

There was an uncomfortable silence. She persisted, not liking the ugly thoughts in her head. "I'm sorry, I couldn't hear your answer."

The dust guy said, "And no answer is required. The Council speaks when it wishes, not to address your concerns."

She studied him carefully. "So in other words, my mother's actions are suspect because of her being drugged even though she went to war for all of you to stay quietly in your innocent sleep, and Sian – who is even now looking after the Hall so that you might remain safe down below and out of the action – is also suspect," she said coolly, ignoring Cody's sucked-in breath, "They are being villainized as not being good enough?"

"It is not for you to speak to the Council like this," the standing vamp retorted in shock. "If this is the result of us sleeping for the last century, then it seems we should have been woken a long time ago."

"It's not. It's a result of being burned, kicked, beat, and having survived numerous attacks on my life and that after having saved hundreds of vamps from death – and yes, humans – I'm being hit by the shock of finding out that the Council still can't recognize value when it's in front of them."

She spun and walked to the door. "As I recall, you can't be reactivated as active Council members without the vote of those current Council members. That would indicate that I need to go and help those Councilmen, see if they are capable of voting you back into active duty." *Like hell,* but she kept that thought to herself.

And she walked out. Anger vibrated through her. How dare they diss Sian and her mother. Sure, everyone knew her mother's actions right now were something that needed to be explained, but at no time did Tessa doubt her mother's motivations. She'd have done and, in fact – did – anything to keep her family safe.

Cody rushed behind her.

Beast, now that she was free of the room, walked at her side again. He had not liked being forced to stay outside. She wondered if Beast was capable of understanding her mood or if it was because he'd been separated from her. Right now, the ridge on the back of his neck stood up, as if he was facing imminent danger, but he wasn't growling.

In the back of her mind, she thought she heard a cry. She stopped. *Deanna, was that you? What is it you wish to say?*

A murmur rustled through her, but not one strong enough to be understood.

While Cody looked on, she stopped and leaned against the wall. She closed her eyes. "Hortran," she said in a low voice loud enough for Cody to hear. "What is Deanna trying to say?"

It took a moment to hear the whisper in her head. *"She*

knows those men."

"Of course she knows them. They are of an age and were all on the same Council."

"They don't like Deanna," Hortran whispered. *"They led a movement to remove Deanna from the Council centuries ago. It was defeated at the time. But now with as many Councilmen down as there are, these men will have more power than ever. That is not a good thing."*

"Will they abuse their new power?" she asked curiously. "And if so, why?"

Many are originals. They lived in violent times like so many of us. Some liked it. Some didn't. And others loved it. These ones loved it. They are accustomed to blood. They demand the real thing.

She sucked in her breath as she stared back at the way they'd come. "Did we just pen the good guys and let the monsters out?"

Hortran's voice faded before her. *Maybe...*
Shit.

❧ ❦

CODY DIDN'T GET the reference to the good guys and monsters, but Tessa was storming ahead as if she had a purpose. "Where are the sick Councilmen?" she asked.

"I'll ask Sian," he said, pulling his phone out. "She'll know."

Tessa nodded but appeared preoccupied.

Sian answered her phone immediately. There was a joyful cry when he quickly brought her up to date. When he mentioned where they'd just come from, she snorted. "Those old geezers had better not try to get back onto the Council. They didn't retire. They *were* retired – willingly or not. They had to be after the last catastrophe with the blood farm. They were given no choice," she said sadly. "They came out of retirement in favor of the facilities the last time we found these blood farms, and it nearly tore our clan apart."

"Really?" Cody was stunned. "I had no idea."

"No, of course not. It was put away, like all dignified Vampire Council dirt," she said in a mocking voice. "Never to see light again."

"Well, some fancy maneuvering needs to be done to keep the old Council from taking it over again." He shook his head, moving quicker to keep up with Tessa. "Where are the sick Councilmen? Tessa wants to see if she can help them."

"They are down in the second level. Most of that floor is filled with injured or recovering vamps. Afterwards, come up and see me," Sian commanded. "We're keeping down the fort up here but could use the extra hands."

"Got it." He tucked the phone away. "Sian says—"

"Got it." She tossed him a quick smile. "Let's go."

He laughed and caught up quickly. "Let's take the stairs."

At the stairwell, he bolted ahead of her and ran up the first flight.

Beast, sensing the hunt, was waiting at the door to the floor when he got there.

"He's fast," Cody said. "And deadly." He reached for the door, and as soon as it opened, Beast started howling.

Cody slammed the doors closed again, his gaze locked on the animal at his side who was even now trying to claw at the door to get through. "What's wrong with him?"

"Not sure," Tessa whispered. "But whatever it is, he wants it."

Cody looked down at her. "Do we let him have at it?"

"Absolutely."

As if hearing the answer, Beast let out a howl. Cody opened the door and Beast hurled himself through.

SERUS PULLED UP to the top of the trees, looking down on the small settlement. He knew the family, or rather he used to know the family that lived here. As he stared at the half-dozen vampire houses built into the trees and cliffs looking to become part of the natural settings, he wondered why he hadn't heard anything in decades. Maybe longer. The patriarch had been killed in the last blood farm battle but had been fighting on the side of right. He remembered hearing something about him having been killed by someone within the family. The details were a little sketchy, but he wasn't the first one to have died in such a betrayal.

The clans were rife with them. Now it was even worse.

There was no movement in the settlement below. Not even heat coming off the houses to give the impression of occupancy. Then again, it was exactly as Tessa had said.

He dropped to the ground and deliberately chose the gatehouse Tessa had gone in. There was something painful about following his daughter's tracks after she'd been hunted and had gone to ground. The thought of it boiled his insides. He also didn't have much time to spend here. Goran needed help. He stood outside facing the hill behind them. Tessa had found an entrance somewhere close by. It didn't mean he had a clear path through, but it should be close.

He didn't have time to go back and find another entrance. As he studied the hillside, his stomach sinking, he realized he wasn't seeing the entrance. Time was wasting.

Gathering his energy, he jumped up to a large rock. As he glided over to land on the roof, he finally saw the entrance.

This was it.

He jumped down to the landing and stopped to give a glance around the empty community before he slipped inside.

GORAN DOVE FOR the closest single vamp. Gas tendrils were already reaching up from the floor. The men below screamed as they tried to climb the walls to get up and away. Goran knew it was just a sleeping gas of some kind to minimize the threat so that a few vamps could handle the large number of men, but it was still scary as shit.

The vamp turned, saw him, and grinned, then pulled out an odd, black, handheld weapon. More of those light weapons. Well, he wasn't born yesterday. These vamps might have tried to take the easy way and avoid the years of learning to fight properly, but Goran hadn't. He'd cut his teeth on disputes like this one.

And like hell they were going to drop him with gas. Besides, he had to be way bigger than the guards here. What was the matter? Were they running out of enhanced assholes now? Were there no others left to fight that they were reduced to using runts?

He hoped so.

He lashed out with his foot, kicking the weapon from the vamp's hand, then followed it up with a twisting kick that caught the vamp's head with the power of his legs and jerked. The vamp went down without a sound. Goran snagged the gas mask off his head and put it on, then turned to study the others. Four were racing toward him.

Right. Neutralize one threat then find four more.

Still, it was only four. If Serus were here, he'd laugh at him and tell him to get serious. They had real work to do.

And in this case, he'd be right.

Goran reached down and grabbed the weapon from the unconscious vamp and turned it on. The spray hit the vamp on the floor. He lit up like a fancy set of firecrackers. Wow.

The others were coming, and they held their own versions of this thing. But now the odds were much better.

He pulled his lips back into a feral grin and hid behind the pillars.

Now they'd get a surprise of their own.

And he couldn't wait.

RHIA WATCHED THE last two of the medical team huddled together like a hawk. "Where are the new arrivals?" she asked in a low tone, keeping the threat imminent but downplayed if they were cooperative.

The younger woman in the back sneered. "Like we're going to tell you," she snapped.

"Maybe I will," the slightly older woman said, stepping back to the side. "I'm new here. I don't want to die."

"Traitor," the young woman said, lifting her chin a notch.

Ian walked closer. Rhia watched him. Would he be able to do what needed to be done? They had all done things they'd never expected to have to. She studied his hard face, the watchful eyes as he gauged the other woman's movements.

"What are you going to do, kill me in cold blood?" the woman vamp spat at him. "I'm defenseless in front of you.

How is that a better regime than the one we are building?"

Ian stopped and frowned.

Rhia winced. It was a tough issue for all of them. They had taken many of these vamps as prisoners, as some had information they could use and there were others who'd been forced into their army and wanted to be saved. But which category did this young woman belong?

Ian gave a shrug. "That will be determined by your actions now. I'm happy to take you prisoner. If you put up a fight and die in the meantime…"

And he reached for her.

She backed up, baring her fangs, then swiped at him.

He shrugged. "Okay, decision made." He pulled a stake out from his pocket and held it under her neck. "I've killed dozens of you so far, one more won't make a dent." She shuddered in place then slumped in defeat.

Pushing her ahead of him, he led her toward where Rhia stood.

They'd almost reached Rhia when the woman pulled something out of her pocket and attacked.

Rhia let her fangs show. The woman backed up slowly.

"Smart, very smart of you."

And Rhia approached her.

DAVID SAT DOWN at the computer, Jewel napping gently beside him. He hated this inactivity. He was on guard duty. He got that. But it chafed, too. He wanted to keep both Sian and Jewel safe, but sometimes it seemed like he could be put to better use.

And maybe while the women slept, he could find something of use in the archives. How did the Council get to a point of retiring a large group of Councilmen, not kill them as he'd have done, and then have the Council decimated to the point that these retirees would be the next wave of power? A position that would allow them to put whoever they needed into power and secure their places at the top once again.

That terrified him. If the Council drew an emergency vote, then none of the ancients he knew would be able to take part as they couldn't get back on time. And that could be a disaster.

He needed his sister to talk to Deanna and find out what they could be up against. Deanna's husband was gone. Many others were either missing in action or drugged to the tips of their toes. Who knew if any of those could be saved or not?

And how could they get proxy votes in place in time? Would they even be honored at this stage?

It's not that he was distrustful of the Council members, he was distrustful of everyone he didn't know at this point.

Should he contact Adamson over his worries? He was still one of the members of the Council that was close enough to come in and vote. In fact, he was here with the elders. He might be able to rein them in. Jameson was another choice as he worked closely with Sian.

Who else was there?

He pulled up the current list and checked them off in his head. Then seeing a tab for inactive members, he brought that list up, too.

And realized that they'd all been called in already.

The Council needed to bring everyone back to elect new members. And as he read the fine print…they needed to do that fast.

CHAPTER 3

H OWLS FILLED THE hallway.

Tessa and Cody stared at each other in shock.

"Not more animals, surely," Cody said. "This floor was supposed to be cleared and safe and people are in here healing."

"I wouldn't be at all surprised." Tessa shrugged. "It will be close now."

Just as suddenly as the howls filled the air, silence cut through their conversation. Taking a chance, Cody poked his head around the doorframe.

Tessa knew Beast was okay. She could sense him, feel him as part of her being. "It's clear." Cody pushed the door open and stepped into the hallway. Tesla followed.

Beast sat in the hallway as charred body parts and ash surrounded him. With that deeply intense stare, he looked at her as if asking permission. Tessa swallowed hard. It was in his nature, but did that make it right? It was in her nature to take blood from the living, and did that make it right? She studied Beast as she walked closer, seeing the bloodlust drain from his eyes. Seeing the mantle of awareness shift down as the danger level receded in his eyes.

It was the rankest smell, yet she couldn't even determine what animal he'd ripped apart because the pieces were so distorted. So much was burnt and the rest was unrecognizable.

"Beast, I don't think you want to eat that. It's disgusting and will make you sick." That gaze never shifted. She winced. "Okay, have at it. But no whining later."

He surged for the piece closest to him. She quickly added, "And please wait until I'm past you."

Beast froze and watched every step she took. As she approached the first of four doorways, she gave a light rap on the door and pushed it open but didn't enter.

Silence.

She gazed at Cody. *What do you think?*

No idea. His voice drifted through her mind. *Can you sense anything?* She was trying to intuit what she was seeing. It was more difficult now as she seemed to be able to connect to so much more than just the wall and floors. She waited for the energy to show up too. When it did finally, she gave a sharp nod and said, "The room is empty."

Cody peered around the edge of the doorframe and took a quick look. Then he took a longer one before stepping back out into the hallway. "You're right. On to the next one."

With Beast back again at her side, and she did not want to consider the tiny bits and pieces that were still hanging to the side of his mouth, they went from door to door and stopped at the second room. This one was full.

"Damn," she said softly, looking at the sheer number of vamps that had yet to recover. Surely there was something she could to do to speed this up. The healer in her wanted them all back on their feet.

"Forget it. There were too many of them for you to help."

"Unless there are some of our Councilmen here?" she

said, frowning as she walked the aisles between the beds pushed so tightly together it was almost impossible to make her way through them. "Do you recognize anyone?"

"I do, but not from the Council. Some of these men we rescued early on, some are more recent."

"Right." She stopped and stared at one man that lay on the bed, seemingly comatose, and yet there was nothing black in his energy. Or that she could see from the initial glance. Rather than go closer, she pulled back slightly and motioned at Beast.

He studied her for a long moment with that deep, golden look and padded closer. The growl in his throat gained in strength the closer he made it to the head of the bed.

If the guy wasn't unconscious, there's no way he'd be able to withstand that threat.

At least she hoped not.

Beast lunged into the man's face and snarled loudly.

Up out of the bed, the vamp who'd been hiding amongst the injured bolted for the door.

Cody reached out an arm, but the vamp tried to swing at him, only to run into Cody's fist.

He reached back to spike the vamp when Tessa cried out, "Wait."

Arm paused in midair, Cody held the vamp by the throat and looked at her. "Why?"

"He doesn't have black in his energy."

Cody blinked at her then dropped his gaze to study the vamp at his feet. "Good guy or bad guy?"

"Good guy," the vamp cried out, his panicked gaze locked onto Cody's face. "I woke up here. I have no idea what happened."

"Tessa?" Cody asked. "Is he telling the truth?"

She walked closer. "You know, I think he is."

Cody lowered his arm slowly.

The vamp shuddered. "Thank you," he said, turning to face Tessa. "I am telling the truth." He looked around at the room full of vamps. "I only woke up a few minutes ago by some horrible noises close by." He swallowed hard, trying to back away from Beast as he approached.

"What is that thing?"

"This is Beast," Tessa said in a terse voice. "He's my pet."

"A pet? No one has pets like that."

"Well, I do," she said calmly, studying the man. "And he's the least dangerous of the three of us."

The man's eyes widened to saucers and he tried to escape. "What is going on?"

"I don't know yet, but if we can figure out who you are and where you came from, that might help us get to the bottom of that question."

"I'm Terry," he said. "My father is…" he swallowed. "Councilman Webster."

Tessa looked over at Cody then back at Terry. "And is he dead?"

Terry nodded. "He is."

"Was he for or against the blood farm?" Cody asked coldly.

"I don't know. He never said." Terry shook his head. "I'm not even sure what you mean by blood farms."

"What do you drink?"

The vamp reared back, a frown on his face. "Blood. What else is there to drink?"

"And how do you get the blood?"

More confused than anything, Terry shifted slightly so

he could look at the room full of unconscious vamps. "Uhm, it's delivered fresh every day." He snorted. "Like everyone's is."

When Tess and Cody glared at him, he cried out, "What?"

"We'll take an educated guess and say that your father was getting it from the blood farms, and that means he's on the wrong side of this war."

"I don't even know what you mean by war," he said fearfully. "I was in Europe and got a strange order from him saying I was to stay there." With a sheepish motion, he added, "So of course I came running to find out what was wrong."

Tessa snorted. "Of course you did. And now you know that your father was on one side of the war and we're on the other."

Cody stared down at him. "But what do we do with him now?"

"I don't know. There aren't many of the enemy left alive."

Terry's face paled beside them. "I don't know what's going on here. What's wrong with the blood farm?"

That the kid had real confusion in his voice was what made Tessa step back. "Are you really so unaware?"

He stared at her mutely.

Stepping in, Cody quickly explained the war the kid had become a part of. Tessa watched the shock, confusion, and distaste when he understood what the blood farm really was, and then the realization of which side his father had picked.

He slumped back to the ground, staring up at the ceiling. "Oh Lord," he whispered. "I had no idea."

"And now that you do?" Tessa asked in a hard voice.

"What side are you going to be on?"

CODY WATCHED THE pain and the turmoil in the young man's eyes as he worked his way through the information. "I'm sorry," Cody said. "It's ugly. It's confusing. It's horrible really. But it's also very real."

"So my father was part of the blood farm." Terry stared at the top of the hallway, his voice expressionless and his face strained. Cody found it painful to see the dawning of the realization as to what his life had been built on.

"Exactly." Tessa said as she walked back to the room full of slack-jawed vamps. Cody watched silently as she stood at the doorway studying the occupants. He smiled when she asked, "Beast, anyone here that isn't like the others?"

Beast whined. Then lay down with his chin on his paws.

"Good boy."

She checked the hallway out, leaving Cody to stand guard over the bed. Terry had a decision to make. One he couldn't make easily. But he might have valuable information that could help round up the rest of his father's cronies so that they could put a stop to this. He'd love to blow the farms to hell, but they had to make sure everyone was safely removed first. As soon as they had that locked down, he wanted to lead the team that made sure these farms and labs became non-serviceable forever.

They'd done that to several of them already, but it wasn't enough. These locations needed to be shut down permanently. And to that end…he studied Terry. "Where did your father work?"

Terry, as if jolted by such a mundane question, turned to look at him. "At Chetek. It is a biodiversity engineering firm."

Cody sat back on his heels. "I know it." He'd actually contemplated going to talk to them in the next year. See what the field was like, the work they did. He was supposedly graduating in a few years. Or not, depending if they could get this mess shut down. And fast.

Any further schooling appeared to be in the hands of fate.

"My father is an accountant," Terry muttered. "Not a chemist. I can't believe he'd be part of something like this."

"And as an accountant, he'd have access to all types of information."

Cody turned to stare at Tessa. She stood at the open door of the next room. She smiled.

"Bingo."

"Bingo what?" Terry asked suspiciously. "Who are you people? How do I know you're telling the truth?"

Ignoring his question, Tessa motioned at the room behind them. "Do you know how you came to be in this room?"

He shook his head. "I came home, but my father wasn't there. I went to his offices but they'd been closed. I wanted to reconnect with a few friends that went to the university here," he said, then took a deep breath, "And I wanted answers."

"Answers to what?" Cody asked coolly from the sidelines. "You didn't know anything to ask yet."

"My father didn't answer my phone calls or respond to my texts. I tried to phone a few of his friends and coworkers but got no answer either. It's like everyone left town."

A sob caught in the back of his throat. "It was a nightmare," he whispered. "I didn't know what to do, so I went to his boss's house. He raged at me. Told me the world was not the same anymore and why had I come home when my father had done so much to keep me safe. He didn't act normal. His temper was horrific."

Tessa nodded and stroked his arm in a soothing motion. Cody didn't have the same patience. Terry's father had been behind a lot of the biochemical weapons they were all dealing with. That couldn't be easy, but Cody had been on the receiving end of them, and that had been much worse.

"He told me to go home again, while I could." Terry rubbed his temple. "I told him I wanted to find my father."

Silence as Terry tried to compose himself. "That's when his boss said he was dead. Killed by other vampires."

He stared at Tessa. "I don't understand how this came to be a war where we are killing our own people."

Tessa studied him. "The story is long and convoluted but in essence, the blood farm needed new humans to hang up and they started stealing people off the streets, out of the homes and schools."

"These people didn't want to donate blood?" Terry asked.

Cody walked over and pulled his phone out of this pocket. He flicked through several pictures and held it up for Terry to see.

Terry cried out in horror. "Are they all dead?"

"No," Cody said harshly, "but they might prefer to be. They were kept alive in a suspended state, their bodies pumping out blood that you consumed. They hung until their bodies finally broke down and their blood is no longer consumable."

"I didn't think such a thing was possible." Terry's voice shook with emotion. "I thought the humans were paid for the blood."

"Yeah, with their lives," Tessa said, standing up. "Then the men behind this decided to snatch other vampires."

Terry laughed. "Right," he said sarcastically. "Like we can use them for the farms."

Cody shifted the pictures until the one showing other vampires hanging showed up. "They were doing experiments on them." He showed Terry several more, including the room with all the test tubes where his brother had died.

The shock sent Terry tumbling down to the floor again. "My father would never do something so…so disgusting." He shook his head. "You have to be wrong."

"No, we're not wrong." Tessa stood at the doorway to the sleeping vamps. "Why do you think these men are all unconscious?" She turned to look at him. "They were going to be reinforcements for the blood farm enhancement program." She shot him a hard look. "They were building an army."

Cody walked over. "Get up. We don't have time for this." He pushed Terry to the open door. "Do you know any of these men?"

Terry, obviously still struggling with the news, studied the men on the beds. "There are some I recognize from the university. I was talking to them when this happened."

He walked down and motioned at six young men. "These men."

Tessa nodded. "You have no idea how lucky you are, do you? We saved these men – you." She walked to the next room. "Otherwise you'd have been drugged up and given whatever brand of enhancements they chose to give you. And you'd have had no choice in the matter. Not even your father's name would have saved you."

"The men who approached didn't even ask," Terry said. "They sprayed us with something and that's the last I remember."

"They are getting desperate. They need more men after we destroyed most, if not all, of the clones they were creating. They are out of men and out of time," Cody snapped. "So if you know anything that would help us, now is the time to say so."

His gaze dull, his face shattered, Terry said, "I have my father's computer at home. When I couldn't find him and things got weird, I hid it in my room just in case."

"And do you know what's on it?"

He shrugged. "Everything. My father always was meticulous with his notes." At that word, the two glared at him. He winced. "I didn't know," he whispered. "I had no idea. He said he was an accountant."

❧ ❧

RHIA FACED THE last woman. Her name tag said Gemma. "Gemma, where do you stand on this issue?"

"Whatever side that will allow me to live," she retorted. "We didn't all have a choice, you know. We were in other jobs before. I worked at the hospital until they decided I was better suited to being here. We were given injections that were to keep us safe. But we're all going to die as part of that keeping safe thing. We're addicted to the drugs. There's no antidote. When I tried to change my job, they said I had no choice. I'd be working here or in a similar facility for the rest of my life. It was the drugs that ensured my cooperation. I get a shot every two days." She shuddered. "Whether I like it or not."

"There might be an antidote," Rhia said quietly. "Our

side is working on it. You're not alone in being drugged against your will."

"The things I've seen…done," she shook her head. "No one on your side will let me live."

Ian snorted. "The things *we've* done – we would prefer to not have done either. But circumstances forced our hand. If you can make a decent case to the Council," he shrugged. "Who knows? They might be lenient."

"Particularly if you help us," Jared said, his voice hard and determined. "You have a recent group of humans brought in. I need to find them."

Gemma gave a broken laugh. "Recent? We have nothing *but* recent groups. They are barely running them through a check. They are so short on supply, they aren't looking for disease or imperfections." She shook her head. "It's been a nightmare this last week."

"Where are they," Jared snapped, struggling to walk to the door. "Show us."

With Ian once again shouldering Seth and Wendy marking the locations on her phone, they walked out.

Rhia kept a firm arm on Gemma. They couldn't make any mistakes at this point.

They were too close to freedom.

As they headed back to the hallway, Gemma said, "The doctor tripped the alarm. There are going to be more guards here soon." She glanced around. "I'm surprised they aren't here already."

"You have to be running out of men soon," Wendy cried. "Surely."

Gemma nodded. "They are doing new experiments on humans to make them fight on our side."

Silence. Jared let out a heavy, gusting breath. "Now that

would be bad."

"Because we need the blood so bad, they've fought doing something like that for a long time, but now, well, they are desperate."

Rhia glanced at Jared. It was one thing to fight off the vampires that had hurt him and his family, but what would he do if he had to fight against other humans armed for war – and ones he knew?

DAVID SURVEYED THE blast that had broken part of the wall. He'd understood Motre's explanation but was still dealing with the aftermath of the shock. How his sister had grown in astronomical, completely non-vampire ways.

He hoped it didn't come back to bite her, but he was afraid that when the war ended, she'd struggle to return to a normal life.

Whatever that term meant for them all at this point.

That she and Cody were a pair wasn't in dispute, but what would they have for a relationship? They'd never had a chance to date, or go through all those wonderfully awkward moments of young love. They'd slammed into something so epic, he imagined it would take time to adjust to.

With Motre's help, they secured the new entrance. "There really was someone upstairs?"

Motre nodded. "And likely for centuries."

"Sometimes I wonder if I know my own clan at all," David said. "It's like everything I was taught was a lie."

"Not a lie, but you were innocent. Naïve." Motre stood with his hands on his hips. "We all were."

"Except those that had lived through it all before."

"And I wasn't here back then," Motre said. "I was in

Europe."

David walked back to where Jewel and Sian were once again running data. This time, the air buzzed with excitement.

"There you are," Jewel exclaimed. "Tessa and Cody found a conscious vamp in the sick bay area. He's the son of an accountant or a chemist – they aren't sure – of the blood farm." She filled them in. "So the laptop has been picked up and they are bringing it here."

"But we don't know what's on it, right?" David clarified. "So this could be great, but might not be?"

"According to Terry, his father kept meticulous notes and only worked on his laptop," Sian said. "So no, it's not for sure, but we're hoping."

The door burst open and one of Motre's men strode in, the laptop under his arm. "Here it is, exactly where the kid said it was."

"And the rest of the house?" Motre asked.

"We're going through it right now."

David listened as the new arrival brought Motre up to date on what they'd found so far.

At least that confirmed what Cody had found. But it depended on what Sian found that would really make the difference.

He watched as she powered up the machine and started searching. Then she slumped back into her chair, a look of joy on her face.

"Names, dates, and locations. If we can cross-reference this information with what we already have, we can hit all the places at once and put this to bed once and for all."

GORAN HATED TO say it, but he was getting tired. He didn't know where the vamps were coming from, but the flow just wasn't stopping. And he needed them to stop. Or he needed reinforcements. Vamps were affected by the gas, as he'd found out the hard way. He'd ripped the masks off several so far and would do it to everyone he could. Drop them in place, then stab them with a stake. So far the system was working, but now they were coming two or three at a time. He dropped over the side as three more came at him. He flew up to the roof where he rested for a moment. There had to be a better way. He swooped down and using his feet and hands, he knocked the men down and ripped off their masks then spiked them.

Thank heavens for the mask. The smell of ash was rank. He flew over the sleeping humans, wondering at how organically weak they were. Still, he'd not fare much better if he hadn't got the mask on first.

He rested on the top of the wall and waited. Had he taken the last of them out or was this his only respite?

A huge figure filled the doorway. Serus. His heart swelled with joy. The old bugger was fine after all.

"Damn well time you got here," he called out. "I finished them all off for you."

Serus's big grin flashed. "You mean I did. I had to come through a wall of men just to get to you." He snorted at the pile of ash lying on the path. "Are you done yet?"

"Oh, I'm done all right." Goran landed in front of him, pointing at the floor covered with the human army. "But these guys need help. They aren't seasoned and way too unsuspecting. The whole lot of them went down in the first wave of gas."

"Damn."

"It's good to see you. Are you sure you should be on active duty already?"

"Ha, Tessa's medicine is very potent." He smiled. "I'm not wearing a gas mask."

Goran frowned. "Is it safe?" Then he turned to look at the last of the men he'd killed and realized they hadn't been wearing the masks either. He ripped it back off his face. "Is that a short window of effectiveness or what?"

"Not necessarily," Serus said. "I think you've been here for a while."

Goran studied the empty second floor hall and the passed-out army. "I have indeed."

"So shall we finally get to work then?"

He slapped Serus on the back. "If you can, then I can."

"Let's call this in and get an update. Then we'll move through this shithole and empty it."

CHAPTER 4

THE LAST ROOM yielded two Councilmen. Tessa vaguely recognized them, but as the Council meetings were something she wasn't allowed to attend, she didn't know the individual members well.

But she trusted Cody and he knew both men.

"How bad are they?" Cody asked, studying the two men. "Can we wake them?"

She circled the beds, seeing the black layers surrounding both men. Deep layers. Multiple layers. "They are not in good shape," she admitted. "I can help them, but the drugs are coursing through their system." She turned to look at the others in the room. "Is there any security in place in case one of the men wakes up on the wrong side of this war? Given the type of drugs we know they've used in the past and the brainwashing, these rooms could become a bloodbath."

"Brainwashing? Drugs?" Terry hobbled forward, his body still struggling to move in a normal manner.

Tessa hadn't noticed any black in his system, but the multiple shocks he'd received could account for his inability to pull himself together in more ways than one.

"There is so much you don't know," Cody murmured. "And all of it bad. Just accept that you'll be able to fill in the holes as we go on."

Terry wavered on his feet. "I don't feel so good," he admitted. "Was I drugged like they were?"

Cody turned to Tessa. "Was he?"

"There were some in his system, but he's thrown them off," she said as she studied the Councilman closest to her. "But not like these guys. They were targeted and given multiple doses, likely of different chemical mixes."

"Why?" Terry asked, confusion coloring his voice. "And why so many?"

"We already explained that to you," Tessa said impatiently. "These guys were either going to get enhancements, brainwashing, or be forced to join the army. Possibly all three."

There was silence behind her. She turned and studied his face. That's when she noticed Beast at his side. Not like he walked at her side, but staring at Terry as if not sure if he should attack or not.

Well, she felt about the same way. Was he an innocent victim like so many others? Or something more sinister?

"Tessa, can you help the Councilmen?"

"Yes, but not sure it will bring them around in time." But they had no choice. She had to try. She sat down on the bed between the two men and got to work. Clearing the top layer of energy wasn't a big issue, but the other layers were more intense. Lots of it was centered on the head, and that was where she needed to focus. She reached into the energy at the brain and started tugging.

Councilman Roberts opened his eyes and stared at her.

She froze. "Hello?" she said quietly. The man closed his eyes again. She relaxed and went back to work, carefully pulling out the deepest, darkest strands. When she was done, she sat back and studied the other man. His energy was slowly improving after the minimal work she'd done on him.

Good.

There was a bit on the side of his head and more over here. With her hands busy and her focus on the men, she managed to filter out some of Cody's explanation to Terry of her actions. She'd become accustomed to people seeing what she did and understanding. But this was new to so many people. Of course Terry didn't understand.

When she was finally done, she stood up and took several steps back where she rotated her shoulders to release the tension of sitting in the odd position for so long. As she finished, the first Councilman woke up.

Roberts stared at her, then frowned. He lifted himself to his elbows and looked around. Then the realization hit him. "Dear God, where am I?"

"Safe," Tessa said. "You were rescued from the blood farm labs and are now in the Council Hall."

His gaze widened in horror. He bolted to his feet and swayed in place.

Tessa studied his physical condition with a dispassionate eye. "How do you feel?"

After taking a deep breath and giving himself a moment to adjust, he said, "I feel okay. A little weak, but that is improving too."

"Good." Tessa walked to the doorway. "Take it easy for the rest of the day so your vampire heritage can bring you fully back to health, but with the drugs draining from your system, you should be fine."

"Wait, where are you going?"

"I need to check on the other rooms. Councilman Baker is beside you. He should wake up soon. Both of you are required downstairs immediately at the Council meeting. You're one of the few members still alive and capable of voting." She spun around to see him. "And make no mistake as to where your vote needs to lie."

"I don't understand."

She nodded. "I know. Cody will fill you in while I check the other rooms."

And she walked out.

I don't like you leaving alone, Cody muttered.

Sorry. I won't be long. But he's not going to listen to me. He needs to hear all this from you.

There was a thoughtful silence as Cody digested that information. *We'll see,* he said. *You aren't as far to the left as you think you might be.*

No, but he doesn't know me. Or what I can do.

I'll let it go this time, he said smoothly, *but you will take your rightful place when this is over.*

Rightful place? she whispered sadly. *Will I have one when this is over? I was odd before. Now? I'm so far away from being normal that I doubt I'll fit in anywhere.*

You will be at my side. That makes you fit in automatically. And if not, then screw them, he said comfortably.

Tessa hated the insecurity in her voice. As if after all she'd learned to do and be, she was still at the same place where she'd been on that fateful day she'd gone to the movies. As she gave Cody a last glance, his gaze warm and loving, she knew she'd moved on from that insecure young girl in some ways.

I wonder if I'll ever feel normal.

I imagine every woman feels like that, Cody said in sympathy. *At least at some point. You've come a long ways so damn quickly.* He hesitated. *I'm just not sure how much.*

She blinked, hearing the vulnerability in his voice now.

And that made her see something else. Of all the things

that worried her about her future – Cody was not one of them. She knew they belonged together. Needed each other and, in fact, likely wouldn't survive without the other.

It wasn't the time for a personal talk. Not with everything happening, but she needed to make time for one thing. She went back into the room, walked closer, slipped her arms around him, and kissed him. And she planned to do so much more as soon as they could. When she pulled back, she looked deep into his glowing eyes and whispered, "When this is over, we need to go away. Somewhere where we can be alone. Just the two of us together. No family, friends, no bad guys."

Heat lit the deep gaze into a passionate fire. She smiled, a smile full of promise, and added, "You pick the place, make sure you can fly us there, and don't tell me where. It can be our retreat – a place we can return to time and time again. If you're interested, that is?"

He slid his hands behind her head and held her firm while he studied her gaze. "There'll be no going back after that. You'll be mine forever. There'll never be anyone else in your world. I won't allow it."

"You're making a big assumption," she said, her heart swelling at the possessive look in his eye. "I think it's safe to say there already is no going back – for either of us now."

SHE SLIPPED FROM Cody's embrace and walked to the other room, leaving his arms aching and empty. He couldn't tear his eyes away until she was out of sight.

A getaway?

A retreat where the two of them could go to be alone? Hell yeah, he could think of a few places. Then frowned. But what type of place? A vampire lair, old-style in a severely awesome, decked-out cave? A modern vamp hotel in another city? He could fly to several, no problem.

Now consumed by the hint of what was to come, he leaned back against the wall and struggled to face the two men staring at him.

"Who was that," Roberts asked. "Is that Councilman Serus's daughter?"

Cody nodded, his gaze hardening as he dared the other man to say something negative about Tessa.

"I've heard some incredible things about what she's accomplished. They sounded like fiction, so I never gave it any thought." He studied all the men unconscious all around him. "But there's got to be a reason why I'm awake and feeling damn good and these men aren't. I'm assuming it was because of her?"

"It was indeed." Cody said. "We need you and the other Councilman back at your posts. The relics, who were somehow brought out of retirement to take their places again because so many of our members were missing, are looking to stay."

Roberts winced. "Not the four elders? They are likely behind this damn blood farm in the first place. How the hell would anyone think bringing them back is a good idea?"

"More to the point, if they do get voted back, how do you ever get rid of them again?" Cody asked.

Roberts shuddered. He turned and gave Baker a shake. "Wake up, Baker. You're needed."

Baker groaned. "What happened," he asked when he could. "My head is splitting."

His eyes popped open quickly when he did understand. "Those old geezers," he cried, "They wanted to bring live sacrifices back into the clan." He cringed. "We can't let them have power again. It took forever to remove it from them."

Cody stared. *Sacrifices.* Jesus. He forgot the ancients were likely stone-aged. "Let's get you to the meeting."

"And what about your father?" Baker asked, taking several tentative steps to test his strength.

"They are out fighting," Cody admitted. "And Rhia is attempting to find her son." At the sidelong looks the other two made at each other, he added, "Sian is also upstairs."

The men sighed. "The ancients we're trying to stop will fight to keep Sian and Rhia off the Council. Sian went several rounds with them before because of Taz." Roberts held up his hand. "He's a good man. No doubt about it, but he's human."

"And they are of course against that," Cody scoffed.

"And anything less than perfect," Baker said. "So Sian's child will never be accepted."

"Except it already is," Cody snapped. "These retirees can disappear back into the woodwork. This is a new world now, and it needs to be one of fairness and acceptance."

The two men stared at him curiously. "That may be, but it's not the way it has been before. Vampires are violent in nature and not particularly careful of anyone else."

"What about Rhia's sisters?" Baker asked. "I think they might be backup Council associates. Where are they?"

Cody stared at Baker. "No idea. I haven't seen them in a long time." But he'd get Sian to track them down now.

"And there could be a reason for that," Roberts said.

Baker asked, "Are there no other Councilmen left?" He named off several, his face becoming more and more drawn as Cody shook his head at each name.

"We need more to overpower these men," he cried. "Just

in numbers alone, we can't make the vote happen without it."

"There are seven if we count the names I've listed and Councilman Adamson."

"He's still alive?" Baker smiled. "Good man. Glad he's made it."

"How many do we need?" Cody asked. "Jameson is here too, although he's the one that brought the elders back — with Adamson's agreement."

At a sound on the left, he turned to see Terry sitting down on the floor looking a little shaky. He studied the young man then realizing he was okay, Cody turned his attention back to the Councilmen.

Baker said, "We need ten to vote in new members."

"And how about promoting the apprentices?"

The men stopped and looked at him. "How many of you are there?"

"There were ten of us."

"And now?"

Cody shrugged. "David, Ian, and myself. As for the others, I don't know, but likely one or two are around."

"Round them up. You can't be fully-fledged members, but you can now be attached to existing members."

Cody frowned. That mess again. He hadn't liked the old system. "Maybe it's time to make changes in that system right now too," he muttered.

"Changes like that require several layers of decision-making and voting."

"So nothing we can do as an emergency measure at the moment?"

They shook their heads. "No. Best is if we have enough members. Sounds like we're two short. And then we need to link the apprenticeships to the existing members that we can start retraining."

He turned to Cody. "We need your father and Councilman Serus back immediately." He motioned at him to leave. "If we call an emergency meeting, they only need six members to vote."

"Don't they have to vote the retirees back in first?"

"Yes, unless we have need of them, as in if half the Council is missing."

"Shit."

❧ ❦

JARED WATCHED THE expressions cross the woman's face as she stopped at a large double door.

Was it safe to trust Gemma? She knew what would happen to her if she betrayed them, but under the circumstances, wouldn't betrayal be expected?

Gemma held her finger to her mouth in a *quiet* motion, then she said, "Follow me. And be aware that there should be two guards in here at all times."

"Why?" Jared asked.

"In case the people wake up." With that note, she opened the door and stepped inside.

Rhia entered next.

Jared was scared to see what was inside. The shit these vamps kept behind closed doors were going to give him nightmares for the rest of his life. But as his vision cleared, tears came to his eyes.

Humans. Dozens of young, bright, healthy students. He should know. He'd gone to school with so many of them.

His gaze whipped along the rows of unconscious kids. So damn many. "What did you do? Empty the school one morning? Call an assembly and gas the gym?"

She winced at the anger in his voice. "They might have done something like that. The principal was paid well for his part in this."

A broken cry erupted from Jared's mouth as he understood the level of betrayal. He raced down the rows. There was Daniel. Joseph. Mags. Tammy. His mind stalled at the numbers. He pulled his phone out. "We need to get the Human Council to send a medical team down here," he said.

"They were supposed to come behind the army," Wendy said. "I heard something about that earlier. Army first. Then medics."

Jared stopped. "Army. That's right, surely both armies should be here by now."

Ian settled Seth onto the floor. "Are they all alive?"

Gemma nodded. "They were going to be the seed to form our new blood farm. Start with young blood, all pure and clean."

Jared spun, the look of fury on his face making Gemma take several hurried steps backward. "They aren't seeds for anything. They are my friends."

She nodded. "I'm sorry," she offered. "The board members don't think of them as anything other than animals."

Not trusting himself to answer her, he turned his gaze back to the rows and rows of innocent kids. Like he'd been at one time too. Until Tessa had saved him.

And now maybe saving these kids would let him pay that forward.

His gaze swept to the third row as he took in the enormity of what they'd found. And froze.

"She's not here," he cried out. First in shock, and then again in anger. "Clarissa is not here."

"Clarissa?" The woman frowned. "There are three rooms exactly like this."

"Three more, so four in total?" Ian asked, collecting and sending information on his phone.

"Jesus. How are we going to get the message out?" Jared asked.

Ian snorted. "And what universe do you live on? The message has already gone out." He tucked his phone away and turned to face the threat.

"It won't matter how many there are," a hard voice called from behind them. "Because no one else will ever know they are here."

CHAPTER 5

TESSA CHECKED OUT the other rooms, but no more vamps were waking up. She could help that process along, but if she did that to so many she'd need recovery time herself, something she could not afford. Better she left these men to recover on their own. She had to get the hell out of here and return to Sian and see what she had planned.

And if that was all good, then she was heading out to find her father. They had a massive clean up to organize. And she was damn tired. She couldn't remember the last time she'd slept. If she had the time she'd do so now, but she had to get the Councilmen back to the meeting and they needed to flush out the son that was the leader in all of this. As for Terry, well, she didn't know what to do with him.

"Tessa?" Cody called her over. "We need to get these men upstairs."

"I know. I was hoping to leave that to someone else so we could join the ancients."

His knowing smile made her grin. "I know, right? We're always happier out in the middle of the action."

"Isn't that the truth," she said with a heartfelt sigh. "Let's go." She motioned at Terry to walk in front of her.

"What's going to happen to me?" Terry said.

"We're turning you over to Sian for interrogation."

"Interrogation?" his voice thinned with fear.

"Questioning," she said humorously. "Sorry, still in battle mentality."

"I think you must live there," he muttered.

"We have been," Cody admitted. "And it's dangerous to slide out of it at this point. We're close to the mop-up stage, but we're not there yet."

Tessa agreed. She nudged Terry toward Sian's office, hoping that they could leave him there. His father's laptop could be huge in filling in the blanks. She just needed the head of this mess locked in. He was powerful, and maybe he was behind this maneuvering going on in Council Hall. She had no idea how the politics worked and didn't want to know either. That should be Sian's domain, because Sian got politics.

Only Sian wasn't in her office.

Right. Turning back the way they'd come, Tessa walked the group into the elevators and pushed the button for where the Councilmen were sequestered.

"How did a teenage vamp get to be so powerful?" Terry asked.

She shot him a look but didn't answer. Out of the corner of her eye, she caught Cody smacking him on the shoulder.

Good.

Then she wanted to laugh. She was upset at his lack of respect and impertinence. Since when had she become an old soul that saw *him* as a kid?

The double doors opened. Cody stepped up first and walked to the Council room. Right. He was welcome in that room.

She stood back and motioned for the two elders to enter. She stood in the open doorway and studied the people there.

Sian sat on the far left side.

"Sian?" she said in a low voice.

Sian walked over.

"Need a moment," Tessa said. She stepped outside, waiting.

Sian followed. "Problems?"

"Not more than usual," Tessa said in a droll voice. "Terry. What do we do about him?" She motioned at the vamp. Standing nervously at the side, his back to them. "He likely has useful information."

"Is he telling the truth in anything he's said yet?" Sian's voice was loud enough that Terry spun to see them speaking about him.

"Yes," Tessa said. "His energy says so."

"Then in that case, I'll find someone to question him." She pulled out her phone and texted several people.

"And how many people are we missing from the Council meeting now?"

Sian snorted. "Too many. We need more. Way more."

"Like who?" Cody asked, now standing in the doorway where he could see them. "Who are we looking for?"

"I think both Triton and Morris could be still alive," Sian said.

"And where would they be?" Tessa asked.

"Morris was in Europe for the last decade. I tracked him down and spoke to him but haven't heard back. And we're on the hunt for Triton. We thought he'd gone on a sabbatical, but we're not sure. I've sent him messages but haven't heard back."

"So there's no one we should be looking for *here*?" Cody asked cautiously. "Do we have confirmation of all the ones we'd assumed had died?"

Sian shook her head. "No," she said softly. "How do we do that unless someone saw them die?"

"Do you have photos of the Council?" Tessa asked. "Not being part of it, I have no idea who was active or retired."

"Neither do I," Cody admitted. "I know those I worked with, but that's it."

"I do," Sian pondered. "There are Council photos in the Hall. One per decade. No one has ever left the Council willingly, so if you go back five to six decades, you'd find all of them shown. And the names are listed below the images."

The elevator doors opened and two men walked toward them. Sian said to them, "Take Terry upstairs to Jameson. He's expecting him."

The men nodded, their faces hard, their eyes locking onto Terry waiting to see how this was going to go.

Terry turned to Tessa and Cody. "Can't you two take me?" he asked.

Tessa studied his energy. The nervousness was real. There was no black in his system. None. That had always bothered her. She just didn't know what she was to read into that.

"The Council Hall is beside Jameson's office," Sian murmured so Tessa and Cody could hear.

"We'll walk up with you," Cody said smoothly, "as we're going that way as well."

Relief settled on Terry's face. "Thank you. I'm really not one of the enemy." He smiled at Sian and turned to walk toward the elevators.

Sian turned to Tessa. "Is he for real?"

"He is and he isn't," she muttered. "There's something going on I don't understand."

Cody froze. "What?"

"He's too clean," she whispered her eyes on Terry's back. "As if he's really innocent. But my mind says that can't be. And maybe this last month has just given me a horrible insight into our species, but could he really not know? And wouldn't his father have protected him even more?"

"Do you doubt his identity?" Sian asked.

Tessa studied the young man walking ahead of him. And something went click. In a low tone, she said urgently, "No, I doubt his genetics."

The two stared at her. "What are you talking about?"

"I think he's a clone. Grown by a lonely man desiring to have a son of his own and raised to whatever version of reality he wanted. I doubt the kid knows anything but what he's been fed…" She studied the super clean energy running through Terry's system and her stomach sank. She'd seen bits and pieces of that energy before.

She whispered in a voice only loud enough for Cody and Sian to hear. "I'm afraid he's less than a year old."

CODY WALKED AUTOMATICALLY behind the three men, Tessa at his side. After Tessa's bombshell, Sian had been called back inside the room and they'd moved down this hallway. Was Tessa's guess possible? Of course it was. And if the chemist had missed his family, then having a second one made sense. And if this was the means he had available and possibly the only means available to him, then it was quite doable. And likely a fascination he couldn't resist trying. The scientist in him wouldn't allow for anything less. The father in him, dying for the son he'd lost, wouldn't be able to resist either.

In a way, they should have contemplated such a thing

happening. But who had time? They'd been in reactionary mode. No one had time to mull over mad scientist experiments beyond those that they had been killing as quickly as possible. And now here was one that gave them a dilemma. Was a clone an ethical issue? Was Terry a vamp like the rest of them? Better? Enhanced? Pure? Did they kill him? Or save him?

Cody wanted to take him out before they found out the wrong way. But then, they should have done so at first meet.

Would he have memories? he asked Tessa quietly in his mind, still stuck on the concept.

Those that he was given. And those he lived since he gained awareness.

"Terry, what kind of courses were you taking in university?"

"Business. My father had hoped to give me an interest in chemistry, but that didn't happen so I went into business."

"Did you like seeing him work?" Tessa asked curiously.

"I don't remember," he said cheerfully. "It was a long time ago."

"Ah, so how do you know you didn't like chemistry. And what about accounting?"

"Just the thought of it is enough to make me want to puke. Father was terribly disappointed. It's the only time I've seen him almost cry." He laughed. "He never tried to teach me accounting. I'd probably suck at that too."

Cody exchanged a glance with Tessa.

See, she murmured.

Still a bit of a stretch, he responded. *One that makes sense, but I hope you're wrong.*

I could be, she said, *but it feels more right the longer I think about it. That fresh innocence. That blithe attitude to life.*

The pain and horror of what's happening. I think his father did what he could to build the type of son he wanted, but clones are only physical clones, not emotional or mental clones. Even with all the programming, it didn't mean he could make his son hate.

Do you think he really avoided brainwashing him though? He had it all available.

It could be there, but maybe not triggered and maybe it was never inputted. Lack of time maybe? Think about it. Up until recently, he had tons of time. Time for his son to grow, mature. Become the vamp he was intended to be like every father wishes for his son. Maybe he hoped his son would adopt his ideals naturally. Maybe the brainwashing is harmful and he didn't want to risk it.

*Then there is the logistics of a son suddenly appearing, Co-*dy said thoughtfully. *So Europe makes sense. In a lab over there. Away from this place. Maybe his father only came here to help out when things blew up.* Cody was liking that theory more and more.

And that way his son is out of everyone's sight. Tessa added. *He might not have even told anyone about losing his first family. This is the replacement. Brought to the right age by science and now filling in the blanks in the same way.*

So the question remains, does he have any information of value, Cody asked. *And can we trust it?* Cody turned to Terry. "Terry, where were you living in Europe?

Terry's smile was bright and sunny. "Germany, near the Swiss border. Love it there. Hope I can go back. We have lots of animals too." His lip trembled. "I'd like to go home."

"We?" Tessa asked. "Who did you live with?"

"My father and I when he could be there." He smiled mistily. "He was forever picking up strays for a few days or weeks then taking them to work when he found people who were willing to help."

"Did he ever do any experiments on animals?"

"Oh no!" Terry cried. "I wouldn't have allowed that."

"How long ago when he started bringing animals home?" Cody asked.

"Hmmm, not sure. A few months maybe? I really loved to see them, even for a few days. I kept two. Stole them away and told him they escaped." Terry's smile was bright and cheery as he shared his secret. "Father was really angry and doubled the security."

He shifted back slightly as Beast turned that massive head to stare at him. "My pets aren't dangerous. They are really cute, unlike…" And he broke off as if afraid Beast would react. He raised his gaze to Tessa and whispered, "Sorry."

Cody caught the quirk of Tessa's lips before she managed to turn away. And now he understood what she meant. It had been a long time since Cody had viewed the world with such innocence.

See, she said.

It's just so damn hard to believe.

They walked to Jameson's office. He stood up when they arrived. Then he shook Cody's hand and then hers and motioned to the chair behind him. "Terry, take a seat."

"Thank you," Terry said as he sat down.

"Jameson, maybe we could have a moment?"

With a raised eyebrow, he nodded, and assigning the guards to keep watch, he stepped outside and looked from one to the other. "What's the matter?"

Tessa took a deep breath. "We think Terry is a recently hatched clone."

RHIA SPUN TO see several more enhanced vampires smirking at them. They were getting bigger and uglier than ever. The scientist in her was fascinated. The mother in her was horrified. As a vamp, she was devastated. How could her race, so old and strong, be reduced to this? There was desperation in the enemy's actions to create such monsters. They were being given too many drugs too fast and with too strong a dosage to force their men to be as big as fast as possible. They weren't thinking of these men's lives or the long-term effects. They were slamming the chemicals into the vamps' bloodstream and shoving them into the line of fire. She understood. They were losing. They had to try everything.

But she was going to rip them apart and spit them out in little pieces – preferably in the form of ash.

With a sidelong glance at Ian, she realized that he was staring at Gemma, a hard twist to his lips.

"Do you really expect these guys to save you," he snapped. "We've taken out dozens just like them."

Gemma's face twisted in anger. "And my brother was one of them. He didn't want to be part of the army either," she said bitterly. "Do you think any of us did?"

"And what, we're supposed to lie down and die because you guys got roped into this? Well, so did we," Wendy snarled.

Rhia looked at her in surprise. She was obviously gaining strength again. Good. They needed her now.

And time to set this into motion. She twisted so her back was turned to the approaching men and checked on Jared, even now standing over her unconscious son. How could her fellow vamps consider humans just another dumb animal?

She was ashamed she had until her daughter showed her

differently.

Her gaze hardened as it fell on Seth. She didn't know what he'd done and how much of it he had done willingly, but she was going to do her best to save him. Even if that meant he was in treatment for a century or two. With their longevity, even that was preferable to death. The Council might want him killed for whatever his part in the blood farm had been, but first someone had to prove what he'd done, and then they had to prove that he'd done so willingly and being in his right mind – at the time.

She knew it was a possibility that she'd lost the child she'd known along the way.

The world was rife with parents who studied their children's actions and wondered how their child could have done something like they'd done. It was more prevalent in human society, but she understood the same phenomena. She'd been naïve these last many decades. Wallowing in the joys of motherhood, and now she was seeing the pain of those same children becoming adults and making decisions on their own that showed who they were really on the inside. She'd been delighted with the man David had grown up to be, horrified by Seth's actions and willing to do what she could to see what that inside man was really like, and then there was her daughter…

Tessa had become someone she didn't recognize.

She admired her. Could respect the growth she'd raced through, but was stunned at the speed she'd lost her little girl. And now she was bonded with Cody, something that she'd never thought she'd see. Tessa was young. Too young. And mostly because she was Rhia's. Other young women started much earlier. Her species was a sexual lot, and she'd hoped to spare Tessa much of the pain of the early broken loves.

Instead, she'd skipped all that and chosen Cody. And then again, maybe there'd not really been a choice. There was a sense of fate to their relationship. It was Rhia who was going to have to adjust when this was over. David had Jewel. Tessa had Cody. Even Ian and Wendy appeared to have a solid relationship.

They were all going to need time alone when this was over to see what each brought to the table when the table wasn't in the middle of a war.

She sighed and stared down at her gloved hands holding multiple spikes she'd taken off the medical staff. She could hear the heavy breathing as the vamps approached. Sensing Ian's gaze, she lifted her head and waited. Then he nodded at her.

She spun, spikes out, and dove forward.

GORAN AND SERUS perched high on the pillars, studying the room below, waiting for reinforcements.

"Do you think they have finally run out of men?" Serus asked.

Serus snorted. "I doubt it." He waved at the ash piles littering the hallway. "Look at this."

"There has been no one in the last few minutes." Goran shifted yet again. "Idiots. What are they waiting for?"

"Us."

Then Serus dropped to the floor and snuck up to the corner. He peered around it. "The hallway is empty. Unbelievable. There really were no more vamps ready to charge."

Goran dropped to the floor then sent texts to Sian and

the head of the Human Council telling them where to come.

They needed two armies now to help out their first one.

Idiots.

Still, when that was done and there was no way for other vamps to get in or out, they could move on.

Serus knew they were both needed elsewhere – not here doing babysitting duty.

He could use a good kickass fight right now. Ever since his daughter had gone missing, his life had been tossed in the air and nothing but anger and anguish was his world now. And how the hell did he find normal again?

His wife was tracking their son who'd somehow taken a wrong turn. His daughter was leading the pack into danger and hellacious events he'd spent his life trying to protect her from. His life had come to a very different place than he'd expected.

It's not that he was against where the pieces had landed, but he was hoping to find a level of comfort with his life as he saw it now. And to think it was just a short time from when he was teasing Tessa about her hair and boyfriends. Now it seemed so long ago.

And yet she was here and so far past that point now it was almost impossible to see the young girl in the woman she'd become. And from the looks of it, his best friend's youngest son could become his son-in-law.

Now didn't that beat all?

When they were younger, Goran and he had joked about it but hadn't ever expected such a thing to happen, and certainly not within the timeframe it had. Young people took centuries to find lasting relationships. Not weeks.

And how did the family go forward after this? Tessa hadn't been away from Cody in days…weeks.

They could hardly continue that way once they returned to normalcy. They both had to attend different schools. They should return to the dating stage of life. Still, that was their problem. He hoped that they walked into their future slower than they'd jumped into their relationship.

Goran slapped him on his back. "Forget about them. The kids are doing fine."

Serus laughed. "If that's the truth, it would surprise me." He twisted to look at his best friend. "Have you ever known those two not to be in trouble?"

"Nope. Keeps life interesting." Goran waved his hand in front of them. "More interesting than our lives at the moment. We've already mopped up, and now we're still sitting here waiting for the humans to show up."

"Isn't that the truth?"

Serus slowed his steps, still alone in the hallway, their voices and footsteps echoing hollowly in the large space. "Do you think they'll make it?"

Goran stopped. "Yes. And more than that, I think it's well past the point of us being able to do anything about it. They have gone beyond anything we have to say. They are more than a bonded pair. They are already one. They just haven't had time alone together to know it."

Serus sighed. "Gonna be hard to let go of her."

"Nope. Because you won't have to. The two of them are cementing the families. Making legal what we already knew and didn't need anyone to tell us – we were always brothers inside. Now this would make us brothers in fact."

Serus laughed and then froze as something whispered through his soul. He smiled, the strain around his heart easing.

Rhia?

CHAPTER 6

TESSA WALKED OUT into the Council Hall. The place was empty. Beast was at her side again. She didn't know where he'd gone for the few moments she'd spoken to Jameson.

He had a self-satisfied air to him. She studied his walk, his high energy. Then knew. "I hope it wasn't one of us."

He shot her a look as if he understood what she'd said. Then let that huge head lower as he walked forward.

"Should be one of the enemy – except they taste yucky. I guess you could use a few more granola bars, huh?"

Beast lifted his head and let out an odd sounding bark. "Come on, let's go to the kitchen. I know where they are kept."

She turned to find Cody following behind and racing to catch up. "Need to go to the kitchen and get granola bars for Beast."

"Why can't he eat like normal dogs?"

"You mean dog food?" she mocked. "I don't think so." She reached out a hand and stroked the huge furry back. "He's a beauty, isn't he?"

Cody laughed. "He is anything but."

"I know, but that's why he's adorable." In the huge kitchen, she walked to the cupboard and pulled out a box of granola bars. "Here we go." She filled her pockets and ripped one open for herself.

She spun around and stopped. Beast stood in front of her, waiting hopefully.

She held out one for him. Beast yipped in joy. She shook her head. "These aren't likely very good for you, but they have to be better than those horrible drugged bodies."

He inhaled the first one as she ate hers at a slower pace. She doled out a second one in smaller chunks, but he didn't appear sated. Then again, neither was she. She opened three more bars and fed two to Beast then ate one herself.

Turning, she found Cody leaning against the doorframe, a smile playing at the corner of his mouth.

"He's hungry," she explained sheepishly.

"I understand." He held up a blood slushie she hadn't seen originally. "I'm on my second too."

She winced. "Right. I should probably have one of those too."

"I'm glad to hear that," he said gently. "I was wondering how many granola bars we'd have to pack for a retreat."

She gave a lusty laugh. "Maybe I'll be hungry for something else."

His gaze smoldered. "We still have to keep our energy up," he murmured, stalking closer, that gaze holding her in place.

"We do," she whispered when he stood in front of her. "But being the innocent here, maybe my information is lacking. I might need to do a little research on the subject."

He lowered his head. "No problem." His warm breath bathed her face. "I'll be happy to be your research subject."

In a low voice, she said uncertainly, "You know so much more than I do."

"No," he whispered. "With you it will be all new and the

little bit I do know, I'll be more than happy to share."

And he swept her into his arms and kissed her.

The floodgates opened and passion rose inside and outside, wrapping them in a thermal blanket that threatened to burn the Council Hall to the ground.

When several chuckles finally penetrated the din of fireworks in her brain, Tessa pulled back to realize they had an audience. She pushed him back gently. "Obviously not the time or place."

"No, but it needs to be soon," he said in a gritty voice. "I need you now."

And keeping his back to the others, he walked out of the kitchen.

OUTSIDE, CODY TOOK several deep breaths, waiting for his body to calm down. Tessa was the only woman he'd met capable of shattering his control. He wanted her like he'd never wanted another woman. He couldn't imagine that ever changing. He had to find a way to get them some time alone. Time to consider their future. He was hardly in a position to support her as he was in school himself. Her family wasn't ready for Tessa to move out. And she was too young for such a big jump. No. They needed to start dating. Go through the motions in the correct order. He didn't want her to feel cheated or to feel like she missed out on something. The Friday gathering he'd invited her to had passed. Hell, he didn't know if anyone there was left around to attend. Once this was over, then maybe they could sort out their lives and meet up with their surviving friends again.

Tessa, well, she'd been at his side for days, weeks, and he wasn't looking forward to the upcoming separation. But as long as they both lived and they managed to get their friends and families out of this nightmare safely, then he would handle it all.

No matter what life threw at him.

And lately it had been throwing way too much at him. He straightened his shoulders and turned, preparing to go back inside the kitchen, when he saw Beast crouched down in the grass as if hiding but alert.

On the hunt.

He slowly turned, his gaze surveying the hill behind him, then the fields of grass around him. The moonlight shone bright, and his eyes easily picked up rocks and hollows as he studied the area that Beast was locked on. He wasn't growling though.

"What's the matter," Tessa asked, coming to stand beside him.

"Beast," he said by way of explanation.

He watched as she closed her eyes and searched in a different way. A way he couldn't. She opened her eyes and they glowed with fire.

"They are coming," she whispered. "This is the attack we've been waiting for."

She was already backing up as she spoke, her movements calm and relaxed for all the world, as if she was still having a nice conversation with him. But there was no doubt she was retreating. Would the enemy see it that way?

He ran to catch up to her and then bolted inside.

She gave a hard whistle.

Beast up and raced – forward.

"Shit, he's heading into the fight," she cried. "He'll get killed."

Cody wasn't sure that was a bad thing, but he owed

Beast already and that would be sad for this animal to come to such an end like this.

"We don't even know what we're up against," Cody snapped, trying to see through the window but still staying hidden.

"I do," she said, her voice soft, deadly. "It's the last of them. Everything they have left to fight with. And it's ugly out there."

Cody shifted to the far side and watched the wave of vamps race toward the Hall.

At the door was a huge bell. He started to ring it and ring it and ring it.

The entire hall needed to show up for this.

And where the hell were the rest of his group? He wished his father were here. They needed the ancients. He didn't dare think of where Ian and Wendy, not to mention where Jared and Rhia, were at. There'd been a vast silence for so long. Sian only managed to get messages through, even though they were only updates and not a full explanation.

If there ever was a time that they needed the troops to rally around, it was now.

David came racing into the kitchen. "Cody, what's up?"

Cody never said a word, he just pointed.

DAVID'S HEART STOPPED as he watched, frozen in place, the black wave moving toward him. "How are there so many?"

"I'd say they opened up the damn lab and let the rats out," Cody snapped, sprinting to the main hall. "There are too many. We have to get everyone downstairs to safety. We need to hide out while we get some kind of strategy in place here."

"I'm on it," David yelled, sending people scattering to spread the message.

He spun around, looking for others to urge faster.

And caught sight of his sister walking to the front door. "Tessa, what are you doing?"

Cody raced past him. "Tessa?"

She opened the double doors wide and stood in the center, Beast once again at her side.

"No," David roared. "There are too many."

She turned to look back at him. "Where are the gas canisters that Bart stole?"

David came to a stumbling stop, his mind racing. Then he saw how that could work. "I'll set it up. Make sure everyone up here is safe downstairs."

Cody ran to the control panel on the side. "I'll warn everyone. They need to be in the three lower floors." He hit the button for the announcement system and ordered everyone below.

David's last worry as he raced to the storage room was why was Tessa still standing in the doorway. She needed to run.

Then his mind was consumed with trying to set up the canisters. Timing was critical.

At least they were where he'd seen them last. The Council hadn't had a chance to examine them yet.

His fingers were thick and awkward with his panic. He snatched up the canister then ran to the boiler room and the air-conditioning system. He had to get these connected fast. At the risk of killing their own people, the others had to be moved down to the lower levels to avoid the gas. It would evaporate quickly, and he could help that along by pushing fresh air out there, but this was all he had to kill off the horde coming toward them.

It was also something he understood in theory – but had never actually tried out himself.

Then again, this nightmare had brought a lot of firsts into his life – and everyone else's too.

RHIA SAGGED TO the ground. Surely this was over?

Is it over? Serus asked in her head, that loving voice bringing tears to her eyes. *Are you done? Satisfied?*

I have our son. I've killed more of our people than I knew the clan had in its population. And every one of those deaths broke her heart.

This is not what she wanted out of life. She would have done anything to avoid this war, but they'd brought it to her doorstep and stole the heart and soul of her child, and she was not going to back down.

I've missed you. I need you back.

I missed you too, but I had to save him. Now we need help. There are rooms full of humans. I have Jared, Ian, Wendy…and Seth.

On our way.

Serus fell silent, but he was still in her head. And her heart. She'd walked such a difficult line this last week, and it wasn't over. She'd have to stand up in front of the Council and justify her actions. But she'd do it all over again if she had to.

Now she had to heal her relationship with her family. Going rogue hadn't hurt just her…

"Are you okay?" Wendy asked, her voice frail. "I can't believe we survived that onslaught."

Ian groaned. "Is this surviving? I feel like I've been skewered and someone pushed all the stuffing out of me."

"If you can talk like that, then you're fine," Jared said in a surprisingly strong voice.

Rhia glanced back at Jared. "I gather from that statement you're okay too?"

He held up two large spikes. "I like being armed."

At his feet was Gemma. Dead and half ash, the stench – like her – rotten to the core.

But the sweat rolled of his face, and she knew he'd come close to losing the freedom he'd fought so long for. "Good job, Jared." She struggled to her feet. "I am so ready to go home and rest."

"Ha," Ian jeered. "As if."

"No, she's right," Wendy said. "We have the people we came to find, more besides, and we've fought several rounds. I can't imagine that there are more here, but going home is the best idea. I'm worried about those at the Hall. I checked my phone, but messages are hit and miss."

Rhia nodded. "I'm worried too, but we can't leave these people unguarded, so we have to wait for Goran and the army."

"Is Goran here?"

Rhia smiled. "Yes, and so is Serus. I've told them where we are. He met up with Goran who brought the human army in, but they raced into a trap and are now unconscious. Goran has a working phone so they've called in backup."

"But they are both fine?" Wendy asked in delight. "That's awesome."

Rhia, stay there. We'll be there in ten. We're that close.

RHIA, TALK TO me. I'm coming, but there are multiple hallways

branching off. Goran keeps walking down endless hallways.

I'm here. Just follow my voice.

Now that the door is open, you mean.

It was always a courtesy as you know. You could open it any time.

I could. But that was a bridge we never crossed.

Until now, she whispered in his head. *Why did you now?*

I have alarms set with you. And knew you were in trouble. I couldn't hear what the trouble was until you'd calmed enough for me to talk to you and for you to hear me.

I'm happy you did. He could hear the heavy sigh in his head. *I do love you, Serus. I know my actions…*

Don't. Don't go there. With everything you've done, I've always known that you were doing it for the right reasons. He's our son. Not just yours. But he won't get a free pass out of this, and we can't be certain that he was coerced into it.

I know. Her voice was sad, broken. *But I have to give him that chance.*

And you — you won't get a free pass either, he warned.

No, and I don't care. Her voice took on a note of defiance. *Most of the Council have no offspring. They have no maternal or paternal instincts.*

And that doesn't work in your favor at this point.

It is what it is. I have Seth. Nothing else matters.

He understood, but at the same time, if she were exiled for her actions, it would impact the Council, the community, but especially her family. He wasn't willing to live without her, and the kids were too young to deal with the ostracization that would happen.

Maybe.

He knew she would worry about it later, but right now she was too tired and not thinking clearly. Then there were the drugs…

The drugs are out of my system. Never to return. I took only a little so that I could remember. Remember where the computers were. Where the database was. Where to go to find Seth. It was all for him. Always for him.

Let's hope it was all worth it, he warned. *They might kill him anyway.*

That's my job, she whispered. *As I'm responsible for bringing him into this world, then it's my job to take him out.*

A door loomed ahead. He nodded to Goran.

Ready for anything, they opened the door to find dozens, no, more – way more, of young humans all lying in beds and hooked up to machines.

"These kids were the seed group for the new blood farm," Rhia said, barely standing on her feet in front of the straggly looking group.

Ian and Wendy had their arms wrapped around each other, slightly behind Rhia.

Jared stood protectively over a vamp crumpled on the ground. Serus's heart raced. Rhia *had* done it.

She'd actually rescued their son.

CHAPTER 7

TESSA STOOD IN the open doorway, watching as the wave of vamps approached. They were minutes out. She knew everyone was scurrying to safety below. It was like a bad movie. She should be slamming the doors shut, but all she could think about was that there had to be a better way.

Sure, David had gone to get the gas and that was a great idea – if the gas gave a shit who got caught up in its spray.

No, there were rumblings in the back of her head that were not clear enough to understand. She thought it might be both Deanna and Hortran screaming at her to run. If she died – they died. And that wasn't what they wanted either.

Back inside, she shut down the double doors and raced up to the apartment at the top. Beast stayed with her. She'd lost Cody, who was helping to search the upstairs and make sure everyone was down safe below.

Everyone but her.

And why is that, Cody asked in her head. *Why is it that everyone is going below and you're going up.*

I can't help but think that if everyone is below and they blow up the building up, everyone dies.

What? He cried out in alarm. *We're deliberately sending them below to safety.*

Then someone, Sian maybe, needs to lead everyone through to the tunnels. In case the building does go down.

She could hear his thoughts spin.

Okay, I'll send everyone forward. If this is going in that direction, it is better to be safe. We do have a lot of injured here though that can't be moved.

I know she said softly. *And that's maybe what they are counting on.*

Motre is searching the various floors and sending everyone below. David has the gas hooked up, but he needs me here so you can tell me when they get into the building.

I can do that.

Are they close?

One hundred meters, less.

Give me the countdown as I'm now standing right beside him.

She watched, knowing the timing was everything. The ground was black as they ran toward the Hall.

Ten. Nine. Eight. Seven. Six. Five.

Several men started to scramble up the stairs, a feral look of hate on their faces. She lifted her gaze to the horizon.

Flyers!

Dozens of flyers.

What? Cody roared. *Damn it, Tessa, get out of there. It's not safe.*

I'm as safe as anyone at this moment, she said.

No, you're not. His voice roared through her head.

Three. Men started to pour into the Hall.

Two. She could see the back end of the black wave. They were almost all inside.

As the last tumbled through the double doors, she dropped down to the front entrance and shut the doors then screamed, *One!*

And she jumped to the windowsill on the first floor and

climbed her way up to where Beast waited for her. Did it work? She watched from the apartment deck, knowing the flyers were approaching. She had already chosen a hiding spot out on the deck, up between the rafters. She moved into position. She didn't know how fast the gas would take effect or if it was even the killing kind.

She hoped so.

Having to skewer all those men would be horrific and emotionally deadly.

But there were dozens of flyers landing around her now. So far, no one had seen her. Beast was inside the apartment and the doors were wide open.

They should see him as one of them.

He was, after all, their creation.

But not all creations were thankful for the master's handiwork. Beast wanted to rip their heads off – he was just waiting for the chance.

She'd happily give it to him, but on her terms. Not a wild bite fest.

Beast snarled.

The vamp closest to him snorted. "They made some really ugly specimens, didn't they?"

As if understanding, the tempo of Beast's snarl deepened. The vamp snorted and walked past. "Good thing they are on our side."

"Still, don't trust them," another flyer said. "They creep me out."

"Not to worry. The specimens die after a few days. They're a weapon with a short life term."

Tessa sucked back her breath. Beast was going to die? On his own? *No*, her mind screamed. *That wasn't fair.*

She'd come to love that dog…wolf…whatever it was.

He had heart. And he was different. She could relate to both of those. And she'd do her damnedest to save him. If possible.

But it would have to wait until they got through this mess. If they got through.

She took a deep breath and locked her arms, making them stronger to keep her in position above the men.

She slipped into her mind and powered up all that energy that she'd accessed before. She could sense Hortran's approval and Deanna's frustration.

They were both waiting for her to do something, but she knew she had to be in the right space mentally to make this natural and…easy.

She'd been running hot when she'd walked through the hallway and wiped out all the enemy. Then it had happened naturally. But right now she hadn't been fighting, wasn't on alert, and…was more tired than she remembered being in a long time.

Therein lay the problem.

Digging deep, she spread her energy outward, thin yet vibrant. She stretched far and wide, connecting to the ceiling, the walls. Where she connected physically, she blended on an energetic level. Then spread out more. Inside the wood, inside the metals, through the air to each of the men below. As she reached for them, she released a deep sigh and released her breath, then flicked each of the flyers in the heart.

One by one, they fell.

Like dominos.

"Whoa, Jake?" One man on the rooftop raced inside. "What's wrong?"

Tessa continued to stretch, to float through the air, intent on sprawling to the skies, feeling a weightlessness in her inner being. She was connected, to nature, to the inanimate objects, the animate objects. Beast lay down on the floor below her. She was careful to connect in a loving way. When he rolled over onto his back, she caressed his belly. His tongue lolled to the side. She pulled down and gave him a warm hug then carried on to the other side where a half dozen flyers were staring down over the rooftop, oblivious to the silent attack behind them. She swept out a long strand of energy and sent bolts into their hearts. One by one, silent and lethal, they dropped to the rooftop. Dead.

From her hiding position, she searched for signs of life. And found her rooftop empty.

She started to lower herself down when something stopped her. She froze, her senses tingling.

Cody was approaching.

Where are you? he asked.

Can you see me?

I can…I see something.

It's me. I'm here, there, and everywhere.

I see a rooftop littered with bodies. Are you hurt? he asked in a sharp voice.

No, she said softly. *I'm fine.*

He landed. She could feel his arrival like a ripple into her energy field as he was absorbed into them, one of her. Part of her. One with her. As always.

She slowly unhooked herself from the roof and stretched, feeling herself, soul, heart moving outward.

Calm. Controlled. Endless.

"Hey," Cody stood in front of her. "You sure you're okay?"

She gave him a sweet smile. "I feel great. Do you know

how everyone is down below?"

"I doubt anyone is left alive," he admitted. "I just hope our people are safe."

"They feel like they are. I can sense life way below us," she said in a low tone as she walked to the edge of the roof. She felt odd. Spacey. Not bad, but light. Connected to the universe around her. And it was so damn special.

"We need to go to the source of where they came from. Are you up for that?"

She closed her eyes and turned in the direction the wave of vampires had come from. The energy was thick and dark but very easy to track.

"Let's go," And she dropped over the roof to the ground several stories below.

"Wait," Cody roared. "You can't fly."

CODY FLEW OVER the edge to the vast space below, his heart hammering in shock. She'd just jumped over. For a glider, that was a crazy ass distance. For anyone else, it was suicide.

"Tessa?"

Her laughter floated toward him. He shook his head. His own knees were crying out at the landing she had coming up.

He flew lower, faster, intent on swooping down and grabbing her before she hit hard, only to find she was floating down gently. She landed softly then called up to Beast, "Jump."

And in shock, Cody watched as Beast jumped off the rooftop apartment with a complete lack of fear. Cody flew up, snagged him mid-fall, and lowered the massive animal to the ground.

"You didn't expect him to land softly, did you?" Cody asked, turning to study Tessa. She had a distant look in her eye. "Or did you learn to fly in a way that not even I can? And then have the dog fly with you."

"I don't know what I expected. I just know that it was all going to be fine. And it was." She smiled. "He might have landed okay, I might have saved him, but neither instance had a chance to happen as you stepped in and changed it."

She pointed to the land behind her. "We need to go over there. There are not many vamps left. And they are hoping this attack has wiped all of us out."

"But it didn't." Cody studied the horizon. "Let's open the doors first and let the gas filter out, then we'll fly over."

"Right." She walked up the front entranceway steps and tugged on the big double doors. Cody stepped up beside her, and together they managed to open them. Instantly, a pale greenish air filtered outward. Cody took one look inside, saw the number of vamps on the ground and some piles of smoldering ash, and jumped back.

"Looks like it did its job."

"Good," she smiled. "Then let's tell the others and leave."

Cody was already calling David. After he told him the good news, he left them with a warning. "We can't be sure they are all dead, so a crew needs to go and make sure, but use masks to protect yourself. We've opened the front door and are now heading to the origin of that army."

"Wait for me," David said. "There are several of us wanting to go."

Cody looked at Tessa, already walking in a circle, arms out, face to the sky. Still, they didn't know what they'd find and could use the help. Tessa, as if hearing his thoughts, sent him a look that made him realize how stupid the thoughts were. "I think Tessa is likely to say that you need to find a way to defeat the Councilmen. We'll bring back those we can, but we're still going to be short in terms of numbers. We need to find out if any of the others are alive still. And if they are – where are they?"

"Right. Stay in touch then."

After he put his phone away, he turned back to Tessa to find her standing with Beast in her arms.

He studied the two of them. "Really? I have to carry both of you?"

She grinned. "I can't leave him behind."

He snorted. "Hell, you can hardly lift him. I can't even see most of your face."

"But he's happy," she said with a laugh. "And that's important too."

Cody shook his head. "Not sure this is going to work."

"It will work," she said in an encouraging tone. "If it doesn't, then I'll have to glide with him beside me."

"Like hell." He scooped her up and the dog, surprised that the dog, although huge and likely to weigh a ton, didn't appear to be as heavy as he looked.

"Where I go, he goes."

Already in the air and his wings pulling strong, Cody contemplated that statement for a long moment. "And does that mean whatever getaway I decide on, I need to plan on bringing Beast along? Because that is going to totally impact the decision as to where we go," he grumbled.

She reached up and kissed his chin and gave a light laugh. "You'll figure it out." She wrapped her free arm around his neck and dropped tiny kisses on it. "Make it a great retreat, okay?"

He gave a happy sigh and nodded. "Will do."

IAN SQUATTED BESIDE Seth. "Do you think he'll be okay?" he asked Wendy in low tones.

She shrugged. "I don't know how he could be," she muttered back, keeping an eye on Rhia pacing ten feet away as they waited for the army to arrive. "He's been drugged many times."

"And some that he might have been willing to take."

Their gazes met. Jared crunched down beside them. "He acted normal when he drove me up to the blood farm but honestly, I don't know what that means for you guys. He didn't act like a psycho vamp."

"Right, but he might not have had much in the way of drugs at that point."

"No," Ian shook his head. "He'd have had quite a few, I imagine."

They frowned and stared at the comatose young man.

"He looks so normal," Wendy said.

"That's because he is normal," Rhia snapped, looming over them. "He doesn't just look it, he is."

The others looked at each other then dropped their gazes.

"You don't believe me?"

Ian stood up tall and faced her. "We saw him in action with Tessa. The things he said, did." He shook his head. "I want to believe that he's on our side, but I just can't see it."

Her gaze narrowed then slipped from one to the other. "Then why help me save him?"

"Because we're hoping there's a way to reverse the drugs and see who he was at the beginning of this," Ian said. "We don't want to see any more vamps die."

A shuddering sigh escaped her chest. "I might not be able to save him," she admitted. "From the drugs or from the Council, but I have to try." Her gaze swept over the trio. "You understand, don't you?" she pleaded.

When silence was her response, her gaze hardened. "Ian, are you really telling me that if that was Wendy on the ground that you wouldn't do everything you could to save her?"

Ian turned to look at Wendy. Then his shoulders slumped. "Absolutely I would."

Wendy gave him a misty smile. "And I would for you, too."

"See," Rhia cried. "It's not difficult. It's called love and trust. If my son is in there, under all that garbage they did to him, then I know he's trusting me to get him out and into the clear. And I'll do it if it's at all possible. If he isn't and he really was so lost as to want to join the ranks of those animals, then it's a hard thing for me to do, but I will dole out the punishment myself."

"No one is going to let you kill him," Wendy cried. "That's your son. That would be horrible."

"If he can't look me in the eye, hell, if he can't look Tessa in the eye and tell her that he's not a part of this and pass her tests, then he can't be trusted. The only choices are to lock him up for centuries – a punishment that I wouldn't want for myself or for him – or to be put to death." Sadness crept into her voice even though she tried hard not to let it. "And that would be very difficult."

"It would have been better if he'd died during the fighting," Serus said. "He's my son too, but if he's part of this abomination, then you know what needs to happen."

SERUS STUDIED THE small group collected around his son. They were still waiting for the army to arrive. His boy looked normal but as much as he loved that kid, he wasn't going to let his paternal feelings blind him to the possibility that he was guilty of the very same things as the other vamps in charge of the blood farm. And that would not have a good end. If his son was involved, then better that he died like Goran's boy had. At least he'd been fighting for his cause. On the wrong side to them, but at least he'd been passionate about it. Believed in it.

As he studied Seth's lax features, he wondered what was going on in his son's mind. Because like Ian, he'd seen Seth act like a very different person that he knew him to be. In reality, they needed the boy awake and Tessa on hand to hear him tell his story. It was sad times when he couldn't trust the words coming out of his own son's mouth.

But inside, he understood that that time was past.

"Easy, Serus. The boy might be innocent," Goran said in low tones.

"You might be able to believe that. *I hope that*," Serus corrected. "But I have my doubts. We saw him in the mine, remember?"

Goran was silent as they approached the group. "I remember," he said quietly. "But if there'd been any chance to save my son, I'd have done it in a heartbeat."

"Exactly. But the longer this goes on, the worse it will be. Better we wake him up now and get Tessa over here. See what the truth is where we'll deal with it privately."

Goran sighed. "Hard but just. I wouldn't want to be part of the nasty Council tribunal either."

"Even worse, we've missed so many of the Council

members that according to Sian, they are setting up a monkey court as it is."

"Something we need to get back for. And fast," Serus acknowledged. "And we need as many Councilmen back to the meeting as possible."

"Right. So Rhia needs to come back with us."

"And any others we can find. But chances are good the ones at the Council Hall are the only ones left alive."

"Unless some are in hibernation or on holidays."

"Sian is tracking those down."

Rhia walked closer. "What's the matter with the Council?"

Serus quickly explained.

"But that's terrible. If those horrible old men get back into power, then all we've done has been for nothing." She turned frantic in front of them, her gaze going from Serus to Goran. "It can't be allowed to happen."

"And we're doing what we can to find the other Councilmen," Goran reassured her. "Sian is working on it."

"There are a lot, and she needs help," Rhia cried. She spun around to look at the crowd of young people behind them. "We have to get back."

"She does need more help. She's needed you," Goran snapped. "And it's likely too late now."

Rhia shook her head. "No, see, I had to do this. There was no other way. Sian will understand."

"Maybe, but there's no time for that now." Serus reached out to grab her hand. "We all have to go back now. To hell with waiting for the army."

"All of us, yes, but I'm not leaving the kids behind."

"We aren't planning to leave anyone behind." Serus motioned at the group behind her to walk forward. "I'll grab

Seth."

"We can't leave the humans here unprotected," Jared said. "They've got to be saved. Many of the kids here are from my high school – Tessa's high school."

Serus froze, thinking about it. "No, we can't leave them," he agreed softly. "I'm not sure how long it will take them to make their way here. The Human Council is sending in teams for the army that is now sleeping off a heavy dose of drugs not far from here."

"Are they sending enough for these rooms full of teenagers?" Jared cried. "I can't go if they aren't safe."

"We'll make sure," Serus promised. "These kids need to be treated by medical professionals. We can't just wake them all up. It will take too much time."

Jared looked around nervously. Serus understood. He was surrounded by vamps, the species that had put all his friends into this situation. "Did you find the one you were searching for, Jared?"

❧ ❦

"No," Jared whispered. "We haven't." he hesitated. "But we didn't check everywhere."

Goran spun around. "There are more rooms. Have you checked every one?"

Jared nodded. "She's not in this area." He walked to the doorway, his heart heavy. "I want to keep checking down this hallway, but Rhia wanted all of us to stay together."

"And she was right," Goran said. "Let me walk down a little ways with you. If there are more rooms, we'll check them out, if there aren't, then we'll be back in a few minutes."

Jared brightened. "Thank you sir, I appreciate that."

Goran groaned. "On one condition. Don't call me that."

With a big grin, Jared slipped around behind the big vamps and darted into the hallway. If he didn't know these two ancients, he'd have been terrified. He was still nervous about getting too close. They were so incredibly strong and capable. Fierce would be a perfect description.

Outside in the hallway, he turned around to reorient himself. Then pointed. "We need to go this way."

Knowing time was tight and that the ancient would have no trouble keeping up, he ran down to the far corner. He'd already made it this far but hadn't had a chance to explore more. At the corner, he took a look down the hallway. There were two doors. He went to the first. It appeared to be a supply room that was more empty than full. That went along with what everyone was saying. The bad guys were running out of supplies – and men.

Not fast enough though.

He turned to the room across, and seeing Goran almost at his side, he pushed the door open.

CHAPTER 8

CODY FLEW LOW across the fields carrying Tessa and Beast. She closed her eyes and enjoyed the moment. It was such a pleasure to fly like this even in these circumstances. In Cody's arms, even with Beast. Poor Cody. He was soaking up the weight of both of them.

She studied the ground ahead of them, but there wasn't much to see. The energy had blended into a large foggy mass. Too many different people. Too many different energies. Too many different actions. And the wisps of drugs that had been visible in each person were completely overwhelmed.

"It's chaos down there," she murmured.

"That's to be expected. A lot of people moved through here."

"I know." She studied the terrain. "Let's land over there." She pointed to a spot above the rise. "If we can look down, we might be able to see better."

"I'll fly lower so we can scan the hillside looking for an entrance first."

"It's such a different view from up here."

"I love it," he said. "I'd do this all day."

"Understandable." She loved the wind in her face, the fresh air in her lungs, and the weightlessness of the flight. To have her body off the ground, to feel that sense of freedom.

It was so damn special.

He flew lower until they were hovering in front of the hill. The hills hummed with energy. It was seriously fascinating. She'd never been able to see any of this from such a view. So much color. So many energies.

"There is the entrance," Cody said. "At the bottom of the hill, there's a large cavern opening."

"Let's go down." She was eager to go inside. She wanted to find the end to this. Looking back at the distance they'd travelled already, she realized that they were likely over the top of the tunnels. If the wave of men had travelled above ground, did that mean that they didn't know about the tunnels or that they'd sent a second wave of people through the tunnel at the same time?

They'd sent David and all the other vamps down into the lower floors and through the tunnels. Something to consider as they entered. If they were on the lookout for attacks, they needed to be watching from several directions. She took a few steps and lowered Beast to the ground. He swiped the side of her face with his wet tongue.

"Ugh, that's enough of that." She backed up and wiped her wet face off. Cody was laughing behind her. She didn't mind the licking so much until she considered what he'd been chewing on lately. Now that was gross.

Trying not to think about exactly that, she walked to the edge of the cavern and studied the darkness inside. Energy flowed in a steady stream. But it was dark, sickly-looking energy. Not the wholesome energy she was hoping for. It meant that whatever was left inside was injected full of drugs. She'd known that would be the case, but the overwhelming cloying smell just added to the evidence. She couldn't see anything but death anywhere.

Her mind centered on the job ahead and with Cody at her side, she entered the darkness.

There was complete absence of light, and with the musty, drug-filled air, she couldn't see anything. She could hear though and it appeared to be more growls and howls than voices. In fact, she didn't think she heard any voices, human or vamp.

"Easy, Tessa, watch out for Beast."

She nodded. When Cody reached out to tug her to a standstill, she stopped and waited. Slowly, her vamp eyesight dominated and sharpened to a clarity that allowed the striations on the cave walls to show up. But the place was empty. Except for the herd of animals that had all been something else and were now…something else again. And in the middle of the pack were ashes…lots and lots of ashes.

"Looks like someone had an argument and lost in here," Cody commented softly.

"Did the animals take the vamps out?" She stared at the evidence before her in shock.

"Science experiments don't always go the way we think they should."

"That is a lot of ash," she said in a noncommittal voice. She didn't want to hurt any animal, but it didn't look like the feeling was mutual. She closed her eyes and drew on the power she'd learned through Hortran. There was no point in making another fight out of this or someone was going to get bitten, or at least scratched. As she understood from the other animals, they had silver to help with their killing spree.

Not good.

Neither did she want Beast injured.

So she had one shot.

She took a deep breath, opened up her arms, and walked

casually through the pack.

The howls grew to enormous proportions then cut off like a knife. She dared not look back. There were dozens more sitting ahead and waiting for her.

Cody walked slightly behind her to the left while Beast walked slightly behind her to the right. And in a steady stream, they carried on deeper into the tunnel, her energy cutting a wide swath through the animals, dropping them where they stood. Sorrow ripped through her. These animals at one time had been glorious in their natural form. She'd have been okay with their new forms even – after all, look at Beast. Only these animals had been turned into killers, and they were in pain. The drugs running through their bloodstream were tearing at their genetics and at the very soul of who they were.

A slow painful death that hurt her to see.

Clouds of darkness weighed in on them. They didn't ask for this. They didn't want this. What animal wanted to be tortured from the inside out? None.

She kept walking.

The animals didn't have time to react as the wave of deadly energy sliced through their systems and put them out of their misery quietly and easily. When she reached the end of the tunnel, her footsteps slowed until she came to a stop. She turned to look behind her. The tunnel was clear of the animal experiments and was now heaped with carcasses.

The stench of death filled her nostrils and clogged her brain. Tears came to her eyes. "Please tell me that was the right thing to do," she whispered, the enormity, the sheer number of animals she'd just killed hurting her.

"It's what needed to be done. They weren't going to live long, and their lives were painful. Then there's the added fact that they were trying to kill us," Cody added on a humorous note. "So all in all, I'd say you did the right thing."

He slid an arm around her shoulders and turned her so she now faced the darkness ahead and not the destruction behind. "Let's keep moving."

She let him lead her forward. When Beast nudged her fingers, she stooped and gave him a big hug. "I'm sorry you had to see that, Beast. I don't think any of those animals could be saved like you. I would have if I could have."

He licked her face, maybe in reassurance. And maybe not. She no longer knew anything except she wanted to make sure no one could ever do this to all those poor animals again.

⚬

CODY NOTED TESSA'S hand on Beast's back and realized he really *was* going to have to make some adjustments to his planned getaway. Beast looked to be coming with them. He was okay with that, maybe. But given what Tessa had just gone through, he knew she'd be extremely upset to think Beast was going to suffer if she went away and left him behind.

Especially after what she'd just done.

He squeezed her close and dropped a kiss on her temple. She leaned into him for a long moment as they slowly walked, then he could see her mentally pick up and gird herself for what was to come.

"Let's get this over with. My parents are in here some-where."

He winced. "Goran will be here, too."

"Let's go find them."

They searched the tunnels for the next half hour, using

Tessa's ability to see different energies. But there was still no sign of any energy she recognized. And no sign of the enemy. Wouldn't it be nice if they'd wiped them out?

He didn't think they'd be that lucky.

Suddenly Tessa raced ahead then came to a shuddering stop. "I can sense them," she cried.

"Sense?" he asked cautiously. "Not see?"

She looked confused for a moment as if just understanding her wording, then shrugged and said, "Sense. Not sure how or who, but I can feel my parents." She smiled. "They are close by."

"Good. Let's hope the whole lot of them are in one group so we don't have to go tearing through the damn place to find them."

"No tearing required," she said in a teasing voice. "We just need to find the way to them." She spun in a slow circle. "It's like they are on the other side of this wall."

"So we need to find a door?" he asked, studying the wall. "More hidden doors."

She looked intrigued at that reminder. "It's all stone, so maybe hidden passageways, but I'm thinking another hallway runs parallel beside us."

"Then let's find it."

❧ ❦

GORAN WATCHED JARED go into and out of the first room, then cross to check out the second door. He stood in the doorway, disheartened, then turned to look back at Goran. "Thanks for coming, but she doesn't appear to be here."

"Let's keep looking," Goran said. "You did well finding all the other humans."

"Not well enough," he said in frustration. "I feel like

we're still missing something."

"What and where?" When Jared looked at him in surprise, Goran laughed. "Just because I'm a vamp doesn't mean I can't listen to what you have to say."

Jared's gaze widened. "Good to know." He hesitated a moment then said, "Back where we found Seth, we went in through large double doors. Not very far from here, but there were double doors on the other side of the room – we didn't check it out, and I can't forget about those doors." He waved his arm behind him, "This just seems to lead out to nothing, so I'd really like to check that operating room out."

Serus stepped up behind Goran. "That's a very good idea." He smacked Goran on the shoulder. "We need to head back that direction anyway as we need to find and bring the army here."

"We shouldn't leave this group unprotected though," Goran said. "I can take Jared and check out this set of doors he's talking about, find the army, and bring them back here all on the same trip. Then maybe we can get our asses back to the Hall before they vote us off the Council."

"Can they do that?" Ian asked, worried. "What about those of us rising up the ranks? I know we're only apprentices but still, if you are voted off, does that mean the apprentices are too?"

Serus's face darkened. "Yes, it does. We have to stop this or you and David and Cody will likely be removed as well, and they'll really have the power to put whoever they want into place."

Goran growled. "They'd love that. They'd be riding high once again. Well, it isn't going to happen," he roared. "Jared, let's move it."

And he grabbed Jared by the back of his jacket and flew

up into the air and down the hallway.

Jared squawked in surprise then laughed as they hit the end in seconds, not minutes. "Cool."

"SIAN, WHAT ARE you looking for?" David stood in Sian's office. They both wore gas masks to protect themselves as they'd returned to the top floor to make sure it was safe for everyone else.

"Deanna left a lot of paperwork behind when she went into hibernation," Sian said. "So did Hortran for that matter. But recently I remember seeing her here and wondered if she'd changed something."

"Change what?"

"As a Council member, she's entitled to suggest her replacement. Although it is technically a suggestion, we always honor it if possible and as long as the replacement is a suitable candidate."

"You're thinking she might have, and that would give the Council a new member?"

"Ratifications only require four members. I think we could pull that off. That would give us one more for the Council then. But I have to find the paperwork." Her voice tapered off as she opened up the big wall cupboard and saw the stacks and stacks of files ahead of her. Some on such old paper it appeared to be written on old animal hides.

David stared, open-mouthed. "I had no idea all this existed," he whispered. "This is seriously cool."

"And it's a serious headache," she muttered. "This is so very valuable, but we're overrun with important documents. I've been asking for a better system, but so far the Council has denied that request."

Jewel walked into the small room. She took one look, and a look of complete rapture washed over her face. "Oh my! Can I help? This is beautiful. I just want to read them all."

"And how do you feel about organizing this mess," Sian snapped. "Because good Lord, it needs to be done. And I need to put my hands on the right documents now."

"Yes," Jewel squealed. "I love this stuff. I'd have been a historian or an archivist if I could."

"Well, we don't have one and someone is needed to take this over. If you're serious, we'll discuss it when this nightmare comes to an end. In the meantime, all of you give me a hand looking for documents that Deanna left behind. It's mandatory when a Councilman retires to leave a writ regarding their position."

The group immediately surged forward. "Any idea what the material would look like so that we can rule out some of these?"

"It's Deanna, and she has little patience with anything modern, but I doubt she'd go so far as to use hide." Sian tilted her head. "Then again, all her original documents were written on those, so not sure."

"Is there any other places the documents could be?" David asked. "You have filing cabinets all around the room."

"And we have another storeroom full, but these are all the recently modified documents that haven't been filed yet."

She gave a heavy sigh, her hands rubbing her rounded tummy. "There doesn't seem to be enough time in a day to do everything. And of course it's been weeks since I even tried."

"I'll start here," Jewel said, reaching up to the top of the shelf. "It looks like there are some possibles in this lot."

"Ha, this whole cupboard is possible," Sian said in a dark voice, "But we need to get at it, so pick a stack and take a look. You're looking for anything that Deanna and Hortran could have written."

"Will do." Jewel reached for the largest stack and took them to the closest table. "If we all get at it, we should sort through this cupboard fast enough."

David grabbed the highest stack and dropped it to the floor, then kneeled beside the pile and started going through the documents. He couldn't believe the names and types of documents he was looking at. "Wills, property transfers, decrees, there's a little bit of everything."

"Yes, but there's no time to decipher most of it. Normally I'd have a pile half this size."

"We'll worry about all the work later, Sian," Jewel muttered from behind her stack. "I'll help."

"And I'll hold you to that."

"So this looks like something possible," Jewel said, holding up an ancient papyrus type of paper. "It's old, and I think I can read her name on the bottom of this decree, but the language isn't something I know."

Sian walked over and lifted the manuscript to see it under better lighting. "It's something… I'm just not sure. Give me a moment to read some of this."

David studied the documents in front of him. This was a vast treasure trove of his heritage. It needed to be preserved. He felt something deep inside stir. Maybe it was pride, a sense of connectedness. He didn't know what it was but he felt…part of something so much bigger. During this war, he'd been fighting to save Jared, then the other humans, then his friends, but he hadn't realized how deeply he felt about his own heritage. His own species. As he sat there, his resolve firmed.

This war needed to end so that their way could continue. They had evolved. They were no longer animals taking what they wanted. They were at the top of the food chain, but that didn't meant they had to destroy all beneath them. The skill to being good rulers was to value and honor those they stood above. Not destroy them.

What good was it to be at the top of the species if there was nothing of value below?

"It's one of the documents we need," Sian said with a catch in her voice. "It's Hortran's decree. Deanna signed as a witness."

"So what else are we looking for then?"

"Now we need Deanna's decree."

"And yet you appear to be very surprised by whatever you are reading?" David asked.

"I am," she whispered. "But in a good way. This is huge, but I can't share it right now. This must go to the Council."

With more energy than she'd shown since he'd arrived, she added, "Now let's find the other document. I must have Deanna's before the Council calls an early meeting."

"They can't call one. They know the ancients are in the field and on their way home."

"Yes, they can, and that's exactly why they'd do it."

"We have to stop them."

"Then keep digging."

SERUS STUDIED HIS wife, his soul mate — the other half of his heart. She looked exhausted. And from what he'd heard on the quiet from Ian, she had good reason to be. She'd been running both sides for days and fighting off the drugs.

"Have you eaten?"

She nodded. "A little."

Ian snorted. "Meaning no." He walked to the far side and rummaged in the big coolers. Serus watched him, appreciating the privacy. It was the first he'd had with Rhia in a long time.

"Have you heard from David," Rhia asked. "Tessa?"

Serus nodded. "Both were fine last I heard from them. David is staying at the Hall, helping Sian keep Jewel close. And Tessa," he laughed, "well, she's someone that I barely recognized. She saved my life, you know."

Rhia gasped in shock. "What?"

"Yeah, I wouldn't be here if it wasn't for her. Not only that, I was stabbed with silver..."

The color faded from Rhia's skin as she grabbed for Serus. "Silver," she whispered, her voice so faint it was almost impossible to hear her. "How is that possible?"

"I don't know," he admitted, "But she grabbed the spike from my side and poured her healing energy inside. And it worked. I was sick for a little bit, but not that long."

Her eyes were huge. "What has happened to our little girl?"

He studied her, realizing how much she'd missed in the last few weeks. On her own pathway, still aligned with the vampire values he honored but chasing to save their son, she'd missed so much of their daughter's magnificent growth. But he hadn't. And he was so damn glad.

"I'm not sure I'd believe it if I hadn't been there myself," he said. "But it's true. She can do so much."

"Yes, but why? How? Is it that Deanna bitch?"

"No, she was doing so much before that already."

Rhia shook her head. "It makes no sense."

"She apparently has a pet now as well," he said with a smile. "Although I haven't seen it."

"That's not good." Rhia shook her head. "She didn't ask."

"You weren't here to ask," Serus pointed out. "And from what I heard, it seems to be that the animal chose *her*."

Rhia stepped back. "We'll discuss this when we get home."

Serus agreed, but he didn't think the homecoming was going to be quite what she had in mind. "You need to get real about Tessa right now."

She spun, that laser gaze on his face. She'd always been quick to pick up on the nuances. "What do I need to get real about?"

"She's not a little girl anymore. She's a leader, the people respect her. They look to her for answers. They follow her. Not because of you or me, but because of who she has become."

"That's good. That's great," Rhia said in delight. "I could see some of it happening. That she could see energy and move energy, help people who are injured..." She reached up and stroked his cheek. "That's wonderful that our little girl has finally come into herself."

"She can do so much more than that now." Serus didn't know how much he should say. He was feeling protective of Tessa and knew that mother and daughter had a cavern between them at the moment. Tessa was not the Tessa Rhia knew, and this new one was a strong, independent woman all her own. But she was young. And leaving home right now wasn't an option, but living at home might not be either. His breath gusted out. Maybe he and Goran should take a holiday and leave the women to work it out.

He kinda liked that idea.

"And you're warning me to give her room?" Rhia asked. "Is that it?"

"Yes, and so much more. She's a woman now. There's no way you're going to be able to fit her back into the little girl mold. While you were out looking for Seth, she grew even more. And you missed many of those steps."

"You're really worried about this, aren't you?"

"Yes," he admitted. "I am."

"Noted." She seemed to pull herself back slightly. "But she's still my daughter."

"And is now more confident and in control than either of your sisters."

She frowned. "That's not necessarily a bad thing."

"No, it's a good thing. I'm really proud of her. But when you see her again, you need to treat her as an adult, a woman."

"Agreed."

She might be hearing the words, but somehow Serus didn't think she was getting the message.

CHAPTER 9

TESSA STUDIED THE stone wall in front of her. She'd seen too many tricks lately to be sure that the wall was rock. The ancient builders seemed to have known exactly what they wanted to do and when to do it because this was a maze that now centuries later was very hard to decipher. She'd love to have blueprints of the tunnels underneath, but she doubted any existed.

Although if they managed to finally get through all of the blood farms and locate the last of the offices and documentation, anything was possible. She knew Ian and David would have a grand time making sure that they found every last look and cranny in the tunnels. Teams could go through all of the farms and make sure they hadn't missed anything and map the tunnels at the same time. The last thing she wanted to do was to leave anyone hanging or hooked up to the drugs. It would be too easy to shut the process down and accidentally kill a dozen or two humans or vamps because they hadn't been rescued in time.

"Cody, I think something's over here." She took long steps that launched her several dozen yards down the hallway and came to a stop where the rock wall was a slightly different color. Cody landed beside her. "What do you think it is?"

"I'm not sure." She shrugged. "But it's different from

everything else along here."

"Energy?"

She walked back a few steps to get a better perspective of the wall. "No energy in the last many days or weeks," she said. "But definitely old energy hanging around."

"How old?"

She walked back and forth in front of the wall a couple of times, trying to understand what it was that she was actually seeing. "I know it sounds silly, but there's like very old energy inside the very dark energy, but none recent." She shrugged. "That again, it's always new when it's different. I have to interpret what I see, and I could very well be wrong. The black energy confuses the issue."

"Drug energy?"

Tessa looked at Cody in surprise. "Maybe?" She turned her gaze back towards the wall. "But it's a different black."

At Cody's silence, she spun and gave him a quirky grin. "I know, right? How many kinds of black can there be?"

"So maybe the question here is in what way is it different?" Cody asked.

"Good question." Tessa walked closer to the wall, her hand out as if she could feel something different. It sounded silly to her ears, but it was a natural movement on her part and she'd learned to go with it. At the wall, she pressed her fingertips against the stone then jerked back in surprise.

"What's wrong?" Cody asked stepping up beside her.

"It's warm," she cried. "Like it's really warm." She walked over to the wall on the side and gently stroked the stone. "It's much colder here."

Cody laid his hand on both walls at the same time, straddling the dividing line. "It is indeed. Now why is that?"

She watched as he backed up and tried to take another

look. "Different color, different temperature." He looked at her. "But still no doorway?"

"Not that I can see," she said tentatively. "But I'm hesitant to open a door made of stone with something behind it so hot it's heating the stone to such a different temperature."

Cody nodded. "No drugs would affect the temperature of the rock, so there has to be a heat source behind it. Are we close maybe to the boiler room?"

Tessa walked down the hallway several steps. "If that's the case, then there should be an access door down here somewhere."

Searching for any possible openings or a new kind of entrance that they had yet to come upon, the two walked several meters farther to find another tunnel opened up beside them. Excited, the two raced ahead and came to a large double door.

Cody placed his hand on Tessa's shoulder in warning. "This is a similar entrance to the boiler room we've already been to."

"Yes," Tessa said. "But is it the same boiler room? You'd think with the several blood farms, one mechanical room wouldn't be sufficient to handle the infrastructure required to move the blood."

"True, but remember, there were guards before so there could easily be more here too."

Tessa gave him a feral grin. "Good. Let's go. I will be happy when we've purged this place of every last asshole available."

CODY AGREED. "DON'T forget we have to get back to the Council meeting with as many Councilmen we can find."

She nodded and pulled open the double doors. "Wow."

The two stared at the vast network of pipes and fluting in front of them.

Tessa said, "I never thought I'd wish to have Bart back beside me again."

"But he is the one that could help explain this to us."

"Then again, there should be several other vamps that can as well." She walked inside and slipped to the right.

Cody stayed close. They'd been attacked and tricked before. They had to be vigilant and make sure that they survived. Too many people thought the war was over and they would relax their guard. That mistake was one he was *not* going to make.

He reached out and tugged Tessa deeper into the shadows. They waited, but there wasn't a sound. If anyone was in here, they could be hiding. "Can you see any energy?"

Tessa shook her head. "Not yet."

"Let's keep to the back wall and do a circle to see if anyone is in here." He stepped into the front and she followed his lead, Beast as always silent behind them. Cody could almost forget Beast was around. Until he sensed the enemy, then Beast would start growling. In a way, he was a better early warning system than anything they had found yet.

From behind him, Tessa said in a low voice, "The place is deserted. I can't sense any activity in recent weeks."

"That doesn't mean that there isn't someone hiding." He looked around. "I imagine a place like this runs itself to a certain extent, but regular maintenance will be required. The machinery will require oil and cleaning."

"And yet with the enemy numbers down, who knows if anyone is around or is left that can handle this type of maintenance. With Bart gone, who else is there to step up?"

Tessa kept her head turned from side to side as she searched the large room.

"Bart didn't work alone. The blood farms required several teams of maintenance men. We didn't target that workgroup, so I imagine there are still many available." Cody stopped and looked around at the massive pipes. "It's hard to imagine that they could have set this all up in the first place. We'll be days…no, weeks, if not months, sorting this out."

He glanced at her. "Still no sign of another entrance or energy that might say there was something hidden?"

She shook her head. "Not yet."

As they walked around to the front again without having seen anyone, Tessa added, "It's like a ghost town in these mines now."

They walked back out into the hallway. Cody looked at her. "We still have no way to get back over to the other side where our friends and family are."

She pointed down the hallway. "Down there. I can sense them."

"Let's go." As they approached the area where Tessa had pointed, they could hear noises on the far side. A single closed door, the only one in the entire hallway, showed up as they turned the corner. With a quick glance at Tessa, Cody reached for the doorknob and pushed the door open.

"It leads to another set of hallways." Cody shook his head. "That's why we could hear them and not see them. This was the connecting door that led through the wall to the two parallel hallways."

Tessa stepped up beside him. "Perfect."

She went to move past him, but Cody held out his hand. "Wait."

She cocked her head to one side and looked at him but

stayed silent.

He loved that about her. No matter how much she grew and learned and developed, she was always willing to listen to him.

When he was sure it was safe and there was nobody lying in wait for them, he opened the door wide enough to let her and Beast through then carefully closed the door behind them.

Another hallway waited for them.

Tessa gave a delighted cry, "I can see the energy of both ancients and," her voice dropped to a whisper. "My brother, Ian, Wendy…and yes, Jared."

At the end, her voice rose again in joy.

Cody frowned. *Jared again.*

Tessa turned with a big smile on her face and asked, "Really?"

His frown deepened, but inside he wanted to squirm like a child. "No, of course not."

But she wasn't fooled. She reached up and kissed his cheek. "Jared is a friend, nothing more."

He gave a sheepish shrug. "I know that."

She dashed ahead, Beast at her heels, toward the energy that she could see.

He walked a little farther behind. Just because the family was here doesn't mean the enemy wasn't as well.

WENDY TRIED TO get along. It was part of who she was. But she wasn't sure she'd ever trust Seth. Not that she knew the man. But now she knew too much about him. She sided with Ian on that matter.

She wished Seth had died in the war and felt terrible

because she felt that way. From where she sat, she could see where Rhia and Serus were having a forceful discussion. They'd been married for so long, been partners for even longer. They knew each other inside and out. But this war had brought a rift between them. Rhia had brought the rift between them.

Wendy had no children but hoped to one day, and as much as she admired Rhia's stance to save her son, she wondered at what point did one actually give up.

Ian walked past her and handed her a large blood bag. She studied it nervously. "Do you think it's safe?"

Ian nodded. "Yes. This is from the employees' fridge."

Wendy turned to study the coolers where he had grabbed the blood from and sure enough, one was labeled "Staff."

She didn't want to take any of this blood, but she was hungry, her energy was low, and they still had a ways to go before they returned to Council Hall. She opened the bag and drank the blood. It was sweet. Oh so sweet. She leaned back against the wall and enjoyed the next sip and the next. No wonder they were fighting so hard to have this. The blood tasted so pure. Then she realized that it probably came from all of Jared's friends.

And her stomach started to curdle.

Ian had passed blood over to Rhia and Serus and had returned to her side. Only she found it very hard to look him in the eye. In a low voice, she said, "I really want to drink more, but the thought that these came from unwilling — friends of Jared's, is just too much."

"It probably wasn't from Jared's friends if that makes you feel better. They are only being processed now." He opened his bag and took a very long drink. She watched the same enjoyment wash over his face that she had felt. "To be this sweet – to be this clean…how can it not be young kids?"

He shrugged. "I don't know, but we have to eat to keep up our strength. We are not safe yet."

She nodded glumly. "I know. I just feel terrible for enjoying it so much."

"And Jared would understand that. He would not hold this against you."

She gave a shuddering sigh. "I hope not."

"Besides," Ian said. "I feel guilty enough for both of us."

Wendy reached out a hand and found Ian's already there waiting for hers. God, she loved this man.

GORAN ENTERED THE same room that Jared and Rhia and the others had been in earlier. The surgical room had been destroyed in the fight, piles of ashes covering the floor. Ignoring those, he walked to the far side of the room, Jared trailing behind.

The boy was smart enough to know Goran could handle anything whereas Jared was going to end up as another victim if he got caught a second time. Or maybe that was a third time. He'd lost track of how many times that boy had gotten into trouble. He was worse than his own boys. Cody had been a hell to raise. Unlike his older brother, who'd been easy. Then again, look where he'd ended up.

Jared spoke up from behind him, "Do you want back up before we go in the other room?"

Goran laughed. "From you?"

He didn't mean to insult the boy. He'd shown more grit and determination and courage than he'd seen out of any human so far. But that didn't change the fact that his body was an easily damaged organic vessel. Whereas Goran, short of silver, would be able to heal and regenerate and be good as new with a little time.

"I'm just worried that we'll walk into something bigger than we're expecting on the other side. And you're alone. I can help a little, but I don't have your capabilities."

Goran nodded. "That's right, but you've done very well so far. Serus will be along if I need him. We'll just have to make do." He shoved the double doors open, and they walked into yet another anteroom that appeared to be a duplicate of the first surgical room. Only this one was empty.

Goran was disappointed. He'd been hoping for another fight. Too much peace was boring. "Nothing's here. Looks like you were worried for nothing."

"Or not." Jared pointed to the far side beside a large cabinet. "There's another door over there."

"Good," Goran said. "Maybe we'll find more action on the other side." He strode over with Jared trailing behind him.

"You want to have a fight?" Jared asked in surprise.

Goran chuckled. "It's not that I'm looking for a fight but if a fight comes my way, I'm more than happy to hit back." He reached for the door and opened it then froze.

DAVID SET THE big stack of documents in front of them off to one side and got up off his feet. Back at the cupboard, they'd been working steadily but had not found the document that Sian was desperate to find. She hadn't explained any more about Hortran's document, only that she needed Deanna's to go with it. He reached up and grabbed another large stack. Seeing that Jewel was almost through hers, he carried it over to her.

"Here, you can start on this pile next." He walked back to the cupboard. "I'll grab another one for myself."

As he reached up, he could see that there was a document jammed into the very back. He stretched up as high as he could and reached into the far recesses of the cupboard. His fingertips just barely managed to grab it. He pulled it forward and the first thing he saw was Deanna's name. He turned to Sian and asked, "Is this the one you're looking for?"

Sian got up from her desk and met him across the room, her hands out and eager to see. Jewel got up off the floor and joined them in the center of the room.

"It's very old," Sian said. "I can't even read most of the text." Sian held it up to the light, her finger moving slowly underneath the words as she read it silently.

David exchanged a questioning look with Jewel. They both waited silently for Sian to make a decision. When she got to the bottom of the page, she tapped it with her finger and said, "Yes."

"Thank heavens for that." Jewel said, turning around to look back at the stacks of paper all over the floor of the room. "I'm almost disappointed. I really enjoyed seeing all these old documents."

Sian laughed. "You definitely need to see me about this after we get back to normal."

Jewel shook her head. "Normal? What is that anymore?" She opened her hands wide. "Do we go back to school now? Is there even a school anymore? What about university? Are there professors left to teach?"

"I know this is hard," Sian said. "But we will regroup. We will start living again and life will fall back into place. It will be different than before. In fact, it is likely to be much better because those of us that will be left will all be aligned in our viewpoints. We will have a vision for how the vampire clan needs to live and to move forward as a single unit. If we can annihilate the enemy, we won't have to face this again but if we leave even one person alive that was part of this organization, one of the heads, then we are in trouble and in another twenty, thirty, or forty years, our children will face exactly what you're facing now." She rubbed her hand over her belly and looked them in the eye. "I will do anything I can to protect my child for today and tomorrow."

"I guess it's easy to see why Rhia has done what she has when you consider it from that point of view."

Sian nodded. "It might be very difficult for some of us to understand, but I have never doubted that she did what she did to save her son."

David nodded. "But that still doesn't make what she did right."

Jewel reached out a hand and slipped her fingers into his.

David grasped her hand lightly, lifting it, dropping a kiss on the knuckles. "I love my brother, but I'm not sure at this point in time that I can trust him. Or that I believe he was innocent in all of this. I want to," he said forcefully, "but I'm just not sure."

Sian nodded. "Keep an open mind and realize that even if he wasn't innocent, he was also young and brainwashed by whatever it was that they were trying to get him involved in. They made him to be one of their own. He would've been included in the secret society. It would not have been hard to turn the young man. It takes a very strong, confident young man to be able to go against all the brainwashing they would've filled his head with. They would've manipulated his thoughts, his feelings, his ego until they had him exactly where they wanted him to be."

"True," Jewel said. "It's easy to judge, but Seth had a whole different friend group and most of those friends were sons of the Councilmen who have died. He'd have been groomed to take a place in the organization."

David frowned and stared down at their entwined hands. "And what do we do with him now, given that my mother is likely to have saved him? But saved him from what and for what?"

IN HIS HEAD, Serus called out. *Goran, what did you find?*

Not sure, Goran replied. *Second operating room was empty, but now we found a room in the back. More humans segregated from the others. It's a big room. Jared is walking from bed to bed and calling out names of those he recognizes. Not sure if Tessa knows, but according to Jared, two of her girlfriends are here. They were rescued from the first blood farm. We thought they were safe back with their families. Jared says he hasn't seen them at school since. But they're here again.*

Jill and Catherine? Serus looked at Rhia, who was at his side. He quickly explained what Jared and Goran had found.

Rhia shook her head. "Those girls were supposed to be safe at home with their parents."

Goran spoke again. *It's even worse than we thought. Jared says Catherine's parents are both here as well. It looks like they went into the house and took everyone that was alive.*

"Jesus," Serus whispered. "Is there no end to this?"

I'm not sure there is, Goran said. *You have to comb through this building and the tunnels looking for more of these poor people.*

No sign of the army yet? Serus asked, Goran.

No, not yet. But they better come soon. Because they need five times the medical personnel that we thought they were going to need. Goran's tone was harsh, angry. *Jared is devastated. He's ready to start doing murder himself.*

Serus winced. *Jared is a good kid. He's been through more than any human I know and yet he still stands strong.*

Yeah, but if he doesn't find his girl, he's going to lose it soon.

She's not there? Serus was shocked. *How many more places could they have humans stashed?*

He's only halfway through the room. She might still be here.

Damn. He needs to move faster. We're out of time. We need to get back to the Council Hall as soon as we can.

CHAPTER 10

TESSA OPENED THE door with a flourish. She knew her family was on the other side. And with no sensation of danger, she rushed inside. Cody was behind her, more cautious than ever. Good, one of them needed to be.

She walked inside and said, "There you are."

Ian and Wendy shouted out in joy, both of them bounding to their feet and racing over to give her a big hug. She laughed and returned the hugs.

Her father and mother ran toward her, arms open. She knew when they stopped and why.

Ian and Wendy both backed up quickly.

Tessa grinned. Her hand slipped down to rest on Beast's muzzle.

"This is Beast," she said. "He was a victim of the enemy, but I saved him and now he has saved me many times."

Cody stepped into the open doorway, his voice loud as he said, "And as much as I hate to say it, he saved my ass once or twice too."

Tessa met her father's gaze and grinned. "Glad to see you're doing okay."

"Of course I'm doing fine." He nodded to Cody. "Good to see you again, Cody."

"Likewise," Cody said.

Tessa heard them talking, but her gaze was locked on her

mother.

"Mom?"

Rhia stared at her, a look of wonder on her face. "You look amazing," Rhia said. "I can't believe how different you look."

Tessa shrugged self-consciously. "I don't really, I'm still Tessa."

Behind Rhia, Ian snorted. "Yeah, that's not true. There's no way in hell you are the same young girl that you were before this mess started."

Tessa flashed a bright smile. "So true, and honestly I wouldn't want to go back to that person either."

She turned her gaze back to her mother, who still appeared to be studying her. "Mom, are you okay?" she asked.

Rhia opened her arms. Tessa ran into them and the two women hugged like they hadn't had a chance to connect in so long.

It brought tears to Tessa's eyes. She brushed them away, smiling at her mother as she stepped back. "I'm so glad to see it's really you inside."

Rhia winced. "I'm so sorry, honey. It's been a very difficult time for me."

Tessa nodded, "For all of us."

Her gaze flicked to her father, a silent question in her head.

He nodded. "She's back to normal."

Relief washed through her. She'd worried that with all the drugs she'd had if they could ever be sure who her mother was again. But she had to trust.

Rhia reached over and picked up Tessa's hand. "I am fine. I'm still very weak and I can feel the last remnants of the drugs inside, but they are almost gone. I just need rest now."

Serus laid an arm across Rhia's shoulders. "Let's get you home."

"Not without Seth."

Exchanging a glance with Tessa, Serus motioned to where her brother lay on the ground.

She crouched down beside him, stunned by the darkness permeating from her brother. "He's completely covered in black," she said in horror. "Mom, did you give him anything?"

"No, of course not." Rhia raced to Tessa's side. "What kind of black are you talking about? I can't see anything!"

"Black energy. Drug energy. His system is completely filled with it." Tessa hated to say it, but she wasn't sure her brother would survive this.

"He was about to be operated on when we found him," Ian said. "He hasn't woken up since."

Tessa nodded, her hands already moving the energy away from her brother's heart. "I don't know that there is anything I can do to save him," she admitted. "I've never seen a case this bad."

Beast start growling from behind her. She looked over at him to see the animal snarling at Seth. "I know, boy. He smells like the enemy."

"He's not the enemy," Rhia snapped, glaring at the animal. "I don't know what abomination that animal is, but if he makes any move toward Seth, I'll kill him."

Tessa froze.

Still crouching, she spun until she could see her mother. But Rhia was still glaring at Beast and not even seeing the look in Tessa's face.

"No one attacks Beast. You call him an abomination?"

she said in a very low tone, too low, she knew. "Then look to your son who has way more drugs in his system than Beast does. Beast at least knows who the enemy is. Seth on the other hand has tried to kill me over and over again."

She swept a hand down to Beast. "Whereas this abomination has saved my life many times."

Now she stood tall in front of her mother, staring her down.

Rhia glared back. "This animal does not belong with us. He's the enemy."

"No, he was created by the enemy," Tessa corrected, "but he is one of us."

Rhia snorted. "Like hell. He does not belong in my house."

"Easy," Serus stepped in between the two women. "This is not the time or the place to have this discussion."

"He's growling at Seth," Rhia protested. "How is that a good thing?"

"Because he is full of the same drugs as all the other enemy he's fought." Serus rubbed her shoulders. "Look, I understand how much effort you've put into saving Seth, now let other people help."

"How much help can Tessa really be?" Rhia waved at the animal at her side. "And then there's that animal."

"Forget about Beast and let Tessa do her thing." Serus gently dragged her back a few feet. "You've missed a lot. At this point you need to trust."

She chewed her bottom lip, undecided. Serus dropped her hand and crossed his arms on his chest. He waited.

Finally, her shoulders slumped. "Fine. Let's see what she can do. But from here, Seth goes straight to the doctors."

Serus snorted. "And what doctors would you trust right

now?"

She looked at him, realization dawning in her eyes. "Can we confirm any are on the good side?"

"Taz." He dropped his arms and held his hands out wide. "Other than that, I have no idea who else."

"Damn."

Ian spoke up from the side. "It's going to take a lot to figure out who is even left behind after this purge," he said. "And then there's going to be a job of trying to fill the gaps in all the professions. As Wendy was just asking, we have no idea if there are even enough vampires left to run the businesses, the Council, or the University."

Rhia said. "We've lost so many people on both sides."

"And that's why we have to make sure that we do this right," Serus said. "We let others go underground last time, and look at where we are at now. We can't let it happen again."

With a defeated tilt of her shoulders, Rhia nodded her head. She turned back to where Tessa was half hearing and half watching them. "I'm sorry for what he did to you. Please don't hold it against him and if you can help him, please find it in your heart to do so."

Tessa, who'd been listening quietly as her parents rage on, nodded. "I would have anyway. Because that's who I am. I don't operate from a core of hatred or resentment or retribution. I'm focusing on good and love. The only way I can do what I'm doing is by being true to me."

She turned her attention back to the very strong core of black surrounding Seth's heart. She dove deeper and pulled, swirled, and swept away black upon black upon black. In her mind, she heard Cody. *Are you okay?*

I will be. What choice is there but to move forward and do what I can do? She shrugged. *It remains to be seen if that's any good.*

JARED WIPED AWAY the angry tears. He didn't want Goran to see his anguish. It's not that he was grieving, but he was so frustrated, so angry it was as if his body had no idea what else to do but cry. He had no target to hit at and the targets that were available were bigger, stronger, faster and a hell of a lot more capable than he was. It so wasn't fair. He stared back at the long rows of unconscious humans. This time, there were maybe three dozen people here, but it looked like a recent collection, possibly already through the processing, maybe into the cleansing part of the system. He didn't know, but he wanted these people out of here and to safety.

Trying to rein in his chaotic emotions, Jared worked systematically through the rows, stopping to stare down at every face, trying to place where he might have seen these people.

When he got to the last row in the very farthest corner, he stopped and gasped then cried out, "Clarissa!" And he ran to her side. A light blanket covered her still form. Her arm was connected to tubes the same as everyone else in the room, her face lax, pale. She was unconscious, obviously drugged, her body taking in even more drugs as he sat there.

He reached up and stroked the loose hair back off her forehead. "Oh thank God, I found you."

From behind, he heard Goran ask, "Jared?"

Jared turned to look at him, a big grin on his face. "It's Clarissa," he said. "We found her."

"Damn, that's good to hear."

Goran didn't enter the big room and in some small way,

Jared was glad. Goran wasn't the enemy, but it's as if this room belonged to the humans and no vampires were allowed. He wished the army were here already. He didn't want to leave Clarissa's side. Tessa hadn't given up on him, and he hadn't given up on Clarissa. In some small way, he'd made atonement.

And he knew that Tessa would be the first to say, "That's what friends are for. No atonement required."

Cody watched the family dynamics play out in front of him. Tessa had bent over backwards to help everyone on both sides of this coin when she could. She was doing her best, but there was no guarantee she could help Seth. She hadn't failed yet, but there was always a first time. He walked over to where Rhia and Serus stood.

"Rhia, I know you haven't seen all that Tessa has learned to do, but you need to give her space. Let her do the best she can. She may not succeed, but right now there is nobody else here that can help her. There may not be anyone left in the Council either." He turned to Serus. "Did you fill her in on the attack at the Hall?"

"I don't even know all that happened. I heard from David and from Sian. They're saying the main Council Hall was gassed." He raised an eyebrow at Cody. "You weren't there obviously."

"Both Tessa and I *were* there," Cody corrected. "Tessa managed to close the front door so the gas killed off all the vamps inside. A good number of flyers landed on the rooftop apartment," Cody added. "Tessa managed to kill them off with Hortran's method she used in the hallways."

He shrugged. "There wasn't much left for Beast or I to

do honestly. Then I carried them both to the entrance in the mountain hillside across the fields from Council Hall. The entrance was deserted and we met no one on the way in." He added, "We did find a second large mechanical room on our way, but it appeared to be empty," he lowered his voice adding, "Except for a nasty group of enhanced animals. Then we followed the passageways until we came here."

Cody twisted to check on Tessa, but she appeared to be focused on Seth in front of her. He turned his gaze back to Serus. "And you and Goran, where did you come from?"

When Serus filled him on Goran's human army, Cody was shocked. "He couldn't stop them?"

Serus shook his head. "Once the vamps knew Goran had survived, they were trying to get at him. He came in through the same doors but flew up and came down on the closest vamp, then took him out and stole his gas mask."

Cody laughed. "Now that would have been fun to see."

Serus smiled. "He did good."

"I was expecting to see him here," he admitted, looking around. "Tessa said she could see his energy," he frowned, his gaze sweeping the room a second time, "And Jared's."

"And as usual she's right." Serus grinned. "The two backtracked to the surgical room where Rhia found Seth. Jared had seen other doors on the far side, but they had no time to look so Goran took him back." The smile fell off his face. "Do you remember Tessa speaking of Jill and Catherine?"

Cody nodded. "Right. Her school friends. They were taken for the blood farm but rescued." He gazed back at Tessa. "Did you ever connect with Catherine and Jill again, Tessa?"

"I couldn't. Wasn't allowed to," she said quietly, never

taking her eyes off of Seth. "I wanted to walk up to the front door and ask to see them, but they now knew I was a vampire and after what had happened to their daughters, I didn't think I'd be welcome."

"That may or may not be true," Serus said. "But Jared has just found both of them, and the parents of one of the girls for sure, in a room where he's gone to look. They have all been hooked up to drugs."

Tessa cried out in shock. "What? No, that's impossible. They were safe."

"And then they weren't safe." Serus shrugged. "There was nothing you could do. The vamps likely took everyone they could find."

From the far side of the room, Ian added, "From what we saw, there are rooms full of your school friends. It looks like the entire school was basically handed over for the blood farm. The medic said the principal was behind it all."

Tessa bounded to her feet. "I have to go see them."

"They are unconscious and hooked up to drugs." Ian walked closer. "I'm really sorry, Tessa. Jared was pretty upset about the whole thing too."

"The principal was an asshole," she snapped. "I never did like him."

"If he is involved, chances are he's been taken to the blood farm too." Serus walked to stand in front of her. "You know that's how the blood farm works. No one is left to tell any tales."

Tessa reached up and rubbed her temple. "I know. They've turned on anyone who helps them."

Cody nodded. "Trust that we will get them all. Focus on Seth, then we will go down to see your school friends." She turned back to her brother and said, "Right. I won't rest until I have the last one in a pile of ash."

Cody heard Rhia's gasp of shock. He studied the look on her face, realizing she had no clue what Tessa had already done and how it made her sick. She wasn't bloodthirsty. She was heartbroken. And wanted to make sure this never happened again. In a low voice, he said, "Remember she's been through a lot."

Rhia wrapped her arms around her chest as if to ward off a chill and whispered. "She's changed."

Serus reached over and tugged her up close. "She has, but don't focus on that. Focus on the magnificent woman she has become. You should be damn proud."

HOW DID ONE reconcile her little girl with the woman in front of her? Rhia knew Serus had warned her. And he told her that no matter how much warning he gave her, it wasn't going to be enough and she should be prepared. Well, even prepared, she didn't understand or recognize this woman.

What she was doing to Seth was one thing, but her attitude, her posture…everything was different, as if she'd aged thirty years and she'd missed those years. And it made her very sad.

Serus was right. She'd been so focused on saving Seth that she hadn't seen the changes in Tessa. She didn't want to gain one child to lose another. And by rights, it shouldn't have to be that way. It'd only been days, weeks. But somehow through this journey, Tessa had matured and grown up and away from her. And the bond between Cody and Tessa was obviously very strong. Her daughter was going to skip the entire dating scenario if she was as strongly bonded to Cody as it appeared.

There's no strongly bonded about it, Serus said in her head. *They are bonded. It doesn't matter how weak or how strong, it exists, the same as yours and mine, the same as Goran and I.*

How can that be? Rhia asked. *I knew they were bonded, but to see them like this. And it's not just Tessa that has changed. Look at Cody. He's a man now. Confident. Determined. Capable. What happened to our young people? Even Ian and Wendy are different.*

War does that, remember?

And what about them in the future? They are too young to be together all the time – aren't they?

Serus replied, *I don't know. None of us can think this moment. They have a lot of decisions to make about their future. The thing is she's made a choice.*

Not yet, she hasn't.

Yes, Serus said in a hard voice. *She has. Deal with it.*

Rhia shuddered. *And Beast?*

I have no idea. But it could be a breaking point for Tessa. Are you sure you want to put that to the test?

She kept her thoughts hidden from Serus, but for her, keeping Beast was a breaking point too. He was a reminder of all the blood farm had done to her family.

The animal might be a victim in his own way, but she was a long ways away from letting that make a difference.

DAVID WATCHED AS Sian ran out of the room. Jewel walked over and placed her hand in his. "What do we do now?" she asked.

"I'm not sure." David looked at the mess around the room. "I guess we should clean up."

"Or we follow her?"

David studied her face. "What are you thinking?"

"I'm thinking it's not safe. Anywhere. For anyone alone. Especially not for Sian."

David hesitated for a moment, then realized she was right and bolted out the door, dragging Jewel with him.

"Slow down, I'm struggling to keep up," Jewel cried.

David instead snagged her up into his arms and picked up his speed. "I don't want to let her get out of my sight."

He nodded down the hallway where Sian was just now turning the corner. He ran faster. "Call her on your phone."

Jewel struggled to pull her phone out of her pocket. He shifted her in his arms so that she had better access.

He turned the corner in time to see the elevator doors closing. "Shit."

He hit the door to the stairwell full force, kicking it just before it would've slammed into Jewel, and bolted down the stairs, jumping from landing to landing to landing. "Do you remember what floor the Council meeting was on?"

"Third down," Jewel said, holding the phone ringing in her ear. "She's not answering."

The entrance to the third floor was ahead. He lowered Jewel to her feet then pushed the door. It was locked from the other side.

With a hard look at Jewel, he backed up then rammed into the door hard. The doors gave way, spilling him out to the hallway. He recovered his footing in time to see several men standing at the elevator, waiting for the doors to open.

He bolted towards them, Jewel at his heels. The double doors opened and Sian walked out. She was immediately engulfed by the waiting men.

"Stop!" David ripped down the hallway toward the closest vampire, tossing him to the ground. The others turned on him. He didn't recognize any of them.

"Who are you, and what do you want with Sian?" he roared.

"The Council has determined that she is a threat," one of the men snarled. "She's to be taken prisoner until the tribunal can address this issue." He gazed at Jewel beside David. "And anyone that helps her will be considered a traitor as well."

"No," Sian cried out, clutching the documents in her arms. "I've done nothing."

"We'll see about that," one of the other men snapped.

The smile on his face sent chills through David's spine. Of course, Sian was trying to protect the Council. They were going to do whatever they could to have her removed. Once they did that, they would slowly take out anybody not favorable to their cause.

That couldn't be allowed. But were these men the enemy, or were they just part of the clan doing their job and not knowing to the truth? He wished he had Tessa here to tell who was lying and who was not. His sister had so many useful skills. Not for the first time, he wished he could learn a few of them for himself.

But then he didn't need her to tell him what instinct was already screaming in his mind. He could see the joy in the other man's eyes. The will to fight. The urge to kill. These men were just plain assholes. He fingered the silver in his pocket, hating to use it, but it would be one way to find out if these assholes were enhanced.

"So what's it going to be, boyo?" said the vampire currently holding Sian in a tight grip.

He raised his gaze to Sian, seeing both the fear and the rage in her gaze. She'd never let herself be taken. Not like this. She had her baby to protect, and he knew as well as she did that these men had been after her before.

A quick glance behind him told him the man he'd knocked out was slowly waking up again.

And that Jewel had positioned herself to take him out if need be. Good, he didn't have to worry about that one. That left three between Sian and himself.

Meeting Jewel's gaze for a quick instance, she gave him a quick nod.

He met Sian's gaze. She narrowed her gaze at him. He smiled.

"Well, if she's a traitor…" David turned with the spike in his hand and stabbed the first vampire in front of him. The man blew up in a cloud of nasty-smelling smoke and ash. David smiled at the other two. "I guess we know what side of this war you're on."

The men launched themselves at him.

Neither reached him. Both blew up in a cloud of ash in front of him. Coughing and waving the air in front of his face, David backed up so he could breathe.

And that's when he saw Sian standing behind the two piles, silver spikes in her own hands.

"You okay?"

She nodded. "But this changes things."

"Do you have a private place where no one can find you until the others get back?" David asked her urgently.

"I'll go to my quarters and lock myself in." Sian said. "I have lots of paperwork to do anyway. I was going to show the Council this first, only I'm afraid it might be a bloodbath now." She gave the two of them a wan smile. "Feel like escorting me?"

"And standing watch, but not your quarters. They will

look for you there," David said, not liking the lines of fatigue on the beautiful woman's face. "You're tired and should rest."

She laughed. "Yes, I'm tired, but not exactly so tired as to need to sleep."

"And how about baby," Jewel asked gently. "Maybe you and baby should have a nap together."

"We'll see," she compromised. "First let's get to safety. Someone is going to be looking for these men soon." She curled up her lip as she stared at the piles of ashes. "We need to clean up the mess, but we don't have time. As soon as they see the ash, they are going to use that as evidence that I'm a traitor."

"Not necessarily." Jewel walked to the small door off to the side. "This is where they keep all the cleaning supplies. I know there's a lot of ash, but we can vacuum it up."

David reached in and pulled out a large commercial system and turned to the women. "Start walking. I'll clean this up and follow you."

He turned it on, only to find it had an incredibly powerful suction. He had the mess cleaned up in just a couple of minutes. Replacing it in the closet, he sprinted down the hallway to catch up to the women. They weren't very far ahead. He snagged an arm from each and urged them forward.

"Let's move it. We need to get out of sight and fast."

CHAPTER 11

TESSA WORKED AS hard as she could to remove the energy from Seth's system. But every time she removed handfuls, more poured in. She didn't understand why. Or how. His body was not responding the way it should have. The way the others did. This was once again something new. She sat back on her heels.

"What is it?" Cody asked. "What's wrong?"

"I can't seem to stop the blackness from pouring in," she said in frustration. She motioned to the full length of Seth. "It's all centered on his chest and abdomen." She stared down at her brother. "I haven't given up, I'm just not sure what to do."

"And that in itself is nothing new either," Cody said. "It seems that we're constantly coming up against something different."

She nodded. An idea hit. She turned to face Ian and Wendy. "Ian? Are you sure the surgery hadn't been done already? Sure that Seth was just going *into* surgery and not coming *out* the surgery?"

Ian frowned, puzzled. "We assumed he was. I think the doctor said he was. But I'm not sure."

Wendy walked closer to Tessa. "Why?"

"There's something going on in his system that I've never seen before." She shrugged. "I just wondered if they'd had time to do something that you might not have known about."

Rhia's hard voice cut through the silence. "Something like what?"

Tessa swiveled so she could look at her mother. "I can't say yet."

"Then who can?" Rhia studied her son as she walked closer. "He doesn't look any different. He still looks the same innocent boy who left the house weeks ago."

"But he's not," Tessa said.

"How do you know that?" Rhia asked in anger. "You might see energy, but you obviously can't see what's wrong with him. So then you can't know what has changed."

Tessa straightened. How did she explain that she knew stuff that she didn't understand and couldn't explain herself? "I don't have all the answers. I have *some* of the answers. No, that's not always enough." She took a step back, letting her mother get closer to Seth.

She wasn't sure she was doing any good as it was. Seth hadn't shown any noticeable difference with her removing the energy from his system.

In her head, Cody said, *You did a lot more to save me. Why can't you do the same to save him?*

Good question, she said. *I don't have an answer for that.*

Inside, it felt like her heart was breaking. Why could she not save her brother when she worked so hard to save Cody?

Did she not want to save Seth? Was she scared of him? Resentful?

Had he hurt her so bad that she wanted him dead even when she might be able to do something about it? Was she such a small person inside?

No, Cody snapped. *Don't even begin to think like that.*

You're a beautiful person inside and out. Maybe there's a reason why you can't save him.

She spun to look at him. *Of course. I don't have the same bond with Seth that I have with you. I followed that bond deep into your center so I could help you. That bond does not exist between my brother and I, and what little bond there is has been broken.*

Can you fix it? Or do you not want to fix it?

I don't know, she whispered, hating the uncertainty in the doubt in her voice. *He's my brother and I should love him, but right now I don't even like him, and there is a part of me that really hates his involvement in all of this.*

And you don't believe he is innocent?

She shook her head. *Not at the end. Maybe at the beginning. I just don't know.*

Do you want him to be innocent? Do you want to give him a chance to explain? Don't you want to know for sure? I'd give a lot to see my brother again. To ask him why.

Of course, she whispered. *But wishing for something doesn't make it so.*

No, but maybe with a new perspective, you can come up with a new solution. Didn't you see other men, human or vamp, where the black just kept pouring in?

Maybe, she said slowly, turning back to stare at her brother. *But in those cases, there was some foreign object inside their body, and that's what had been causing the blackness.*

And maybe this is just a more advanced version, Cody suggested. *For your sake and everyone else's, please take another look.*

Ignoring the confused looks of everyone around her as they tried to understand what she was doing, Tessa circled Seth's body then dropped to her knees across from her mother. She started at his feet and looked well below the darkness, trying to see if there was something – anything – that would be causing this energy. She worked her way slowly up past his hips and his belly, stopping at his ribs. Instinctively, she laid her hand on his chest and this time picked up an odd pulse. She could sense it from deep below the energy. She didn't know what it was, but it was there.

Excited, she ripped open his shirt, realizing he was dressed in pants and some kind of gown over his shoulders and belly.

As soon as his belly was exposed, everyone gasped.

In a harsh voice, Rhia asked, "What is that?"

Tessa let her fingers gently stroke the edges around what appeared to be a slowly healing wound, but in the center sat something metallic, slowing the healing process down. She wasn't even sure that the tissue would be able to heal over the inanimate object. And that's obviously what the surgeon had been hoping would happen.

"I have no idea." She studied the object in fascination. "It has a pulse, as if it's sending out waves or beats."

"What do you mean, Tessa?" Cody asked. "What kind of beat?"

"A pulse." She held the palm over the metallic object and whispered, "Boom, boom, boom."

"Like a heartbeat," Wendy asked. "Or a bomb."

That brought more cries from Rhia. "Get it out of there. We need to get it out."

"I agree, but I'm not sure how to take it out." She didn't want to touch it. It had evil scientist crap written all over it. "I'm afraid forcing it out will cause more harm than good."

"I don't think there's a choice." Cody pointed at the healing skin. "Another hour and it will have closed up completely, and no one would know. If you weren't taking another look, it wouldn't have been found in time."

Serus said, "There's no guarantee he's going to survive anyway."

Rhia reached over and grasped her hand. "Please, if you can take it out, then take it out."

"I can take it out," Tessa said gently. "But I can't guarantee how he will heal afterwards because I don't know what it is attempting to do."

But Rhia wasn't listening. She was staring in horror at the metallic object. "It's another one of their nasty toys. Please take it out."

Tessa glanced up at Cody, a question in her eyes. He nodded. She took a deep breath and centered herself inside. *Deanna, Hortran, if you are there, please help.* Silence. Then again, what else had she expected?

She exhaled gently and held both hands over the top of the object, sensing the pulse building and building. She lowered her hand, trying to pull the pulse and disperse the pulsing energy. But nothing seemed to work. She laid her hand atop the object, trying to sense what it was.

As soon as she touched the cold metal, she knew.

Anger slid through her. It was a bomb intended to take her brother out and who was around him at the time.

Maybe with a remote device to trigger it, maybe not. Maybe it ran on time. Maybe Seth knew about it. She had no idea, but she had to stop it before everyone she loved and cared about died right now. Because she was pretty damn sure that it was going to blow up if she pulled it out.

Realizing nothing was working, she said in her mind, *Cody, it's going to explode. I'm not sure if it will be now or in five minutes or five days, but it's going to.*

Cody crouched beside her, studying the object. *Are you sure?*

Yes, she whispered. *I'm sure.*

She took a deep breath. *I think pulling it out will make it self-destruct.* She hated the nerves galloping in her stomach, the tremor in her voice. She barely managed to hold her hand steady above the object, and only because she didn't want to worry all the others.

This is not for you to do alone. Cody said, reaching for her hand. *We need to find a way to save this. Can you draw the power away from it?*

No.

How about the opposite then. Fill it to the brim with energy and short it out.

She brightened. *That might work.*

She started to pour energy through her left hand and then her right hand. Centering the beam on the object, pounding it with these waves and waves of energy, she drew from her feet, from her body, from her heart and soul. And then when that wasn't appearing to be enough, she pulled from Cody.

Cody turned to the others surrounding them and said, "Everyone make a circle and hold hands. Tessa needs energy quickly."

Everyone formed a circle around them, encircling Tessa. She was only dimly aware of their physical actions but recognized the surge of energy when her father placed his hand on her shoulder. And still it wasn't enough. She poured and she pulled and she poured and she pulled. Finally she could sense a weakening within the system. The start of something…hopefully it would be enough to destroy this.

Then that too slowed down. She twisted, looking for

something else to help her slam energy into this thing.

And then Beast stepped inside the circle of vamps and straddled Seth's legs. In a surprise move, he placed his jaw directly on top of Tessa's hands.

Sizzling filled the air then sparks flew in all directions. Followed by a funny pop then…nothing.

In the silence, she could feel the energy drain from her hands. She turned to look at those gathered around to help. "Burnt out. You can back up now."

Beast lifted his head and shuffled back slightly. Tessa raised her hands and stroked him on the back. "Thanks, Beast."

Beast made a snuffling sound and pushed his head into her hand.

Rhia leaned forward but still stayed away from Beast. "Are you sure it's okay now?"

Tessa laughed. "It's safer now than it ever has been."

Cody said, "Tessa thought it was a bomb, possibly with a remote detonator. We won't know much more until we get that device back to the lab and get it analyzed."

Silence.

"That's terrible," Wendy cried out first. "How could they do that?"

"And did Seth know?" Ian asked. "Surely this wasn't done with his approval?"

"No, he wouldn't have," Serus said. "This is the best proof of his innocence yet. There's no way he'd have become so indoctrinated he'd have given up his own life for the cause."

Rhia let out a cry and reached for Serus's hand. "I'm so glad we found it. We could have lost him." She turned to Tessa. "Can you take it out now?"

"I think so." Using her nails, she plucked the offending item out, cutting the bits of tissue that were already trying to enclose it, then held it up in her hand for all of them to see.

It was smaller looking now that it was free. It was a thin, flat disc. Innocuous-looking. There was nothing on the outside to indicate what it was for. But she could no longer sense anything alive inside – energy or otherwise. Cody picked it up from her hand to examine it, leaving her free to turn her attention back to Seth's gaping wound.

But, now that the foreign object was removed, Seth's body was already starting to heal. "He'll be fine now," she said with satisfaction.

Cody asked, "What about the dark energy that's poisoning him?"

She looked up at him and smiled. "I can remove that now too."

And she set about doing just that.

CODY WANTED TO laugh. He loved it when Tessa managed to pull off a magical trick that no one else could see coming. In this case, it was gratifying to see her mom's reaction. Rhia still saw Tessa as a little girl, and Tessa had grown well past that. In order to have good relationships with the family, he knew Rhia needed to accept Tessa for who she was, and then she needed to take that next step and accept Cody as her life mate.

He thought his father would have an easier time of it. But there was something about that mother-daughter bond that he didn't quite understand and couldn't access because he was male. Rhia needed to work it out. Because Cody wasn't giving up on Tessa.

Then there was the disc in his hand.

And how is it that Seth came to be implanted with one of these nasty little things? "It could be that it has another purpose and it would only blow up if it was being removed."

"What type of purpose do you think?" Serus growled. "It doesn't make much sense to at all."

"I know, but they have done so many things that we never considered already." Cody slipped the item into his pocket. "We'll take it back and see what our specialist can find."

Ian snorted. "Are there any left?"

There was a sad silence as everyone realized how many professionals have been killed in this process. Serus said, "I sure hope so. If nothing else, David might be able to find something."

"In that case," Ian said. "I want to be there with him."

Cody grinned. "You just want to be involved, don't you?" he teased his friend.

"Especially if there's electronics involved," he admitted. "I love computers."

Serus smacked him on the shoulder. "Looks like you're going to get your wish."

Cody watched as Tessa's movement slowed. It appeared like she was almost done. "Tessa?"

Tessa bowed her head for a moment, as if pulling in her energy and looking for a second wind. She was so capable of so many things now that everyone tended to forget that she needed to rejuvenate herself.

"How are you doing?"

She straightened, her hand going to the small of her back, but she gave him a bright smile. "I'm fine, especially now. It looks like I got the bulk of the energy out." She turned to her father. "Can you carry him?"

With a quick nod, her father stepped closer then bent down and lifted his son into his arms.

Cody admired the ease of his movements as he picked up the man. When he was as old as the ancient, he hoped to have the same amount of strength that Serus had. In fact, Serus was damn healthy. Then the vampires tended to be a long-lived breed. Plus he'd been at the receiving end of Tessa's healing efforts, which no doubt helped. Providing no assholes from blood farms were after them. He turned from his musings to see Tessa striding out of the room. He raced to catch up. "Hey wait," he called. "Where are you going?"

She spun in surprise. "I'm going down to where Jared and Goran are. They said Jill and Catherine were there. I have to go see if I can help them." And she picked up the pace.

Cody dashed up beside her. "Did you even consider where Beast is?"

She came to a stop and turned. "Where is he?" She searched the hallway. "He was right beside me when I was working on Seth."

"No, he was right beside you up until we all broke apart and then you started working on Seth alone," Cody said lightly. "But I think you'd like to see where he is right now."

She dashed back to look into the room and stopped in the doorway. Slowly, a smile dawned on her face.

Cody stepped up behind her and whispered, "I think once Rhia understood that it was Beast's actions that allowed you to finally kill that electronic device, she decided maybe he wasn't quite so bad after all."

In fact, from what she could see, Rhia was making friends with Beast. And didn't that do her heart good. She watched her mom gently stroke his back and his head as she whispered something quietly in his ear. Beast seemed to be receptive. Then he caught sight of Tessa and he bounded towards her. Inordinately pleased, Tessa bent down and gave him a big hug.

Cody could hear her whispering to him. "I'm sorry, Beast, I forgot to say thank you." She gave him another big hug and straightened and flashed a smile Cody's way. "Thank you for letting me know." She nodded in the direction of her mother. "It does help."

❧ ❧

GORAN WATCHED AS Jared sat on the bed beside Clarissa.

"Do you think she's going to be okay?" Jared asked.

Goran didn't know what to say. He wasn't given to positive sentiment, but the boy needed something. It looked to him like most of these people were relatively new arrivals, but as some were here for the second time, he wasn't sure what their chances of recovery were. "You know they will get the best medical help available."

Jared twisted so he could look at his face. "That does not sound very positive."

"She'll do much better if we can get Tessa here."

"And just why is that?" Jared asked. "The Tessa I knew in school didn't have any of these abilities."

Goran shrugged. "Who knows? At the same time, why question it?"

He watched as Jared gently stroked Clarissa's arm. The boy had a soft heart. Maybe that was a good thing. Maybe not.

"Did you know Tessa well?" Goran asked as he couldn't help worrying that maybe Jared was wanting a relationship with Tessa. As far as he was concerned, Tessa belonged to his boy.

Jared smiled. "As well as I knew any girl in school," he admitted. "She was pretty then, but she is seriously beautiful now," he added. "Only she wasn't scary back then."

"Scary?" Goran prodded. "Why is she scary?"

Jared shot him a dark look. "Seriously? Look at what she can do. How many people has she killed? She didn't even think about it. It came naturally to her. And then there's the fact that she's really gorgeous," he added. "That's very intimidating. She's capable, deadly, and a knockout."

He shook his head, staring back down at Clarissa. "That's scary. Not sure I'm up for that." He straightened and looked back at Goran. "Not that I was ever in the running. She's all about Cody."

"They are a good match," Goran admitted. "And I'd be proud to have her in the family." An odd sound beside him had him spinning around on guard to see a flustered Tessa and a grinning Cody standing in front of him.

Goran beamed. "There you are." He laughed. "And make no mistake, I meant what I said."

She stared at him for a long time, and he wondered if he'd crossed some kind of line.

Then she raced towards him and threw herself into his arms. Goran wrapped her up in a hug and held her close. Against her ear, he whispered "I never had a daughter but if I had, I wish she'd been like you."

Tessa pulled back and looked up at him, tears in the corner of her eyes. "That's the nicest thing anyone's ever said to me." She reached up and dropped a kiss on his cheek. Pulling back, she saw the room full of people and her bottom lip trembled. "How could our species do this to another that's so like our own?"

"Times are changing," Goran said, letting her go. "But change has not been fast or easy. Many of us are used to doing things the old way. And we have very old viewpoints. Humans have only ever been food up until recently."

He watched as Cody walked over to Tessa and put his arm around her shoulder, tucking her up close against his chest. He was so happy for his boy.

Cody said, "It's up to us to show everyone else the new way forward." He motioned to Jared standing and staring at them and said, "That you and Jared had a friendship and that we have helped the humans and didn't slaughter them is already a massive change." He rubbed her shoulder gently. "We need to take this one more step further. It's not going to be that hard or that difficult, but we must purge first and then start fresh."

Goran added, "But doing the purge also means convincing everyone left behind that this is the best way for everyone going forward. That will not be easy."

She nodded. "But first we have to see what we can do for these poor people." She turned to face Goran. "Have you heard from the army at all?"

He nodded. "They should be here in another five minutes or so."

Good. She walked over to where Jared sat and laid a gentle hand on his shoulder. "I'm so sorry, Jared."

"It's not your fault," he said, but he looked as if he was struggling to say something else when the words rushed out. He kept a wary eye on Beast but managed to ask, "Can you help her?"

With Cody at his side, Goran watched as Tessa studied Jared's friend. Then she reached down and gently disconnected the tube in her arm and with some kind of weird brushstroke movement appeared to be pulling something away from her arm and out from her body.

Jared never said a word.

Goran looked over at Cody, a question in his eyes. Cody smiled, patted his shoulder, and said, "Let her work. And better that she works before the army gets here."

Goran could understand that. "In that case, I'll go stand watch."

And he walked up to the hallway on the other side of the surgical rooms. He checked both directions, but so far there was no sign of the army.

He called back, "I'll let you know if they're coming."

DAVID CLOSED THE door behind Sian and Jewel and locked it. The room they were in was one of the Council's private meeting chambers. He didn't know whose chambers though. Neither did he care. Chances were the Councilman was no longer alive anyways.

Sian collapsed on the couch, her hand on her belly, obviously shaken. Jewel crouched beside her.

"Can I get you something, Sian?"

Sian shook her head. "No, I'm fine."

"No, you're not fine," David said. "But we have to figure out what to do next regardless."

"How long do you think we have before they come looking for us?" Jewel asked.

"Not long," Sian said. "They were sent to pick me up. When they don't return, they will know that something is up."

"Do you have any idea what we can do?" Jewel asked.

"We need the other ancients. They are the ones that can help stop this," David snapped. "They would be back here already if they understood what was going on."

Sian gave a light laugh. "I don't think they have any idea how bad the situation is."

"Then we need to tell them," urged Jewel. "This has gone beyond anything we can handle without them."

Sian pulled her phone out and tried to call Serus. But the phone just rang and rang and eventually went to voicemail. She shrugged. "This is about the third time I've tried. They have to be deep in the mountain because the reception cannot get through."

David sent text messages to Ian and Cody. "Maybe, but that doesn't mean nothing is getting through."

"Even when they do get the message," Sian said. "Chances are it would to be too late to get back here and save us."

"Save us?" Jewel asked. "Are you thinking they really are trying to kill us?"

"At this point, yes." Sian tried to straighten up in the couch then winced. She relaxed back down again, both hands wrapping around her belly. "I need to contact Taz, let him know what's happened."

Jewel handed her the phone that had dropped when she'd shifted position and said, "Call Taz and warn him."

Sian nodded. "Right, he's going to be in danger too."

"Even more so," David suggested in a gentle voice. "He's been instrumental in recovering as many people as possible from the blood farms."

"And as the father of your baby, he's going to be one of the first they go after once they have you captive."

Sian shuddered. "I won't want to live if Taz dies."

"We aren't going there," David said in a strong voice. "And neither are we going to give these assholes another chance at you."

"We may not have a choice," Sian said in a defeated voice. "It seems like no matter what we do, there's just always more of these guys showing up."

Jewel patted her hand and stood up. "That's why they are making mistakes. They're desperate," she said. "We've got them on the run. We can capitalize on that. We're almost there. It figures that it would be the Council that we'd have to take on last."

Sian laughed. "You are right there. The Council has run this clan since the beginning of our time, and now we're trying to make changes. Of course they are resisting." She nodded, pleased. "And you're right on something else, we just have to stand strong until our own reinforcements return."

The phone call to Taz took longer than a few minutes but after assurances that she was fine, she hung up with a smile on her face. She shifted her position so she was lying more horizontal. "On that note, I think I will have a nap."

She closed her eyes and as Jewel watched, she drifted off to sleep.

CHAPTER 12

"**T**ESSA?" CODY CALLED. "Time to go."

She turned to see Cody and Goran talking with the human army that had arrived several minutes ago. "Do they have medical personnel here to help these people?"

"They have one team here now and have just called in a second team given the high number of victims in need of care." Cody motioned at her to come faster.

Sensing an urgency she didn't understand, she got to her feet, patted Jared on his shoulder, and walked towards Cody. When she was close enough, Cody asked, "How are Jill and Catherine?"

She smiled. "I think they'll be fine." She nodded to the medical team that was standing and waiting. She couldn't resist checking out their energy to make sure everybody here looking after these people were safe. They were supposed to save these people, not hurt them further. Thankfully, there appeared to be no black energy in any of their systems. Cody ushered her out into the hallway and then with a grasp on her hand moved her quickly towards where the rest of the family was waiting.

"Oh, I hadn't realized everyone was ready to go."

"Not only are we ready to go, but there's been another attack on Sian. This time from within the Council itself."

His whisper was so low she wasn't sure she heard it out

loud or in her head. She spun in shock. "What?"

"Shh." He urged her forward. "The Council has decided that Sian is a traitor to the clan. The Council ordered her to be taken as prisoner until such a time they could deal with her."

"She is not a traitor," Tessa said hotly. "That's ridiculous."

"We know that, but that's the Council's maneuvering to get her out of the way."

"We have to get back there and help her."

"Exactly. We're also trying to contact the other Councilmen and get them back in time. It looks like Goran might need to fly over and pick up a couple."

"How long will that take?"

"Too long." Goran growled. "They are all over the world."

"Can't they cast votes electronically?" She asked. "Given the circumstances, you should."

"I agree with you," Goran said. "But I only understand the minimum of this technology explosion from all of you kids."

Serus added, "And that is something that many ancients are missing. Councilmen tend to be centuries old with no access or interest in learning technology."

"We've come up against this before," Cody said. "It's difficult for the younger clan members to understand, but many of the ancients don't have computers or cell phones and have no wish to learn to use either."

"In this instance, we may not have much choice," Tessa said. "We're out of time."

"Sian was working on bringing everybody back before this incident," Serus said. "We can only hope that enough people were contacted and capable of returning."

It was Ian that popped up and said, "They also have to care."

Outside, it was still dark but dawn was coming very quickly – scarily quickly.

"We have to hurry," she cried. "Or we're going to be stuck here too."

She turned again and glanced at all the numbers around them, but before she realized what was happening, Cody had swooped down and picked her up, already carrying her through the air.

"No, wait," she cried. "We have to take Beast too. He'll try to follow us and die in the sunlight."

With a heavy sigh, Cody swooped back in, not quite landing but hovering just above the ground.

"Beast…" she ordered. "Jump!"

Beast took a flying run and jumped straight into her arms. Cody sagged in the air as he absorbed the hit, but then he recovered and was up flying stronger than ever toward the Hall. She peered over Cody's shoulder to try and see how the others were doing. She didn't want anyone to be left behind.

"Forget about them," Cody said. "They will be along in a few minutes."

"I just want to make sure that we are leaving nobody behind."

"They will work it out."

She turned to stare at the Council Hall coming up very quickly. "They should be able to run this distance in time anyways," she said, feeling better.

"Yep." Cody landed gently on the front stairs. Immediately, Beast jumped off and Tessa was able to see much clearer with his big head out of the way.

"Do we think it's safe?"

Cody laughed. "Maybe that's a question I should be asking you," He studied the wide-open front door. "I can smell something in the air, but it's not strong and I don't see the discoloration in the air that we saw earlier."

"The gases have dispersed." She walked back and forth in front of the front doors, assessing the danger level. "I think it's fine." Boldly, she stepped inside.

❧ ❧

"HEY, WAIT." DAMN her. She always would walk where angels would fear to tread. "Don't you think we should run some kind of test or something?"

"No," she said, "look."

There in front were two vamps Cody recognized from the maintenance crew. "Oh, am I glad to see them."

The men were too far away to speak with, but it was obvious what they were doing as they loaded up the bodies onto big carts while Cody stood and stared. Together, they picked up six men and proceeded to wield the cart out back. From the looks of it, they'd been at it for a little while. The left-hand side of the Hall was pretty cleaned up while the right-hand side was full of bodies.

"Jesus, did we do all this?"

Cody turned and saw Tessa trembling. He tugged and pulled her into his arms. "Remember, we had no choice. It was them or us."

She bowed her head and snuggled in close.

He let her have a moment to collect herself. In fact, he could use one or two himself. It was a pretty gruesome sight right now. There were at least thirty dead men on the side. How many more had already been carried out? The Hall was huge and everywhere he looked, there were more bodies to be collected.

It was a strange silence as they stood and realized the impact on the clan. He suspected their numbers were cut in half by now. It was very disheartening. So many friends and family members lost. At the sound of wings behind them, Cody twisted to see his father landing on the front step. With a big grin, Goran walked inside and froze.

"Dear God," he whispered. That was it, nothing else, but his jaw worked as if he wanted to say more and couldn't find the words to express his thoughts.

Cody understood. While they stood there in shock, the others slowly arrived. By the time the group was together again, the two men had returned with their cart and started loading up more dead bodies.

Rhia gasped in horror. "Oh my God, what have we done to ourselves?"

Tessa answered, "Annihilation."

Cody stepped back and gave her a little shake. "No!" He looked at the others and said, "That's not true. It *would* have been annihilation, now it's our salvation. And let's not forget it's not over yet. Come on, let's go." And keeping a firm arm around Tessa's shoulders, he led the way to the elevators.

He wondered how long it would be before Tessa realized Jared wasn't with them.

SIAN OPENED HER eyes and didn't recognize where she was. It took a moment for the memories to fill her mind again. Dear God, they'd been trying to take her prisoner.

Panic threatened to overwhelm her once again. She reached down and stroked her belly. *It's okay little one. I will protect you.*

Why was it when she'd been attacked on the street she'd turned into a warrior woman, but now that she'd been attacked inside her second home, she hadn't been able to summon up the same fierceness?

Instinctively, she knew the answer. The first attack had been from the outsiders. The second attack had been from within her own Council. They had the power to make her life a living hell. They had the power to put her to death. And to destroy Taz and her unborn child.

That's when she realized a different truth. The Councilmen that were doing this were not from inside her own Council, they were outsiders that had infiltrated the Council.

They weren't her people. They were the enemy – once again trying a different attack. So far it was working.

She was terrified.

Her phone buzzed. She lifted it to read the message. And smiled. "Everyone is back in the Hall."

"Good. Warn them," Wendy said. "Or they will be taken prisoner too."

"Especially Rhia," Ian said. "And if they have Seth, it's a guarantee that they won't make it anywhere. Better they get into the tunnels and come up that way."

❧ ❦

SERUS ANSWERED THE phone call and listened in shock and amazement as Sian explained what was going on. "Right, we'll go into the tunnels then work our way up. When is the meeting?"

Sian said, "I have no idea. I don't dare show up until it is safe."

"We're heading your way." Serus tucked his phone into

his pocket and turned to the rest of the group. "We're going to take the stairs down and use the tunnels. The Council is hunting us all. We need to get out of sight, fast."

Tessa spoke up. "Then we're not going in through this area. We'll go in from outside." She turned to look at Cody.

Cody nodded. "It's the only way. Let's go."

Serus shook his head as he realized how much the kids knew that he didn't. "Okay, let's go fast."

Ushering the others ahead of them, they slipped down the hallway and out the back door. It was only as they heard the door close behind him that Serus thought he heard shouts and he realized that they'd been recognized. "Move. Move it, *move it.*"

Tessa led the way up the hillside and a tower opening that he had no idea existed, but he was willing to follow. When she disappeared from sight, he knew she had the right idea. Minutes later, the whole group had dropped down to the tunnels under the Council Hall.

He stopped and stared. "How is it I never knew this existed?"

"Is this where you found Victor?" Ian asked.

"This was where we realized someone was living in the apartments above the Hall. We could see him above. It's after that we found out it was Victor." She raced through the tunnel, looking for the passageway that would lead off. She called back, "Did Sian tell you what floor she was on?"

"Yes, she's on the third floor." Still carrying his son, Serus followed Tessa to where there was a network of staircases. "It's truly amazing."

"Yes, it is." Cody said. "We can explore later. We don't have time now."

Serus wasn't going to argue that point as Tessa led them

straight up and he could see markers on the various doors as they climbed higher and higher. When she hit the third one, she opened the door and stepped inside, holding up her hand for everyone else to wait. A moment later she poked her head back out and said, "It's safe."

Serus studied the doors. "We don't know which one they are in."

"I do." Tessa walked straight to the third door on the left-hand side and knocked. A moment later, the door opened and she raced inside.

Within seconds, the whole group was once again together.

∾ ∾

IT HAD BEEN an easy decision to stay behind. Jared didn't want to leave his friends. And he couldn't keep up with the others. Now they were heading into a fight that in no way was he equipped to help out. If they'd asked for him to come and give them a hand, he would've been more than willing but the truth was, he had been forgotten in the chaos. The army was here, so he was safe and he would do what he could to get his friends back home in one piece.

"Jared, do you have any idea how many are here?" One of the medics asked, holding up a clipboard.

Jared walked closer and realized that the men had started to write down the numbers and a basic description of the people. Of course none of the patients in the beds had ID anymore.

"No," he said, "but let me help."

The man gratefully handed over the clipboard and said, "Something basic to help us ID them, that's all we can do."

"I can do so much more," Jared said. "I know many of

these people here." He nodded to the students behind the man. "Many of them are my friends."

The medic gave him a big smile. "Then give us names and a description if you can. Make sure everybody is accounted for. We'll identify them with the same number on the clipboard," he said. "That way we don't lose track of who is who when we get the back to the hospital."

"Any idea where Taz is?" Jared asked.

The medic shook his head. "No, I think he's on his way here, but I know that his wife has been attacked so he could be heading to Council Hall too."

Jared winced. "That's too bad. Sian is good people. And so is Taz."

The medic nodded. "We don't have a problem with any of the ones we deal with. The trouble is not everybody on their side likes that they are helping us. They are in the middle of a war all on their own right now."

"Yeah, that's why I was happy to stay here," Jared said, waving his arms at the room full of his own people. "It's not only safer now, but I understand humans."

"So true." The medic laughed. "Then as we're short-handed, let's put you to work."

CHAPTER 13

"I CAN'T BELIEVE everybody is finally together again," Tessa cried in joy. She walked over to her brother and gave him a great big hug, one that he returned with great affection. She leaned back and looked up at him, a beaming smile across her face. "I'm so happy to see you survived."

He reached around and hugged her tight. "Same here, sis."

Motre walked in just then. David laughed and said, "Motre's been telling us all about the blast and how you saved Cody." David studied her face intently. "Are you that good now that you can haul somebody back from the dead?"

She gave a bright laugh. "Hell no." She shook her head when her brother didn't listen but continue to stare at her, a question in his eyes, as if she'd tell him the truth if he looked hard enough. "Honest. Cody was given a choice apparently."

"And I wonder about that," David said.

"Hey, we all do," Sian said from the far corner of the couch. She waved at Tessa through the crowd. Tessa raced over and gave her a great big hug too.

"I'm so glad you and the baby are doing fine," Tessa said, feeling the same old anger spiking up inside. "I can't believe they attacked you. Your own people."

"They didn't really," Sian said. "They were going to escort me to a personal prison."

"Let them try with me around," Tessa snapped. "No one is going to hurt you or the baby."

Serus and Goran stepped up behind Sian. Goran said, "What we have to do first is figure out how to stop these guys from taking over the Council."

Tessa stopped and looked at them. "Were they before your time on the Council?"

Goran puffed up. "Do I look that old?"

She sniggered. "Maybe…"

He narrowed his gaze at her, but there was laughter in their depths. She was happy to see that things were a little lighthearted, at least for a moment. They would get back to having to fight for their lives soon enough.

Sian said, "I contacted four Councilmen," she said. "I heard that one had passed on that we did not know about. That was Bush, he's gone."

Serus shrugged. "I barely even know the name."

Tessa asked, "Really?"

Her father nodded. "He's been retired for centuries."

"One was on his way to come back and help. That's Triton, he should be here soon but I haven't heard anything from him."

"Triton is a good man." Goran said. "He'll be on our side."

"He will be if we can find him," Serus said. "If you know that he's a good guy so quickly, then the other half of this nightmare will also know that. And they will pick him off before he has a chance to meet us."

"Then we need to have a team to meet him," Motre said. "Any idea how far he is? Could he already be here at the Hall?"

"It's possible," Sian said. "I was expecting him a few

hours ago."

Tessa took a step back. "I bet he's already here. And I bet they already have him."

"Then we're going to find him and anyone else they are holding, and we're going to take him back," Motre said, walking toward the main door.

"Wait," Sian said. "I heard from Morris. He's on his way as well. So you need to keep an eye out for him as well."

"Morris is a good guy too," Motre shook his head. "What's with all these guys traveling? They should stay home where they are needed."

Goran asked, "What about the fourth man? Who was that?"

"Privy," Sian said. "I managed to contact his family, but no one has seen him in a long time."

"He might be missing, or he might be part of the blood farm. He was one of the ones that we had a lot of trouble with before. He backed out and walked away from the clan at that point in time." Serus crossed his arms over his chest. "That's it? There's no one else to call on?"

"There are, but I couldn't reach anybody." Sian's voice faded slightly with fatigue. "I've been trying hard but not getting anywhere." She lowered her voice. "I'm afraid the other Council members may have taken them out before I could reach them."

"That would mean that the blood farm was expecting this. That they were planning and were prepared for this takeover," Cody said, anger making his voice vibrate.

"And of course that's nothing new," Tessa said calmly. "We've seen a lot of planning, a lot of preparation, and a lot of infrastructure in place ready to expand to do more – be more. All they needed was to get rid of those of us that would fight them." She shrugged. "What a good way to do it. Make the Council all on your side and slowly get rid of those that are against you."

"At least I know who to look for," Motre said from the doorway. "I'm going to see if I can find the missing Councilmen."

Tessa watched him leave with misgivings. She didn't like to think of anyone going it alone right now. She wanted to volunteer to go with him but was torn, wanting to stay to protect Sian.

David walked over. "Motre, I'll come with you. We should stay paired up in case one of us runs into trouble."

Motre nodded. "Am glad to have you along."

"Wait," Tessa cried, inspiration striking. "Do you have any idea where you are going to go look for them?"

"No," Motre said. "Any suggestions?"

"Yes, go down two levels. We passed a hallway that would have made a perfect prison. There was energy on that floor, but not any I recognized."

"AND BE CAREFUL," Cody warned. "We are expecting an attack."

David threw him a cocky grin. "We will. Anything is better than sitting here and doing nothing."

"Best if we can find the missing Councilmen. Then all of us can go as one group to the meeting." Serus glanced over at Rhia and Sian. "No one should be left alone at this point in time."

Sian gave a broken laugh. "I have no intention of going anywhere without you." She shook her head. "It was very distressing to have my own people turn against me."

Rhia sat down beside her and picked up her hand. "I'm so sorry I had to leave you."

Sian gave her wan smile. "It's okay. I do understand why you did what you did."

"And you're probably one of the few that does," Rhia admitted. "The maternal instinct is not and never has been very strong in our species."

Sian went to say something then hesitated.

"What is it?" Rhia asked.

Cody walked closer. If something was bothering Sian, they all needed to know.

Sian gave a tiny shrug. "It's nothing really, I just..." She looked uncomfortable.

"Spit it out, Sian," Serus said. "What's bothering you?"

Sian looked up at Rhia and Serus. "Where are Rosha and Gitorria?"

Goran crossed his arms over his chest and frowned. "I have no idea. In as much as I would like to think that they are part of this mess. I don't think they are."

"No, they are not," Rhia said. "They both left as soon as the trouble started. The last I saw of them was when I was in the hospital. At that time, they were planning on leaving before they got mixed up in any more of this."

"Typical of them. Besides, they both spent most of the last two centuries in Europe anyways." Goran opened his arms and added. "As much as we could use the extra help from those two, I'd never be quite sure whose side they were on, so I wouldn't trust them now."

Rhia turned and frowned at him.

Goran didn't back down. "Admit it, Rhia, they've been involved with how many doctors in the last decade. Make that century? They've had nothing but affairs with medical people for the last God only knows how many years. I would not be at all surprised if they've had a few modifications done themselves."

At that, Rhia went to open her mouth in protest but she caught Serus's look and her shoulders slumped. "I can see they may have had some modification," she admitted. "But no more than many other women their age. They'd be trying to look good for longer. Not trying to be better or bigger or stronger."

That brought smiles to both Goran and Serus's faces. Cody just shook his head. Vampire women were seriously gorgeous right through until becoming ancients. There was no need for beauty modifications.

"Maybe contact them to make sure that they are in Europe and not part of this mess or not caught up in this mess," he suggested. "Then we can forget about them." Cody paused then added, "Does anyone know what happened to Darren and the other vampires that were hung up in the first blood farm?"

Everyone looked at him. As he suspected, everyone had forgotten about them.

"Weren't they taken to the vampire hospital?" Goran asked. "But of course that's a problem in itself."

"There's a list in the office," Sian said, "of all those that were rescued. But it was a short list. I don't think it's been updated after the hospital massacre. At this point in time, there's no way to know who is alive and who is not."

"Did we get everybody out of the hospital?" Cody asked. "Do we know that for sure?"

"Yes." Sian's tone was confident enough to satisfy Cody.

"Okay, so if the hospital has been cleared and we're not sure if there are more vampires in the blood farm or not…

Where is everybody?" He started to pace the small room. "There should be thousands and thousands of us. Why have we not drafted them to be part of this army?"

"We have," Goran said. "There are hundreds helping us."

Cody came to a stop in front of the small group. "And the others?"

Goran shrugged. "It's possible they're just hiding. Not every vamp wants to fight. Obviously many vamps are still trying to keep families and businesses intact." He opened his arm and waved at the door. "Consider that they were still taking young students from the university. They didn't wipe out the university or all the students that attended, so in theory there are still many there."

Serus looked at his son. "We do not want everyone involved. We don't want them to even know how bad this is. It's very important that we pull out the key people and try to keep the infrastructure of our society functioning."

Cody wasn't sure that was possible. "I like that theory. I'm just not sure it's viable."

Rhia said in a gentle voice. "And that's because for you, this war has taken over every moment of every day. There are tens of thousands of vamps out there who have no idea what's going on. Some have gone to sleep for a week or a month. Others are busy living their lives totally unaware of the war. Without any involvement in the fresh blood market or dealing with areas where the kids had gone missing, or the Council, how would anybody know?"

Cody threw himself onto the closest chair and sprawled his legs out. "It just seems so far-fetched that we would be dealing with this as intensely as we are and yet so many thousands of our own peers are walking through this nightmare blind to what's going on."

"And that's the way it needs to be," Sian said. "It's very important that this be handled in a methodical order so that all the vamps know that we are in control dealing with this problem."

Cody stared at her in frustration. "And are we?"

Her gaze was shuttered as she stared at him. "I have to believe that we are," she said. "I know that this is a time of great stress with a takeover bid by the old Council, but as we defeated them last time, we have to believe that we can do it again."

Wendy spoke up for the first time since they arrived in the room, "I don't understand how they think they can take over the Council," she said. "Unless they have some of the enhanced army to overpower us." She stood up and walked closer. "Given the number of us versus the number of them, why would you have to listen to them at all?"

"It's the way things have always been done," Sian said. "The rules were established centuries ago."

☙ ❧

WENDY LOOKED AROUND the room. "Doesn't that mean it's time to give the system an overhaul?"

Beside her, Tessa laughed. "It so is."

"Now you young ones just wait," Goran said. "This system's suited us fine for a long time."

"That's because you don't like change," Cody said. "But it's good timing with the purge that's happened."

"That doesn't mean that the change can happen instantaneously," Sian said. "We would still need to establish the rules of the new order."

"Which we are not going to be able to do," Tessa said,

"if the elders maneuver their way back into power. If these old Councilmen do get back on, change will happen, but it won't be change any of us are happy about."

Wendy wanted to laugh as she watched the elders exchange glances. They were so resistant to anything new. She couldn't really blame them. They *were* ancients. This was the way things had always been done, and it worked for them. But they were on the cusp of a new direction. The old ways were not going to be acceptable anymore. The problem at this point was how to make the change happen fast enough to suit them.

It also had to happen fast enough to save Sian, Rhia, and anyone else the old guard determined to be traitors to the cause. She knew Sian and Rhia would never do anything against the Council or the clan – not willingly.

"You do realize that by making that suggestion, you would be classed as being a traitor as well?" Ian asked.

She turned to watch the man in her life as he approached, his long lanky form more mature, standing taller and straighter than she'd ever seen him before.

"Yes, by the standard of the old Council, as they would judge Sian to be a traitor. This discussion puts all of us on the same side." Tessa shrugged. "And? It changes nothing."

"That's treason though," Goran said. "Where would all this end if we don't monitor ourselves?"

"Would you like to see the elders work their way back into power and start the blood farm again?" Tessa asked.

Goran shook his head. "Never." He moved to stand behind Sian. "It took a lot to get rid of them in the first place, and now they've turned on Sian and Rhia. Where will that end?"

"It won't," Serus said. "Unless we stop it."

Wendy watched as the two ancients studied each other, likely having a silent conversation the way she knew they could. She wouldn't be surprised if Tessa and Cody weren't discussing the matter themselves as well. She wished she and Ian could, but so far they hadn't been so blessed as to find that type of a connection. She kept hoping.

"The worst-case scenario right now is the Council deems all of us traitors and we're given a death sentence." Ian said it simply and factually.

Wendy shivered in horror. "I'm glad you said worst-case scenario."

Ian walked closer and wrapped his arm around her, holding her close. She loved that they were able to show affection now in public as everyone knew about their relationship. She slipped her arms around his waist and hung on. His worst-case scenario was pretty damn bad. She didn't want to think about it.

RHIA SANK BACK into the couch. This Council was going to be the death of them all. She'd been prepared to lose her own life to save Seth, but at this point she knew they were all going to be grouped together as traitors.

And that wasn't fair.

She couldn't imagine that fate for any of her children, yet she knew that Tessa would be at the top of the list. Seth wouldn't be given a chance. Only David might survive, but not likely. They would all be put to death.

And that she couldn't let happen either.

"Suggestions?" She let her gaze land on every one of the people that had been beside her since this journey began. That David and Motre weren't here just brought home the fact that everybody involved would be put to death, not just those in the room. What did the enemy care if yet another few hundred good vampires died? They'd killed so many more than that already.

"How can it be treason if they are the ones that are killing us?" Tessa asked. "They'd be the ones in the wrong."

"And that's a very good question. If they've mounted a coup to take over the current Council, which is a possibility, they are the ones that should be put to death." Rhia nodded, liking that. Trust the young people to have a very different viewpoint. "I think we are struggling because we're coming from centuries of obedience and allegiance to the Council."

"But we don't know what the elders want for sure though," Cody said. "They said they've been forced back into service because so many of our people have been killed. What if it is true that they don't want to be here?"

"Then let's ask," Tessa said. "And if they are happy to retire, then let them." She gave a fierce smile that encompassed the group and added. "If, however, they are guilty then…" her fangs sharpened, "We take them out."

Rhia wondered when her daughter had become so bloodthirsty. Having killed more people and vamps that she cared to count herself, she could just imagine how doing the same affected her daughter. She didn't want her to become numb to the fact that they would be taking more lives.

That she won't do, Rhia my love, Serus said in her mind. *She has cried for the deaths of so many, yet she still stands strong.*

I hope you're right, Rhia said. *She was such an innocent before this, and look at her now. She's a battle-weary warrior.*

That she is. And I'm damn proud of her for it.

It's not that simple, Rhia protested. *She's just a schoolgirl, yet listen to the words that are coming out of her mouth.*

And that's because she's looking for a way to save her family and friends – exactly the same as she has done many times since this mess started. She's no longer a schoolgirl. She's a seasoned warrior.

"I don't think any of them should have to die unless they are planning to kill us," Tessa said. "But I won't back down in a fight. If they bring it then we will take it, turn it, and fire it back at them."

She stood up and walked toward the door. "In fact, I think sitting here waiting for them to take action is hurting us."

Rhia watched as Cody reached out a gentle hand and snagged Tessa's arm, tugging her back. "Slow down, we are waiting for David and Motre, remember?"

She made a funny face at him, making Rhia smile to see the camaraderie between the two of them. Cody wasn't afraid of Tessa and that was a good thing, but neither was he dominant and overbearing, and that was a better thing. It was obvious there was great affection between the two of them. And that was wonderful.

See, I told you, Serus said.

She wanted to shake him. *Yes, you told me, but I needed to see it for myself,* she whispered.

And now you have. Okay, so he was a little on the smug side with that one, which he deserved. At the very least she wouldn't worry so much about Tessa and Cody at this point in time.

Good, then let's find a solution to this damn problem instead, Serus said.

Just then, the door opened and Motre and David walked back in, escorting two very confused and shaky-looking vampires.

Sian jumped to her feet. "Oh my, you actually found Councilmen Triton and Morris."

DAVID LAUGHED, FEELING triumphant. "Tessa was correct. They were two floors down in the hallways. The doors were locked, but there were no guards. Both men were in the same room."

Sian walked in front of the two men and studied their features. "How are you feeling?" Triton lifted his head and stared at her bleary-eyed and still a bit unfocused. "I feel like shit. What the hell happened?"

Morris added, "And why the hell were we treated like that when we came back to help?"

"And fell into enemy hands," Sian said gently. "I'm sorry about that. I hadn't realized the treachery had infiltrated the Council to such a level." She motioned to empty chairs. "Please, sit down, you look a little pale…"

David helped the men to the chairs. When they were seated, he took up a place behind them and listened.

Rhia asked, "What happened to you?"

Triton said, "I was walking from the parking lot up to Council Hall when I was greeted by four men who said that they were guards and would escort me to the Council rooms."

He shrugged, "But they escorted me straight to that room and locked me in." He looked over at his co-prisoner and said, "Several hours later, they brought Morris in to join me. I tried to ask them questions. Ask what they wanted. When I could be released. They never said a word and just slammed the door shut and locked it."

"Were you given any drugs?" Tessa asked. "Any injections? Anything to eat or drink."

Morris said, "We were offered bottles of some kind of liquid, which we both tried and decided was terrible." He looked over at the first vamp and said, "So neither of us drank very much."

"And that's a good thing," Tessa said. "As it was likely drugged. You appear to have some side effects happening, but not very much at all."

"Drugs? Side effects?" Triton murmured. "I knew things were bad, but I hadn't realized they would be this bad. I wish I came home weeks ago."

Rhia gave him a wry smile. "We wish you had too."

"Just how bad is it?" Morris asked.

Goran, in his inimitable style, said, "Bad."

"Thousands of our people are dead, and half the Council is either dead or missing," Sian said. "They have brought the forced retirees back into service on the Council. If we don't have enough members to cast a vote amongst ourselves, then they will be placed back on active duty. I don't know if any of you remember the fight we had to get…"

"Those guys, they were all over the blood farm issue last time. Weren't there some rumors about live sacrifices too?" Triton shuddered. "They should have been put to death then."

"It's hard to imagine that they could ever return to power again," Morris agreed. "I'd forgotten all about them until you just brought them up."

"So had I," Serus said. "But they already tried to brand Sian as a traitor and have her imprisoned until a tribunal could determine her fate."

"What!" Triton bounded to his feet. "How do they get off doing something like that?"

"It came as a surprise to all of us, but if they are calling her a traitor, you know that they are branding the rest of us as the same." Rhia waved her arm at the new arrivals. "Except in your case. They are likely going to wait until they can determine which side of this war you are on. If you choose their side, you will get a chance to live. If you choose our side, then you will die."

The color bleached from both vamps' faces. "Shit."

They looked at each other and then back at the group around them.

"I know where I stand, where I have always stood," Triton said. "I never did believe in the blood farms."

"And I was part of the group that put those Councilmen out to pasture last time," Morris added. "So my fate has already been sealed."

Both men slumped into their seats. "It never occurred to us that we would be in a life or death situation by returning."

Tessa said, "Be glad that you had a chance to be free and escape all the war so far. We've taken care of all the enhanced nasty experiments that the blood farm has created. Now it's down to the power struggle in the Council."

"And Victor's son," Cody added.

The men stared at her.

"Enhanced experiments?" The first vamp shuddered and said, "Don't explain, I don't think I want to know."

"You may not want to, but I think you need to know," Goran said. "Because you're going to come up against a few if the old guard has some still tucked away." He turned to look at Tessa. "Where is Beast?"

Tessa gave him a frown. "He's not that bad," she protested.

Cody laughed. "Yes, he is. But now that we've all come

to understand how big a help he can be, he's forgiven for being big ass ugly."

As if hearing his name, Beast got up from the corner where he'd been snoozing and padded closer, a deep questioning growl coming out of his throat.

"Jesus, what is that thing?" Morris cried out in horror. Both men climbed to the back of their chairs as Beast approached.

David found that he appreciated the men's reaction. He wasn't a big fan of Beast either. But neither had he had a chance to get used to his presence, whereas Tessa and Cody appeared to be totally okay with this monster in their midst. In fact, Beast appeared to be extremely affectionate with Tessa, if the nuzzling and banging his head against her hand to get her to scratch it meant that. He watched as his sister bent down and gave Beast a hug. He really was like a puppy.

Just a monster version of a puppy.

Tessa, still squatting, turned to face the man. "He's one of the blood farm experiments. Not content with giving enhancements and special drugs to humans and vamps willing and unwilling, when they ran out of recruits for their army, they started doing the same thing to animals."

David watched but realized neither men were accepting of that explanation. "They really were doing these type of experiments on everyone," he emphasized. "Human and vamp and animals."

The two men twisted to look up at him as if asking for confirmation. He nodded. "It's a sad fact, but it's true."

"That is just despicable," the first vamp said. "How could they do that to our own people?"

Cody stepped up. "It started by seducing the young men and women into thinking they weren't good enough. Then they offered drugs and enhancements that would make them fly, when they couldn't fly. Make them walk in sunlight when they couldn't walk in sunlight. Make them do and be so much better than they were… but the truth is, they weren't able to prove any of those claims. And after the enhancements they became hooked on the drugs they were fed, which just become stronger, more twisted, and eventually they became these misshapen, deformed experiments. And of course they were also cloning vamps."

Morris stared at him in shock. "But cloning is not allowed," he cried out. "It's against clan law."

Goran snorted. "I really don't think they asked for permission."

"And that's why your vote is going to be very important," Rhia said gently. "Because the same old assholes that we got rid of for this decades ago are now trying to get back into power, and I'm afraid if they succeed, then they have the connections to start this all up again."

"They are already planning to rebuild," Tessa said. "Think about it. This puts them back in control and back where they can make sure that the blood farm that they helped create now has a governing body that approves of it."

Her smile was grim as she caught David's gaze.

He could see the determination in her gaze to end this. He added, "And anybody who doesn't agree… well…there won't be anybody who doesn't agree, because they'd have killed them all."

Tessa walked towards the door, Beast at her side. "And now that we have everyone together, we must join the meeting as a group."

"No, wait," David said. "We saw six vamps and a couple of the older Councilmen, at least I'm presuming they were elders in a discussion during our search. They broke up as we approached." He glanced at Motre. "And the vamps were big and healthy, but I didn't recognize any of them. Motre, did you?" Motre shook his head. "No, none of them." David nodded. "I'm afraid that they're going to have vampires waiting for us."

David stepped into the center of the group where she could see him better.

"Tessa, before we go there, we need a plan."

"And more men," Ian suggested. "What about all the foreign dignitaries and their men? Are they still here?"

Sian said, "The clans all over the world are facing the same threat. Any of the men healthy enough to travel returned home to fight their own battle, and those left behind are still unconscious." David studied the occupants of the room. "Once again, it's just us here left to fight."

CHAPTER 14

TESSA SLIPPED QUIETLY into the tunnels surrounding the Council Hall's new meeting room. She had no idea that this set of tunnels even existed until Sian brought up one of the blueprints she'd found in the office.

"If there's going to be any of the enemy waiting, they will be in here," Sian had announced. "I suggest those of you that are not part of the Council hide in there. If we run into trouble, then you'll do what you do best," she said with a big smile, but showing teeth, "And ride to the rescue if needed."

And that's how Tessa, Wendy, Motre, Jewel, and Beast were now walking through the tunnels. It had been decided that as they were part of the Council but at a much lower level, David, Ian, and Cody needed to go into the meeting as well.

As much as she hated to think of Sian being up against the Councilmen, she was no longer alone and Tessa knew that her family would protect her. She very much wanted to hear the conversation though.

Motre was ahead of her. She'd been following slightly behind when he made a sudden sharp movement. She raced forward to stand beside him. There she could see a group of vamps standing and staring through some kind of a window.

"Any idea what they're watching?" she whispered.

Motre shook his head. "No, but I can guess."

"I suggest we find out." She brushed past him and with Beast still at her side, she sauntered towards the group. "Hey, what are you looking at?"

The men turned to face her.

Even in the shadows of the tunnel, she could see the dark energy in their bodies, in their hearts, and in their souls. "Nice, guys."

She waved her arms to encompass the whole group. "Interesting that all of you chose to take drugs and enhancements to make yourselves better. Were all of you so *lacking* in self-confidence before that you needed the boost – even though it's short-term and fake?"

Shocked surprise washed around her, even from her friends behind her. This was going to be a job for her and Beast. She hadn't come here depending on them to help out.

"What are you talking about?" the closest vamp asked. "Who are you, and what are you doing here?"

One of the men in the back called out. "Don't listen to her. She's one of the traitors." He muscled through the group to stand in front. He looked at her with a sneer. "Your days are numbered."

Tessa laughed. "What about your days? Do you realize that your life is ebbing away right now? That the drugs inside your system are only good for two days and if you don't get more drugs, then you die?"

The vamp shrugged. "We'll be getting lots of the new drugs, so it's not going to be an issue."

"Except for the fact that we closed down the labs," Motre said at her side. "And you won't be getting your drugs in time. How do you feel about that now?"

"You're lying. Besides, we're not depending on the drugs from here. Our drugs come from Europe. They are pure.

They aren't the corrupted ones from here. There was a mad scientist running loose in this place." He motioned at Beast beside Tessa. "He must have made him. What the hell? How messed up is it?"

One of the other vamps in the group snorted and said, "That's okay, we'll take care of him for you."

And he stepped forward with a spike in his hand.

Tessa studied him like he was some kind of an odd specimen. "Nobody touches this animal," she warned in a soft tone.

"Yeah, or else what?"

She smiled. "Or else I kill you."

"You and whose army?" The man with the spike chuckled. "I don't think that animal will be much help to you."

Motre laughed back at him. "I guess you don't know who she is, do you?" He motioned at Tessa and added, "Particularly if you're not from around here."

"We're from Europe, so no, not particularly," one of the men leaning against the hallway said. "We just got in this morning, not that it matters." The vamp eyed Tessa up and down. "You don't look to be anything special."

"Oh, I'm not. And because I'm not," Tessa said with a big innocent smile, "I'll give you this chance to live. But only if you agree to return to the nightmare where you came from."

"I think we should find out all the information on the European lab before we let them go home again," Wendy piped up from behind her.

Twisting slightly, Tessa nodded and said, "A good point." She turned back to the men sneering at them. "So you can tell us everything you know and I'll let you live. Or you could not cooperate and then you'll die." She shrugged.

"I really don't care either way. I didn't bring any gas masks for when the nasty ash starts flying though."

"And in close confines like this, it's going to be really gross," Wendy muttered. "Maybe I'll retreat back to the hallway until you guys are done."

"Me too," Jewel added.

Tessa didn't look back at her but did offer her a suggestion. "Good idea, stand watch and let us know if anyone else comes."

Then she took a step forward. Two men in the front straightened. "Hey, we've got no quarrel with you."

"You haven't explained what you're doing here," Tessa said in a lighthearted tone. "And of course, no one has volunteered any useful information at this point."

"You don't really expect us to, do you?" one of the men asked in disbelief. "It wouldn't be worth our jobs."

"I hear you," she said. "And I'm sorry because it looks like we're on opposite sides in this war. It would be easier if you did know who I was," she admitted. "Then I wouldn't have to kill anyone to prove to you that I can."

She studied their energy and realized that the man leaning against the wall was doing so because he was weak. His physical body was already breaking down. She pointed to him. "You're already dying. That's why you are leaning against the wall. You don't want the others to know how weak you are."

He straightened. "I'm just tired. I don't like flying."

"And the last dose of drugs was weaker. Your system is slowly dying off."

He shook his head. "That's not true. It can't be true."

"It is. I can see the black running through your body, taking your life force with it."

"You're lying," he scoffed. "No one can see all that."

"Am I?" She took a step closer. "Lift your hand and hold it out steady."

In a moment of bravado, he did as she asked. Then stared in shock at his arm, now shaking like crazy.

"See, it's already started. And there isn't anything anyone can do to help you. At least not here."

"Why not here?" he asked, his voice shaking with the truth.

"Because the drugs here are no good. If the drugs you have in Europe are better, then you might be okay if you get a full dose fast enough."

"Why were you given only a partial dose?" Motre asked.

"They were short on it," one of the other men said. "They are shipping more here for us as we speak."

"Oh good, then you only have to wait until the drugs arrive. Maybe you'll make it after all." But as she studied the look on his face and the depth of the poisoning, she whispered, "Or maybe not."

"She's lying. Don't let her get to you. We did hear about her. She's the one they warned us about."

The men frowned as if turning the information over in their brains. They turned their attention toward her. "She's pretty young for all we heard."

"Ah, you did hear about me, did you?" She smiled. "I might be young, but what you heard is likely to be the truth."

"No, it's not," the dying one scoffed. "Besides, it doesn't matter."

"We're letting them turn our attention away from what we are supposed to be doing. Get them," someone in the middle of the group ordered. "Shut her up permanently."

Tessa laughed. "Bring it on, boys."

She took a step forward as two of the men started to walk towards her. Beast, always eager for a fight, jumped forward, snarling. "Easy, boy. We have to give them a chance to back off first."

"There will be no backing off here," snarled the man closest to her.

Tessa looked each of the two men in the eye and gave a final warning. "This is your only chance to stop. If you take one more step, then I will kill you."

But no one was in a listening mood.

The two men rushed her.

Tessa settled into a wider stance and raised one hand. In a small space like this, her only trouble would be in keeping the energy flare confined to the two men. Studying their energy, she flicked the first one in the heart chakra, hitting directly beneath the darkness and into the actual organ – he stopped in place and crumpled at her feet soundlessly.

The second man hit the brakes to stare down at his comrade and then glared at her. "What did you do?" he screamed.

"Only what I said I'd do," she asked calmly. "I warned you." She nodded at the man on the floor and smiled, but it was a grim smile, a hard smile. "He was your example. If you take another step, you will join him."

The vamp shook his head in shock. "That's not possible," he cried. "It's a trick." He crouched down beside his fallen friend and shook the man's shoulder hard. The vamp rocked slightly but didn't wake. Slowly, as if realizing he really was dead and somehow the unbelievable had become believable, the man straightened, but this time there was anger and hatred in his gaze.

"That is my brother." His fingers went into claws, and he barely restrained himself from reaching for her.

"That *was* your brother," she said, her gaze hard as she watched him, waiting for the attack. "And have no doubt, you will join him if you come after any of us."

The man turned to look at the rest of the vamps behind him urging him on.

"Get her," the leader ordered. "She can't get all of us at the same time."

Instantly several of the men raced towards her. Tessa held up her hand and flicked her fingers four times. Each time she hit a man in the heart chakra. Each time the man fell to the floor, dead.

Energy buzzed around her. She took a deep breath and exhaled, releasing some pent up energy in a harmless manner.

The first man still stood, as if not believing what was happening. She understood. But it didn't change the fact that they always seem to learn the hard way. "What's it going to be?" she challenged. "Life or death?"

Too bad her species were knotheads.

They didn't learn easy or fast.

A new wave of men, she had no idea how many, rushed towards her. She didn't have as much time as last time so instead of fine-tuning hits to the heart, she just slammed energy to their chest area. It wasn't as clean and maybe not as fast a death, but it was more effective in close quarters.

Again the men dropped in place – dead.

This time the vampire closest to her backed up, holding his hands up in front of him. "No, no no no. This can't be." He turned to run and came face-to-face with the leader, who was glaring at him.

"Did you see what she did?" he cried. "We don't have a chance."

The leader snarled, "You have no choice either way."

Tessa couldn't see what he did, but the result was the same. The vamp who'd retreated blew up in a cloud of ash. He'd chosen life, but his boss had refused to accept the decision.

As ash covered the nine dead men on the floor, she studied the leader on the other side. "Is this really the end you wish for you and your friends?"

The leader was snapping in rage. "I don't know what you're doing or how you're doing it," he said, "but we came here to do a job, and now even I can see behind my order's actions. You cannot be allowed to live. You are a danger to us all."

"Really?" Tessa studied him like he was a bug. Which to her he was. Something to be squashed. Something to never have to deal with again. "Interesting that you would say that," she said. "Because in reality, you're the one that shouldn't be allowed to live. What I do, I do naturally. I was born this way. What you do, you can only do with drugs and enhancements. I might be a quirk of nature," she worked her lip in a sneer, "but you're an abomination of nature."

A movement behind him showed one other vamp, a younger, slightly slimmer version of the leader. She sighed. "Do you really want your son to die too?" Then she frowned. "Or is he a clone like Terry?"

The young kid from behind called out, "Do you know Terry?" His voice held that same quivering mix of innocence and hope.

And Tessa realized that he likely was the same. In a softer voice, she said, "Yes, I've met Terry."

"Is he okay?" the young man asked in worry. "He's my friend."

Tessa nodded. "He's fine. Maybe I'll get a chance to take you to him when this is over."

She flipped her gaze back to the leader and quite possibly the father of the young boy. "Is this the way things are done in your world now? No need to have babies anymore?"

"It's none of your business." He turned to the boy. "Go back to Bruno. Tell him that you are both to go home."

The young man protested, "You said I could stay with you, Father."

"Don't argue," the father snapped. "Bruno will look after you. He'll keep you safe."

"But…" The boy seemed to know better. He turned and started to walk down the tunnel. He stopped and cast a look back at his father. "Are you going to be okay?" he asked, his voice trembling.

"I'll be fine," the father answered.

Tessa studied him. "So you don't care that the boy will have no father? You're still planning on attacking?"

"I came here to do a job. My loyalty has never been questioned; that can't change now."

Motre walked ahead so that he could stand beside Tessa. "You don't have to do this. Haven't enough men died by now?"

"I have no choice, don't you understand that?" He stared at them in frustration. "I can't just surrender."

"Why not?" Tessa asked in a quiet voice. "There had to be a reason for bringing your son into existence. Is it so easy to let go of that bond?"

"I would do anything to save my son."

"And how does dying help him?" Tessa studied him,

trying to understand. She understood doing anything to keep someone you loved safe, but how did throwing himself into a fight he couldn't win solve anything?

"I want to keep my son safe," he replied. "As long as we're talking, he's had a chance to get away."

"What's to stop her from going down that same hallway and taking out Bruno and your son after you're dead?" Motre asked. "You've seen her in action. If we want it, your son will die."

"No!" He stood undecided, trembling from the conflicting need to look after his son and yet do his duty. Tessa watched and waited. Even if he did surrender, she wasn't sure she could trust him. He had black energy in his system, but it wasn't as deep or as dark or his body is deteriorated as the other men. "Have you just recently started taking the drugs?"

He nodded. "In Germany, we've had a resurgence of disease, something we haven't seen in centuries amongst our clan. We were hoping the drugs would stop the progression."

"Disease?" Tessa asked in surprise. "What's wrong that your bodies can heal themselves?"

The sick vamp shrugged. "Nobody knows. That's partly why we started the new cloning project." He twisted so he could look down the hallway and make sure his son had left as instructed.

"The drugs were not meant to be enhancements as much as a cure to stop the disease from killing us." He shook his head in disgust. "Then the scientists went crazy."

"And the cloning?" Motre asked. "Or was that to purify the DNA again so that more vamps could be born without the health issues?"

"Exactly. We've kept it secret from the other clans, but

our numbers have been decimated by disease."

"This is fascinating," Tessa said. "I'd be much happier about the drugs if they were used to serve the health of the vampires. There are no health issues in our clan at this point," she said. "But they were building an army of mutants to overpower the rest of us."

In a low tone, Motre asked, "Do we know that for sure about the disease?"

She shook her head. "No. How could we?" She studied the vampires on the floor, but there was so much darkness in their energy it was hard to tell from this point if they had health issues or not. "No one has said anything about such a thing yet."

"Maybe they couldn't," the other vamp said. "We weren't allowed to speak about it. It was against clan law to let the other clans know. It would weaken us in their eyes."

"And yet that's not something that you can keep secret for long." Motre walked forward two steps and stopped. "So what's it going to be, a life with your son? Or your son having a life without you?"

"I want protection from the rest of the clan," he growled, anger emanating from his frame.

"Interesting. Are you saying it's your clan that's behind this?"

The other vamp shook his head. "No, but they have joined in to get the benefit of the drugs." He shrugged. "Your clan — the blood farm half — were trying to overtake the clan, all the clans actually, and this was part of our agreement with them. We join, but we get the drugs to stop the disease. And the technology for clones."

Tessa looked at Motre. Motre looked at Tessa.

She shrugged. "Fair enough. We'll do what we can."

"That's not good enough," he snapped in anger. "I want your word."

Inside, Tessa was delighted with this turn of events.

Motre said, "I give you my word, but I don't think it will be our clans that will be the issue. Whoever you are working for here will be the dangerous one."

He half-turned to gaze into the smoky window and said, "I didn't like this from the beginning, but our people needed the drugs. The Council decided that there was no other way."

"Then we'll see what we can do."

Tessa motioned the vamp to turn around and move back towards Wendy. As he passed Beast, the animal snarled at him.

In a lightning move, the vamp turned and stabbed Beast with a stake through the side then turned to them. "Beast." Tessa cried out in shock, dropping to the floor at his side.

Motre jumped in front of her and stabbed the vamp. Seconds later, in a cloud of dust, he blew up and slowly fell all around them.

Tessa barely noticed. "Beast," she cried. "Oh Beast."

Her hands were already pulling the silver poison from his body, her fingers sliding into the open wound and pouring energy inside to heal him. She didn't know if she could save him, but she had to at least try. He'd saved her life several times. She could do no less.

Beside her, Motre dropped to his knees. "Can you save him?"

She shook her head. "I have no idea."

She wiped away the tears and continued to work.

CODY OPENED THE door to where the new Council meeting was being held and stepped inside.

"Why did you enter without permission?" said one of the elders as he made some attempt to rise, only to fall back into his chair from the effort.

Cody studied him dispassionately. Why he was even involved anymore? His days were over. What good would any of it do? It's not like they had drugs for longevity.

He froze. That's exactly what some of them had been working on. Is that why these old geezers were here? Were they afraid that they were going to die on the cusp of drugs being discovered that could extend life forever?

"I'm sorry, I wasn't aware the meeting had started," Cody said in a deferential tone. Behind him, the rest of the members streamed inside and took their seats.

The elders were too shocked to respond. Jameson sat up, his mouth open in surprise as the room filled. Roberts and Baker were there, big welcoming smiles on their faces.

"Of course they wouldn't start without us," Serus said. "Because that would be a breach of Council trust. We'd have to suspect those involved of ulterior motives if they did that," Serus said, taking his place at the table.

Cody retreated to stand at the back wall with David and Ian. This was a power struggle, but it didn't involve them. They were only needed if there was a hidden army somewhere ready to pounce.

From his position, he could see the shock and the anger on everyone else's faces at the suggestion.

Serus spoke up again and said, "As you can see, we have more than enough Council members now. You may go back to retirement, thanks so much for being willing to step up."

The men started shaking their heads collectively. In one

voice, they shouted, "No."

It was the strongest voice he'd heard out of them so far. Of course it took all four to make it happen.

Goran pounded the table in front of them. "Yes. You do not belong here. We got rid of you once, we will get rid of you again."

The dust elder spoke up in a quavering voice, "You cannot do this. We have already ratified the vote against those two *women*," he spat out the word. "They are no longer part of the Council."

Serus laughed. "You can't ratify anything. You aren't fully pledged Council members yet. You're just dusty, angry, old men trying your stupid little tricks. You are not part of this Council. Your ratification does not stand."

He stood, turned to the rest of the table, and said, "All in favor of keeping Rhia and Sian on the Council, speak now."

Instantly, a cry rose from everyone at the table, "Yes."

Cody tried to see if there were any dissenting voices. But he didn't see any other than the four elders.

Serus turned to the dusty old man. "You have no say here. Go back to the hole wherever they dragged you from." The door opened and Adamson walked in, shaky and pale but strong enough to show up for his vote. Cody was glad to see it. He roared. "What kind of monkey business is this?"

He turned to Cody and Ian and David. "You may leave. This is Council business."

Not one of the men moved.

Furious to the point of not being able to speak, Councilman Adamson spun on the Council members. His eyebrows shot up at the sight of the four men. "Elders?" he said in a cold, formal voice. He turned to the others when the elders stayed silent and said, "Just what is going on here?"

Goran and Serus stood up and faced him. "What's going on here is that there will be no more maneuvering from these four ancients back onto the Council," Serus snapped. "The Council still stands as always. There are enough surviving members here that these elders can go back to the hole they crawled from."

"Good, deal with it then." Councilman Adamson glared at him then turned his gaze on the members. "Jameson, what's going on?"

"The same as before you left to lie down," Jameson roared in disbelief. "I have been trying to preserve this Council by finding enough people to keep our government alive and well before chaos reigned."

The dust elders turned on Sian. "You are part of the same mutation problem as the blood farm. How dare you give birth to a half-human, half-vampire child?"

Cody took a step forward from the wall, ready to defend Sian. Adamson turned on him and hissed, "Remember your place."

Sian, still standing from where she had been before, smiled at Cody but motioned him back and whispered, "Thanks."

Then she turned back to the elders and said, "It's nice to know how you really feel." And she sat down, completely nonchalant.

Adamson stared at her in surprise. "What, that's all you have to say?"

"Nothing he said required more," Sian said. "One of the first things I plan to do is vote to have them removed permanently from the Council." She smiled at him. "So we never have this problem again."

Cody almost laughed when he saw the look of surprise on Adamson's face. And the respect.

Adamson opened his mouth to speak, but she held up her hand. "Stop. I know everything you're going to say. We need them. We don't. We need reserve Councilmen that aren't playing secret games with hidden agendas."

The dust man stood up beside Adamson. "This is outrageous."

And that started the yelling match.

From where they stood in the back room, Cody had never seen anything like it. It appeared that one side was yelling at the other and the other side was yelling right back. He turned to look at David and Ian, and all three of them were completely shocked. They'd never seen such unbridled behavior before. The Council was known to talk forever about a single issue, and they had witnessed heated arguments before. But nothing like this.

David whispered, "Do we do anything?"

Ian shook his head. "Hell no. I want to videotape this and put it up on the Internet."

Cody almost laughed, but this was serious. Too serious. And he wasn't sure what to do, if anything.

"This is a monkey court." David leaned against the wall again, crossing his arms as he eyed the argument going on with disgust.

"At the moment, it's just anger," Cody said. "But it can turn very quickly to something more damaging."

"It's too bizarre. Nobody would believe me." Ian turned to the other two. "I have my cell phone on me." He pulled it out of his pocket, switched on the video, and started filming the nightmare in front of them.

Cody thought of stepping in the middle of the chaos to

calm the meeting down when the dusty guy shot to his feet and roared at the top of his lungs, "Guards!"

David straightened at his side and Cody stepped forward, alert. What guards? The door behind the Council table where everyone sat opened, but no one rushed in.

The Councilman looked like he was ready to have a heart attack, he was so angry. He let out one more cry, "Guards! Get in here."

A roar exploded from the open doorway and a ferocious animal burst through, soaring in the air to land in the center of the round table.

There were screams and cries of horror as everyone pushed their chairs back and rushed to safety.

With everyone flattened against the outer edges of the room, Cody studied the animal. It *almost* looked like Beast. It *almost* sounded like Beast. But it wasn't Beast. Or wasn't Beast as he knew him. In his mind, he reached for Tessa.

Tessa, are you there, honey?

Coming now.

Sharp footsteps approached from outside the door. Just as he was about to call her again, someone appeared in the open doorway.

Tessa.

JARED SAT DOWN beside Clarissa's bed in the hospital. He was exhausted. They'd spent hours working, trying to remove all the humans, and finally he'd left when Clarissa had been taken out. The medic had let him hop into the back of the ambulance and sit with her.

She still hadn't regained consciousness.

He worried away at his lower lip as he studied her features. She didn't look any different. She should though, shouldn't she?

The door opened. Jared stood up and realized it was Taz.

"Taz?"

Taz turned to face him, a smile breaking free. "Hello, Jared. Damn, it's good to see you." His gaze shifted to the bed. "And Clarissa. I heard the news, but it's nice to see the proof for myself."

"Yeah, it's going to be a while searching that place to make sure we have everyone."

Taz nodded. "We've got good numbers coming in, and with a list of those recently missing, we're hopeful we'll find them all."

"Wouldn't that be nice for a change?" Jared waited then asked, "How is Sian?"

"In trouble again," Taz sent him a smile. "But the gang have rallied around her so with any luck, she'll be fine. If not, I might need your help to bust her loose." He laughed.

"Anytime," Jared said. "Anytime."

CHAPTER 15

"BEAST, GET OFF the table." Tessa strode into the room, her gaze swiftly moving from face to face. When she ascertained that Cody and the rest of her friends and family were safe, the set of her shoulders eased slightly. She tilted her head in acknowledgment to the Council, but her gaze turned and locked on the dust man. "Not who you are expecting, by any chance?"

"What is the meaning of this?" The elder's voice roared, but with a thin waver in it. "How dare you enter the Council meeting?"

Tessa laughed. "I dare much at this stage of my life."

She waved her arm at her friends and family standing quiet, watching. "It's good that all my friends and my family are still safe." She spun in a slow circle, studying the group. She knew this was going to be a slightly delicate situation. And she wasn't into doing delicate lately.

This was important to get locked down and finished. "And speaking of how dare I, I understand that you are no longer a member of this Council, and you therefore no longer have the right to be here. I'll be happy to escort you back to your chambers." And she smiled, showing her fangs.

The four men rose up on their haunches, anger, resentment, and fury spitting from them. They turned to face each other, then back at her. "What have you done with our guards?"

"Oh, they were your guards? Interesting." Tessa turned to motion at Motre standing in the doorway behind her. "Perhaps Motre here will explain what we found in the tunnel waiting for your instructions."

She motioned at Motre to enter the room. "Motre?"

Motre stepped inside. "We entered from the hallway in the tunnels below to find eleven men and one young boy standing watch through these fake windows," He motioned at the glass that had a painting etched into them. A fake-looking window to make the stone room look bigger and more open. "From where they stood, it was obvious these men were watching the proceedings."

Goran growled.

Serus hissed.

Tessa smiled.

Motre continued, "When they tried to take us out, Tessa gave them a demonstration of what would happen to them if they refused to back down."

"And just what kind of demonstration did she give them?" snapped the dust guy.

"She killed one." Motre smiled. "But the men didn't believe her, so they kept coming."

The second elder stood in outrage. "Did you kill them all?" he cried. "They were good men."

"Yes, they were." Tessa tilted her head to the side. "They were also from Europe on an agreement with the blood farm that they could receive the drugs that they needed to kill off a disease rampaging through their clan." She heard the shock murmurs around her but ignored them.

She didn't dare take her eyes off these four old men. "So they were your men? Which means you are associated with the blood farm." She took one step closer. "So why is it I shouldn't kill you right now?"

Silence.

"Tessa?" Cody walked over to stand beside her. "Maybe killing them is not necessary."

"One of the guards tried to kill Beast," she said in a low tone. "Stabbed him in the side with silver."

She could feel Cody's start of surprise and from those around her. Cody shifted so he could look at the table where Beast sat snarling. He was different now. Instead of that dark coat, there was a light gray, almost a blue tinge to his color. "What did you do to him? And *is* this Beast?"

She tossed him a light, sorrow-filled gaze. "How could I let him die after all he's done to protect me and mine?"

Cody ran his hand through his hair, staring at what appeared to be a bigger, stronger, more otherworldly-looking Beast before them. In a low whisper, he said, "Jesus."

"What do you mean you couldn't let him die?"

Tessa turned that laser gaze on the old Councilmen. "I saved his life," she said simply. "He's bigger, better, and stronger because of the healing energy I poured into him."

"You can heal?" one of the other elders asked eagerly. "We were supposed to get drugs that would double our life span. Make *us* younger – stronger."

"You mean can I help you extend *your* life?" She shrugged. "No one, including the blood farm, has magical drugs that will keep you alive longer. They may say they do, but all we have seen are drugs that kill you faster."

"No, that's not true," one of the other old Councilmen said. "They promised us that they had developed new drugs. Secret drugs. Ones that worked but weren't going to be made available for everybody. We've been waiting for decades."

"And you believe them?" Cody asked.

"Interesting that you would choose such a thing when supposedly you're all purists living on real blood. Existing the way you used to in the olden days that were so much better than the new ones. And yet, here someone offers you a magic pill to live longer and you jump at it?" Tessa asked, struggling to keep the mockery out of her voice. It's not who she was, it's not who she wanted to become, but these men were pissing her off.

Easy, Tessa, Cody said. *They've already been voted off the Council. There is no way for them to take charge again now.*

Unless they kill everybody in this room. She turned and looked at him. *Have you considered that?*

Cody frowned and studied the men. "It's not likely at this point in time," he said out loud.

She shrugged. "The only way for these four elders to regain their position and power on the Council again is if they killed us all off." She paused, her hard gaze going from one to another. "As they already have done to the other members." She snorted. "Eleven guards? Why would they need such heavy manpower?"

Silence.

"And as the elders couldn't put their plan in place without some inside help, at this point, the question is who else in this room is on their side?" she asked, her gaze slowly turning from one member to another. She knew in her heart it could not be her friends or her family. It would break her if she was wrong, and she wasn't willing to go there. She'd seen no sign of duplicity with any of them. She hated to think that Motre was involved. But she'd been forced to consider the possibility recently. Thankfully she discarded the idea.

That left six Councilmen. Roberts, Baker, Triton. Morris, Jameson, and Adamson.

One who'd been here with the old Councilmen since the beginning?

"Are you sure it's one of them here? Cody asked in a low voice.

"Yes," she said. "He has to be here."

"You don't know anything," one of the elders snapped. "You're on a killing spree. The bloodlust has got you. You won't be happy until you've annihilated everyone. That makes you worse than the ones you are killing."

Inside, Tessa could feel her shoulders cringe and her heart squeeze. She didn't want to listen to the words as they poured over her. It's not who she was. But was it what she had become?

No, Cody said. *Don't even begin to think along those lines. You've only done what you have needed to do to stay alive.* He reached out and put an arm across her shoulder, tucking her up close.

She gave him a shuttered look. *He's right in many ways.*

No, he's not. Motivation is everything. He glared at the elder, then added. *Besides, that's not the issue for right now.* Out loud, Cody said, "We need to bring this to an end. If you know who the traitor behind all of this is, please tell us now."

"She doesn't know anything," the dust guy said. "She's just guessing."

"It's obvious the four of you are once again involved in the blood farms that got you kicked off the Council before," she snapped. "Now even more so. You're involved in the drugs and experiments on vampires this time. The penalty should be much worse. It's one thing to hurt all the animals, the humans, but it's quite another to hurt your own clansmen."

"Our lines have become weak. The strain diluted. They are disposable. They should never have been allowed to exist in the first place." The dust guy was almost spluttering with rage as it consumed him. "I've been killing vamps like you since time began. Whenever there was bad blood, there is corrupted DNA." He shook his head. "Our genetics have been diluted to an unbearable mockery of our original souls. *You* have no right to live."

"Interesting." She turned and dismissed him with a flick of her fingers. She knew it would piss him right off. Sure enough, she felt the rush behind her.

She spun and faced him.

"Tessa." Cody tugged her back behind him. "I'll take care of him."

Neither had a chance to do anything.

Beast leapt from the table, launching himself onto the elder. The elder spun to face the new threat, silver spikes threaded through his fingers. Beast's attack sent them both tumbling to the ground.

The elder tried to lift his arms to stab him when Beast sank his teeth into the Councilman's neck.

Just like the nickname she'd given the elder, he turned to dust before her very eyes.

She lifted her gaze to the other three Councilmen, staring at the remains in front of them. Shock, horror, and yes, anger on their faces. Inside, her soul cried for yet another unnecessary death. They could have retreated, but they wouldn't. Why?

A second elder stepped forward. "None of our people

should have to die by a creature like that."

"You would prefer to die by my hand?" Cody asked.

"You're nothing but a child. Do you think we don't have ways and means of killing that you don't know about?" He blustered. "We are centuries older than you. Hell, I'm probably a thousand years older than you." He flicked his fingers around the room. "Than all of you."

He pointed at Beast. "That is an abomination I will not let live."

Beast, as if instinctively knowing a second attack was coming his way, turned his glowing eyes at the elder.

"I wouldn't try that if I were you," Tessa snapped. "But if you think to take him on and win, then so be it."

The elder dropped his gown and huge, spidery-thin wings opened up behind him.

Tessa heard Cody's gasp, and she realized that this must be one of the ancients of his line. How difficult this must be for him.

Why would these men not retire gracefully back into the hole they had come from again? Then again as they had killed many of their own clan, why should these men be allowed to survive?

Except she herself was sick of death too…

To that end, she gave them one more chance. "If you agree to go back to where you came from and have nothing more to do with the Council and with the blood farm and all that it entails," she offered, "we will let you live."

The Councilman charged. In his fingers was yet again some kind of splayed instrument intended to kill.

"I wouldn't do that if I were you," she said one last time. "Silver will not stop Beast."

"What are you talking about?" the elder said, rocking

back on his heels, stunned by her words. "How is that possible?" He shook his head. "Of course you lie."

Beast turned as if to come to Tessa's side when the elder threw himself at the animal, claws and spikes fully extended.

Beast turned, flipped up in the air, and came down on the back of the elder, sending them both to the floor. Then in one smooth move, Beast bit his neck.

Instantly ash filled the air as the drug-filled body burnt to a crisp. A horrible stench filled the air. Left behind in the middle of the ash pile were two finger-spike sets made of silver.

Coughing, the aroma beyond worse in the small, contained room, Tessa turned and walked toward Motre, who had returned to guard the entrance. There she breathed deeply in the hallway, trying to clear her lungs of that horrible stench. In a low voice, Motre asked, "You okay?"

She nodded. "Why don't they learn?"

"Because they aren't willing to give in." Motre shrugged. "None of these men have seen anything like what you are able to do."

He motioned at the two stunned men staring at where their fallen comrades had been. "Look at them right now, they don't understand the shift of power and how fast it happened. Give those two another chance, then I suggest we move on."

As she turned to look back at the room, Goran and Serus both stepped up. "You've done enough, Tessa. We'll handle these two." He turned back to the men. "Before you retire, we need something from you. We need names. We need locations. We need everyone involved."

The smaller of the two men curled his lip at him and said, "Or what?"

"You've already seen what," Goran snapped. "So make up your mind fast. We have other traitors to catch."

The elder studied Goran's face, but he didn't back down.

Tessa would have missed that little shift in the smaller elder's gaze if she hadn't been watching so close. It was only a tiny flick before returning to Goran's face. But it was enough.

She twisted to see who the elder had glanced at.

And smiled. Now she could finish this.

She turned her gaze back to the elders.

The two men looked at each other, nodded, and in a move that surprised everyone, they stabbed each other in the chest.

Instantly the room was filled with nasty, cloying, sickening, drug-filled ash.

Coughing and groaning, everyone raced to the hallway.

Sian called out, "I'm calling a recess until we can get this cleaned up."

"Everyone stay close. No one leaves the tunnels." Tessa grabbed Motre, and the two of them raced to the front entrance to stop anyone from leaving.

Tessa turned to see where Cody was. *Cody, where are you?*

In the middle of the pack. Why?

This is perfect for an attack from within. It's one of the six other Councilmen. Grab our fathers and keep watch. I have Motre and Wendy here at my side. Rhia, Jewel, and Sian are coming towards me. Take David and Ian and pin the others in the middle. Oh, and behind you could be a vamp and another young boy like Terry. We never did find them.

What?

I didn't have time to keep looking. I was trying to save Beast. Motre ran down the tunnel, but we couldn't see them either. I suspect they returned to Europe as fast as they could, but I can't count on it. In fact, I'm sure I can sense them hiding, terrified.

The maintenance men arrived quickly, having been on hand after being alerted with the first elder going to ash. They went in, vacuumed, and set up the fan within twenty minutes. When the group all filtered back into the room again, she did a headcount to make sure they were all still there. Yes.

She pulled Motre to one side. "You want to go and see if you can find the boy and the other man that were missing? Borg or Bruno, I think his name was." She shrugged. "Maybe take a few men with you, just in case."

"You don't need me here?"

She shook her head. "No, you're good to go." Motre grabbed the two cleaning men and took them down the passageway. Once they'd gone around the corner and disappeared from sight, Cody turned back to her and said, "So he's not involved?"

She smiled, "Thankfully no, he's not." She reached out for his hand and walked into the room, the last two to enter. "Motre is what we always expected him to be. A good guy."

Jameson laughed. "Of course Motre's a good guy. We all are. We got rid of the four guys that were behind all this." He walked over to the chair where he'd been sitting and picked up his notes. "We have a hell of a lot of work to get through. Any chance the meeting can return to normal?"

Sian and Rhia exchanged glances, then both turned to look at Tessa with questions in their eyes.

Adamson said, "And the sooner the better. I'm still not

feeling very good. Those drugs are wicked."

"They sure are, aren't they?"

Adamson raised his gaze to her. "My body is healing, but it's pretty slow."

Tessa studied the energy around him, his body, and thought about what a great camouflage drugs made.

"Interesting that you chose to get another dose of drugs to hide the black in your soul," she said calmly. "It was actually very smart of you."

Adamson reared back slightly. "What are you talking about?"

Cody stiffened at her side. "What?"

Tessa smiled. "You're Victor's son. The head of all of this. You had me fooled for a while when Gloria tried to kill you. But that worked in your favor. And ever since, you've been on board with the group of us trying to stop the blood farms, which enabled you to find out how far we had gone. How much information we learned. How many blood farms we'd taken down." She shook her head. "Smart of you to set up your own attack to hide your involvement," she said calmly. "Of course with all the drugs, I can't tell you're lying, which is why I didn't believe it at first. Besides, you always spoke with such passion – I couldn't see the lies in your passion because they weren't really lies – as you believed them so strongly."

There were gasps of shock and surprise all around her.

Ian cried out, "What? I thought it was Jameson for sure."

"What?" roared Jameson. "Why me?"

Ian looked at him. "Because you were so adamant in bringing the elders back into power."

"Only because I was trying to keep the government running, and for that we need the Council. If we had no Council members, then we could not get any type of law system back in place," he protested. "I knew that the elders would be difficult, but I figured that if we could at least get those men on board, we could figure out who else to raise up through the ranks."

He opened his arms wide. "We got rid of those men once, so we could get rid of them again. But I had to keep the government functioning while the rest of the clan was in self-destruct mode."

Tessa heard the conversation, and she understood it. She didn't dare take her gaze off of Adamson. His eyes had locked on her, ready to take her out without a second's hesitation.

"What gave me away?" Adamson said, not even trying to hide the truth. "I was sure I was safe."

"In a way, you were. And in a way, you were at the top of the list since Gloria."

"You're lying," Adamson snapped. "There's no way you knew back then."

She could see she'd insulted him.

"Oh, I had a strong suspicion back then," she grinned, "but then you were being helpful, so I wasn't so sure. Besides, at that point in time we had no idea about Victor at all." She studied him curiously. "He was the real head of the blood farms, wasn't he? Did you have anything to do with him?"

"He was." Adamson shrugged. "And no. Why would I?"

"He died to save you, you know that?" Cody added. "He'd have done anything to save you."

Adamson snorted. "No, he'd have done anything to save the blood farms. There was no paternal love there at all. He didn't give a damn about me. Especially in the last few centuries when I wouldn't follow his bidding."

Adamson crossed his arms and leaned back against the table. "What I wouldn't have done to have had your DNA in the lab." He shook his head. "Such a waste. Even Beast as you call him has DNA that we need."

"Need?" Tessa asked. "Maybe I should be asking about that part first."

"Europe's in trouble," he said abruptly. "There's disease in the clans. Something we've never seen before, and we were trying to help them when things went a little haywire. Victor had always been working on the pure lines strains of DNA on his own. He was hung up on perfect vamps. But through those experiments, we found some of the drugs produced enhanced the DNA." He ran a hand through his hair. "When the European clan came to us having heard rumors about our new drugs and DNA lines, they asked for help. It was the first time we'd had an opportunity to do so. To help another of our own species.

"Believe it or not, but that was my passion. Helping them. Not creating a super race," he said in disgust. He dropped his hand and stared at everyone. "That's what I wanted to focus on, but I was up against everyone else. They were already preparing to turn the other clans. Clean the lines and make them pure again. I was looking for a cure. They were looking for perfection."

He turned his gaze onto Beast. "If we had your cooperation and his, I think it would have been amazing to see what we could do."

"You mean if you had more animals to try your nasty experiments on?" Tessa shook her head. "Beast has been through enough."

Surprisingly, Adamson nodded. "Oh, I agree with you. The animals were never my idea. Once we started working on these drugs, the European clans started testing animals on their side. Once there was any progress in any direction, it seemed like everyone jumped on it and turned an animal into some new kind of a nightmare. And progress over there made people here crazy to beat them with their experiments."

He smiled, but it was a tired smile. "Of all of this mess, the only thing I really wanted to work on was finding a cure for our people."

"And yet not our people," Goran snapped. "*Our* people are fine."

"The disease is spreading." Adamson shook his head. "There are several in our clan inflicted with the same disease now."

He stood up and paced the room. "It's a hard thing to admit that our vampire heritage is failing, whether it's from inbreeding or not," he said. "Our ability to heal is not as strong as it was."

"I know it's hard to accept, but one of the causes they put down to that is the lack of pure nutrients." He waved his arms to where the four elders had sat. "Blood."

"Hence the blood farms," Rhia whispered.

Adamson nodded. "Yes. But like all good things, the bosses got greedy. Victor got greedy. And plans became too big. If they had stayed with paying humans to donate, it would have been fine." He turned to face them. "But the disease continued to grow, even on those that were only fed pure blood."

"I don't understand, what was Gloria about then?" Goran asked.

Adamson gave him a wry smile. "How many relationships have you had, Goran? How many relationships ended nicely? She was heavily involved in the blood farms. I was in the labs. We were already on the verge of a break up when I realized she'd been using a lot of my research to set up more blood farms. Whereas, I was fighting to bring health issues out in the open so everybody could help solve the problems, instead she was busy using my information, and my money apparently," he winced, "to set herself up as one of the board members of the blood farms." He shook his head. "Then she wasn't even satisfied with that and was quite prepared to take me out to satisfy her plans."

Goran snorted. "Of course she did." His tone was quite commiserating. "Been there a few too many times myself."

Tessa looked over at her father and the others. "What do you want to do now?"

They all looked at each other and shrugged. "No idea," Serus admitted.

"I have a suggestion," Adamson said. "Instead of killing me, let me work."

Cries rose around him. He held up a hand. "I understand your concerns. I never wanted anything to do with the experiments. Or the blood farms," He stood tall. "I do want to find a cure for our people. The disease may not have hit here very hard, but it has hit," he admitted. "It's only going to get worse. It is something I can do to contribute. To give back."

"And how would Victor view that?" Tessa walked closer to stand in front of him. "It's not what you were raised to become."

"And that's one of the things about genetics that we are learning," he said, his voice wry. "We can put the cells together. We can put the formula on paper, and we can follow it through in the lab, but there is something unique about each and every combination that we do this with. The surprise is always that the person has free will and a unique personality with their own thoughts. They make decisions and choices that we didn't expect."

He looked around at the others as he slouched back down again, his arms crossed.

"I understand that in your mind I should be put to death," he said. "A part of me agrees with you. Another group of you would probably prefer that I lived in a cave for the next several centuries, hoping that I suffer for all that I have made others suffer, and you'd be right. But there are very few people with the knowledge and experience and skills that I have to help our own people. So I suggest that I be removed from the Council and be sequestered away and under close watch. Have my lab experiments officially regulated and let me work. Let me see if I can find a cure."

"And if we find out you are creating more blood farms?" Serus asked. "Or creating more monsters?"

"We do need pure blood," he admitted. "Vamps heal better with it, but I suggest we return to volunteer donations. Pay the humans for their contribution. And again regulate it. Set up a governing body that will look after this to make sure the humans are treated decently and that they are willing."

Silence.

"There are thousands of our people already gone," Wendy said in a faint voice, but the hopeful element shone through. "We don't need to kill anyone else, do we?"

"Tessa, look what we found," David spoke from the doorway. Beside him stood the same young man that Tessa had met earlier, and at his side was another man, slightly older but very similar-looking. So similar she knew he had to be a clone, but an earlier version. There was still a fresh innocence to the look of him. His system was also drug-free.

Nice for them.

She turned to Adamson. "What about the clones?"

Adamson smiled and nodded a greeting at the two new arrivals. "They were created in Europe. That's where scientists first started as a way to combat the disease. It took decades before they found a system that worked." He tilted his head and studied the two men. "They're beautiful, aren't they?"

"Just like Terry," Tessa said. "How many are there?"

Adamson shrugged. "Half a dozen, maybe a dozen. Not many. I'm glad to hear Terry is okay. He's a good kid."

His lifted his tired gaze to study them all one by one. "That's something you're going to have to take up with all the Councils. Just because in our clan the good guys won does not mean the other clans were as successful at fighting off the takeover bids."

"There are many things we're still going to have to clean up," Sian said. "That alone is going to take years."

"And I can help you with that," Adamson said quietly.

"If we trust you," Rhia said. "After what you did to my boy, I'm not sure I'll trust anyone again."

"I had nothing to do with him," Adamson protested, "but I'm happy to do what I can to help him heal. It's the least I can do."

Tessa knew that her parents' vote would be to give Adamson a chance to help. He'd have to be watched carefully. Guarded. But if the clans were in trouble, he might be one of the few left who could help.

He nodded at Tessa. "Kudos to you for the massive

strides you've taken forward. I sure as hell wish I knew how you became what you've become."

Tessa studied him. "So do I, but as I will never be a participant in your lab," she said, her voice hard and cold. "I guess we'll never know."

CODY WRAPPED AN arm around Tessa's shoulders. He wasn't sure if it was support for him or for her. He studied the man he'd have like to have called a friend – up until now. It was hard to accept the betrayal. He looked different now. No longer conflicted. No longer as dark, as old, having seen too much. As if this was a relief. To finally be free of the duplicate life. And likely the heavy chains from Victor.

"Can you call the rest of the blood farm goons off?" he asked Adamson.

"No." Adamson shook his head. "I never did command them. That was all Victor's side of life. However, I can tell you where the rest of them are – if there are any left." He stared at Cody and Tessa, the two standing so close together. "You two have been extremely efficient in wiping out most of them."

"Not efficient enough," Tessa said, "if there are any still around."

"Where are they?" Sian asked. "We need to know so we can round them up. We want to shut this down and know that it's never going to rise again."

"Goran and I can take a run out and make sure that we have the last of them." Serus looked over at Goran. "Right?"

"I can't believe there are any left still running," he said, shaking his head.

"If you wait a day or two," Adamson said, "there won't

be. With the drug flow interrupted and no one left capable of making more, all those on it will die within days."

That brought a surprised murmur from everyone.

"We'd have to make sure that we find all the supplies and completely destroy all the drugs so that no one else can start the operation up again." Sian brought up her computer. While waiting for it to load, she looked over at Adamson. "And we need to know where the drugs are in Europe."

Adamson's face shut down slightly, then he gave a clipped nod. "I don't understand where or how, but Terry, Bruno, and Marcus will have more information for you. But you need to be gentle with them. Their memories are a year old, not centuries old."

Cody studied the young men shifting nervously now that the attention was focused on them.

Marcus asked, "Where is Terry?"

Sian spoke up again. "I sent him to meet with Jameson." She turned to study Jameson.

"And we delivered him to Jameson," Tessa said, turning to look at the Councilman who was leaning back, his feet up on the desk, his eyes closed as if trying to catch a nap. "Jameson, where's Terry?"

He opened his eyes. "Likely still asleep on my couch."

"I'll have someone bring him down to us then," Sian said.

"Thank you." Marcus looked around. "Is there a place to sit?" he asked in a hesitant voice. David brought a chair for them.

"Are we going to get through any of the work that's on our list?" Jameson asked. "Or is there still so much to discuss here that we need to push that off for say forever…" he said in a disgruntled tone.

Adamson spoke up, "You also need to consider that if I'm no longer on the Council, my seat needs to be filled."

Everyone turned to look at him. Cody frowned. "Sian, are we okay without Adamson's seat?"

"I hate to have disposed of the four elders, and now we find out that we're still going to be short with Adamson's removal," Tessa said.

"No, we will be fine. We try to keep an uneven number of active Councilmen at all times so that there is never a tie vote on an issue," Sian said. "But having said that, we do have many empty seats that need to still be filled."

"Why not keep the Council numbers down. It would be easy to keep track of who's who." Rhia got up from her chair and walked over to stand close to Serus. "We didn't even notice that so many were missing because they were picked off one by one. And so many don't show up for the regular meetings that we didn't notice their absence. If there was just a dozen, fifteen, even twenty, it would be much easier for everyone to recognize when someone was gone."

"True, that is something that can be discussed later." Sian got up from where she stood and pulled something large out from under the desk. Old manuscripts.

Cody could feel Tessa's surprise.

"Those are lovely," she said impulsively.

Sian smiled. "They are indeed. They are also very important."

"Why?" Tessa asked.

"Because we have a very unique situation here. Both Hortran and Deanna exist within you, but with no physical body. They both held seats on the Council, although Hortran was rarely here."

Adamson snorted. "He was *never* here."

"He's a Ghost. And that was part of the appeal." Goran snorted. "Besides, his position was also very unique and he was uniquely suited for that as a Ghost."

"In what way?" Cody asked. "I've never seen him at the Council meetings. But then I'd never seen Deanna either."

Behind him, Ian and David repeated the same thing.

"Nevertheless, they were both members. And as many of the Councilmen who retire do, they left behind written decrees as to what was to become of their property and their position. Power is very important to a vampire." She laid the manuscripts on the table. "In some ways, what they have done may surprise you and in some ways, maybe not."

"Deanna has left all her property possessions and if the Council wills, her seat on the Council, to another Leant." She lifted her head and studied the people around her. "She left her seat to Tessa."

"But that is outrageous," Jameson said, glaring at Tessa. "Sure, she's done a lot of things, but she's never been trained. She can't hold a Council position. She hasn't even been an apprentice. It's never been done."

And that started more arguments as Rhia turned to defend her daughter. Cody listened to the arguments back and forth for letting Tessa on the Council.

It's not what I want. You know that, right?

He smiled and kissed her temple. *I know that, but somehow this has to be resolved.*

That's easy. Let me go back to school and finish up so I can go to university.

And what would you study, Cody asked curiously.

She tilted her head and said, *Council law.*

His eyebrows shot up in surprise. "Really?" Shocked, he spoke out loud. He'd never have guessed she'd want to go that route. But it made sense. She was always cheering for the underdog.

She nodded. "I want to make sure something like this never happens again. In order to do that, I have to know more. To learn more. To be more," she said passionately.

She spread her arms wide, and Cody knew she wasn't thinking of all the people watching them curiously. "The reason this happened was so many people were in the dark. Oblivious to what was going on around them. Living their own lives independent of each other as is our nature. Only the Council brought them together, making it both a strong and weak point of our clan. That can't continue. We need to have a watchdog. And I want that role," she admitted. "We need to liaison more with the humans. And I want to be involved. We need to keep an eye on our older, less active vamps to make sure they are doing okay. And I need to see that is happening."

"Exactly what I need to speak about next," Sian said with gentle firmness. "There was a reason for Deanna's request, and she was obviously in cahoots with Hortran over this."

Everyone turned to face Sian.

"Now that I have your attention, I suggest you all take a seat and let me read this to you."

Obediently, everyone took a seat at the table, even Wendy and Jewel. Motre chose to stand at the entrance, on guard as always.

Cody turned his attention to Sian.

SIAN PICKED UP the manuscript and said, "This is my last decree. I'm soon to see my last day on earth. A life well lived, and long lived. Not an easy one nor a friendly one, but there were enemies everywhere. Throughout these many centuries, I have walked beside Deanna. We have not always agreed. We have not always fought. There were decades where we barely talked. But now that we come to the end of the road, I see so much that still needs to be done. The blood of our ancestors is no longer the blood of our future children. And this is the way it should be. We need to adapt or die. Our race is not immune to human diseases, human greed, or that quest for perfection that seems to permeate vampire clans."

Sian lifted her head and looked around the room, then she continued. "Tessa has Leant blood in her. But she has more Ghost than many of the ghosts I have seen and worked and walked beside. I hope I managed to stay long enough to teach her our ways. She would be the most apt student. Deanna has chosen her as her replacement on the Council. Depending on when our last breath flows from our bodies, she may yet be too young for such a position. It's also not the right position for her."

A murmur rippled around the room as everyone stared at Tessa. Sian caught her gaze and gave her a small smile of reassurance.

Tessa slumped into the chair and stared straight ahead. As usual, she'd take whatever it was coming straight on.

"However, it's a necessary step, as it's a requirement for her true purpose." Sian smiled. Everyone leaned forward in confusion, voices rising in a wave. She held up her hand. "Let me continue."

She turned back to the manuscript. "When my position on the Council started over eight centuries ago, it was one of the most important positions of all. Everyone else wanted that power position. But in my eyes, it was more important than power. For many centuries, I was faithful and I did my best, but as I failed physically, I also failed in my position. Young blood is needed to take over. Young blood who understands not only my ways but Deanna's ways. In order to take my position, one must already be a Council member. So I'm requesting that Tessa take my place. She will need to do the training that goes with all Council positions. She can start as a junior so that she works her way up, but it is Tessa and Tessa alone that can hold this position on the Council."

Sian laid the manuscript on the table and continued to read. Cody listened as she raised her voice over the shocked cries. "For those of you so young and so new to our ways, you may not know what position I hold. I am the gatekeeper. I am the Ghost. I am he who is always there, who knows, who sees, who understands, but who also must be the force that says *no,* we are not going there. Our clan has lost its soul. It's badly in need of a conscience. There is no other as uniquely qualified as Tessa. As Deanna has left her all of her worldly goods, I too leave Tessa all of my worldly goods. She carries my soul even now and well past the time that I will be gone. However, that connection will hold forever. My position is also unique in that it is not a request. This is an order from the grave if must be.

"My replacement, the new conscience of the clan, the gatekeeper to all you do, the head of the regulatory body that will watch over all areas of this clan to make sure we stand true to ourselves."

The room erupted in shock.

Sian raised her hand for quiet so she could finish.

"Yes, she's young. Yes, she's female. And yes, she is untested in these roles, but she is not untested in all these concepts. At each and every stage, she has stepped up to the plate and shown that she is the right person for this job. I have wandered this planet looking for someone else to take my place."

Sian took a deep breath, then finished with, "It's only now that in my death that I have found her. One of my last physical acts was to write this and place it where it would be safe. May your lives be blessed."

Slowly, Sian lifted her head and looked around at the shocked, silent faces. None more shocked than Tessa.

And waited.

CHAPTER 16

TESSA WAS FROZEN. Inside, she was screaming at both Deanna and Hortran. *Don't you understand? I can't do this. Not alone.*

Whispers rippled through her mind as Deanna and Hortran spoke, but their words were faint.

And firm.

You can do this. It's what you are meant to do, Hortran said, his voice the strongest she'd heard. *I will stay as long as I can to train you. And you can tell them that, but they won't understand.*

They won't like it either. This is a huge responsibility, she said. *I'm not sure I'm up for it.*

You are. There was such conviction in their combined voices, but she could hear how faint Deanna's was. *Is Deanna okay?* she asked, worried.

Hortran's smile whispered through her. *She's fading a little more every day. She will be there for years until one day you will wake up and her presence will be gone. But remember, you have access to her history. To her memories. You have the information you need to do this. As you do mine. You will be fine.*

And if I don't want to take this on? she asked, her voice strained. *Besides, what if they don't let me?*

Let me speak to them, Hortran commanded.

She gasped. *How am I supposed to do that?*

Jameson bounded to his feet. "This is ridiculous. There is no way she's capable of doing something like that. She's a child. She's not even done her years as an apprentice or as a junior Council member. Hell, before this mess, we all knew she was never going to be accepted on the Council. Now she's supposed to skip all that and take one of the choicest positions." He snorted and collapsed back into his chair. "All because of a dead man's writ. I don't think so."

Silence.

It's as if no one knew what to say or do.

Tessa sank lower in the chair. *See what you started. They will never let me do this.*

They will. They have no choice. They are bound by law.

Until they change the law, she snapped.

Morris stood up and held out his hands. "I guess I missed a lot while in Europe that a child is now decreed as the gatekeeper?" He shook his head. "I'm not saying that I'd vote against it—"

"Hell, I will," Jameson snapped.

"But it's a little hard to vote *for* it," Morris said, "while I am lacking in all the background. From teenage vamp to powerful vamp, that's a huge step." He sat down, careful to keep his gaze away from Tessa.

Triton stood up. "I guess I have to agree with him." He turned to face Tessa. "No insult to you, but we don't understand."

Tessa nodded, but she didn't say anything. What could she say?

Her gaze glanced over at Adamson still in the room. Why hadn't he been led away? She frowned at him. He smiled at her. What did that mean?

Baker stood. "I've heard of a lot of the rumors. I'm the beneficiary of her healing abilities. Some of the rumors I've heard about her seem very over the top, so I can't say for real how I feel about them. But I actually come down on this issue on her side. We do need a conscience. We do need somebody to watch over us. I don't feel like it should be one of our generation. I think it should be new blood. The younger generation, those in this room in particular, have seen so much more than we did at their age. They have a whole new way of thinking. And I think that's important. We have to do whatever we need to do in order to stop this from happening again."

He sat down abruptly. "That's all I wanted to say."

"It's just too ridiculous," Jameson said. "Hell, I would've understood it if maybe Sian was given the job. She seems to oversee so much of the human and vampire relations as it is. That makes sense. But to put Tessa in such a position? No."

"Good thing you're only one vote then, isn't it?" Serus stood up. "She's my daughter. But she's also an incredible woman. My vote is yes. She has always been the heart behind this. It was because of her conscience, her caring, that soul of hers that heals and wants to help that drove us forward and kept us in line the whole time. I don't know how she has learned to do everything she has. I want to call it a miracle, but I know that it's through her own need to save her friends and family that's made it all happen. We must also not forget that the position always came with several assistants. In this case, maybe that would be enough to help her learn the ropes. She'll be put in the line of fire – and so far, she's demonstrated that's where she excels."

Serus sat down.

Tessa listened in shock as her friends all stood up and

made a case in her favor. Still, the vampires that were against her taking this position were very vocal. She wasn't sure she wanted the position. It was uncomfortable to be the center of attention all the time, even more now. Everyone stared at her, glanced away, and then couldn't help but turn back again. Even Motre, and she knew he had no stake in this.

There was a whisper, almost a choking cough in her mind.

What? she asked Hortran, *What did I say?*

There is some mystery behind what you just said.

What? she said, her instincts now starting to rise up. Casually, she glanced over at Motre yet again and then away, only this time she came up with a new perspective. She sat quietly, letting the impressions glide through her. He'd been a guardsman for one of the Council members, hadn't he originally?

In a position of trust.

But the Councilman had died. And now for the first time she wondered…by whose hand? Was he a good guy, had she missed something? No. It couldn't be. She knew him. Who he was. So why the suspicion now?

Beast was lying in the corner behind her as her thoughts started to stir, and he rose up on his haunches and let out a low howl.

Several of the people in the room turned to look at her, fear bouncing from face to face.

Cody asked, "What's wrong with Beast?"

Tessa dropped her gaze to the table. "Easy, Beast," she said, lowering a hand. Beast walked over obediently and shoved his muzzle into her hand for her to pet him. She tossed Cody a smile. "He's fine."

Obviously not. He's picking up something from you.

She'd have to watch her thoughts if that little bit alone was enough to put Beast on guard.

Cody's thoughts whispered through her head. *Or not,* he said. *He makes a great guard dog. We might be out of danger, but we will have to be careful for several more days, if not months.*

She nodded but kept her voice quiet. Silent. She stared down at the palms of her hands, her nails already extending. Forcibly she tugged them back, her mind racing to figure out how to sort through the stressful fear that said she'd missed something. How could she know for certain?

Because she knew no one would believe her. Not without proof.

Inside the back of her mind, she sensed Hortran's approval. *I need help to sort this out,* she cried. *How can I be certain of my suspicions?*

You're on the right path. Now follow it like you always have done.

Energy. She could follow the energy.

No, she couldn't. She slumped back into place, her hands now shaking. It didn't look any different than what she'd always seen. Or did it? She took a quick look.

Are you okay? Cody asked quietly.

No, I'm not. I'm just not sure what to do about it.

About what?

She didn't know what to say.

It was too bizarre. Too far out there. She gave a half laugh. Listen to her. How could this be *too* far? Everything in her life was too damn far. This just fit right in.

But she had to be sure.

She stood up from her chair and excused herself. She raced past Motre and out of the room and down the hallway, her stomach heaving in denial.

"Tessa," Cody called, racing behind her. "Wait up. Look, you don't have to take the position if you don't want to, you know."

"Yes, I do," she cried, her mind already consumed with this new fear. "That's got nothing to do with why I'm upset."

She spun and faced him. "Go back. I need you to make sure no one gets out of that room."

And she turned and bolted down the hallway.

"Wait," Cody snarled behind her. "You're not going anywhere alone."

She twisted so she could see his face. His dearly beloved face. And screamed, *Please. You're the only one I can trust. Lock down that room so nobody gets in or out. Promise me.*

As if he understood the urgency, he nodded, already turning back towards the room. *Call me if you need help. I can send Motre your way.*

As if…

Tessa threw herself through the doors leading to the stairs and made several jumps to the second floor. Now she was here, she could take the time to investigate the energies she'd seen here earlier. She felt them there but she hadn't known, couldn't have imagined what might be going on. But the fact that it was here Motre had found Morris and Triton that made it the best place to be checking.

At the double doors leading to the hallway of the second floor, she stopped trying to still the panic inside, then pulled the doors open and jumped through.

Silence.

And darkness – except for dozens of glowing eyes.

She slowly lowered her hand. In her mind, she called for

Beast. His muzzle connected with her fingertips. She gently stroked him as she let her eyes adjust.

Not that she needed to identify the animals ahead of her as the animals started to howl. The hallway was full of cats. This was where the cats they had met earlier came from.

"Well, Beast, it's just you and I. Ready?" Beast growled low in the back of his throat, his muscles bunching up, ready to spring. Tessa pulled on deep from the energy inside.

If there was ever a time that she needed help, it was right now. This was it.

This was the last defense to pull down.

The last secret to reveal.

The last horror to be exposed.

And she had to do it now before all was lost.

And not one person would believe her if she tried to explain.

With Beast at her side, she launched herself forward, her claws out as she flung energy from side to side to side to side. One cat lunged on her back from behind. Beast jumped and ripped it off her back, then had it to the floor and pinned in seconds. She didn't have time to stop and look.

Two more snuck in from behind. She spun and kicked and threw out energy as far and as fast as she could.

And still they kept coming.

They couldn't be allowed to stop her. She'd have loved to have left them alone, but it wasn't possible.

Not when she needed to know what was behind those damn doors.

And not when they were still coming at her with tooth and claws.

Finally, trembling, with fear and with anger, she stood, alone.

She spun, searching the darkness for Beast.

And heard a satisfying crunch.

"Gross, Beast. Just so gross."

Shuddering at the sight, she turned her back on the ecstatic animal and faced the closed doors in front of her. She didn't want to be right.

She wanted to be wrong.

She needed to be wrong.

Anything else was just too horrible.

She closed her eyes and took a deep breath. And reached the first one.

She threw the door open and sucked in her breath. Instantly she closed the door and stood with her forehead against it, trembling. Please let that not be what she thought it was. *Please.*

She walked to the second one, slightly better prepared but hoping she'd be wrong. And opened it.

Tessa pushed the door open wider. Her hard gaze mentally took a search of the inhabitants, her gaze going from face to face before slowly closing the door. Now her mind spun at super speed. She moved to the third room.

She opened the third door.

Dear God.

She'd been right.

She'd found what she was looking for.

Motre.

And he wasn't alone.

DID YOU MEAN it? Cody asked as he ran back to the meeting and carefully closed and locked the door behind him. *You only trust me right now?* He tried to do it in such a way that no one would notice, but of course that didn't work.

Motre frowned at him. "What's the matter?"

He shrugged. "Tessa," he said by way of explanation. It was all he could do. Hell, he didn't know anything else. *Tessa? Talk to me.*

Can't, a little busy now, she cried. *Just fought off a hallway full of crazed vampire cats.*

Jesus, what the hell are you doing? he roared.

Finding the truth – finally.

Silence.

Are you saying there is more to find out, he asked cautiously. *Surely not.*

Keep your features calm. Because this is going to be a doozy. She sighed. *No, better I just bring them. Hold on for just a few minutes. I'll be there as soon as I can.*

"Cody, let me out," Serus snapped. "I'll go find Tessa."

Cody stood firm, hating to be in this position. But he also trusted Tessa. "No, sir. She'll be back in a few moments. No one is to go in or out until then."

"What rubbish is this?" Goran roared.

Cody gave him a look that shut him down. "Like you, I'm only following orders," he added with a humorous note.

"Is this the life you want?" Goran asked incredulously.

"I do," Cody said softly. "And you should be so lucky as to find someone else for yourself, Father."

"Harumph, like that's going to happen." But he settled down slightly.

"There was that cute little nurse downstairs," Cody said, trying to keep the conversation away from everyone leaving. "Ask her out."

His father got a faraway look in his eyes. "Maybe I will at that."

JARED DOZED IN his chair. The hospital had been a flurry of activity as the rest of the high school kids were brought in. Between hysterical parents and other kids swarming the building, there'd been enough pandemonium to raise the dead.

But not Clarissa. She was still unconscious.

He got up and paced the room. Then when he tired of that, he stopped and stared out the window. He couldn't imagine what kind of people – humans – would have been involved with this supply line. There was still so much to sort out. And he wanted to be involved if he could. The real issue were the victims, where they were now and if they were getting the care they needed.

Lots of care. Taz had stopped in several times and always said the same thing, "She'll wake when she's ready. Not before."

And Jared had to be content with that.

An odd noise had him turning to study the bed.

And found her struggling to open her eyes.

He raced to her side. "Hey, take it easy. It's me, and you're safe."

"Jared," she cried in a soft voice and opened her arms. "Thank you for saving me." And she hugged him tight.

CHAPTER 17

ER HEART WAS still racing, panic still firing through her bloodstream. She bent down and quickly untied Motre's bonds. "Take it easy, Motre. I don't know how long you've been here, but your system is suffering."

"I've been here too damn long," he whispered. "Thank God you found me." He tried to stand up but was so weak he fell to the floor again.

"Shit," he said. "I'm weaker than I thought. I need to feed."

"And I don't have anything here for you." She placed her hand on his chest. "Maybe this will help," and she pulsed energy gently through his body, giving him enough strength that he could move. Her strength.

Instantly, he started to look better as his body filled out slightly as more of the energy ran through him, giving him a livelier look. "I know this is a short-term measure. But hopefully it will get you out of here. Then we can get you some blood."

She helped him to stand up. "Take a few minutes, let your body adjust, and see if you can stand up and walk."

"I'll be fine. You go deal with the others." Tessa straightened and walked over to where Councilmen Morris and Triton lay. Both unconscious, but the good news was she didn't see any drugs running through their system. She bent down and repeated the process, pulsing energy gently into their heart chakra.

Both men woke up and stared at her in shock. "What happened?"

She shook her head. "I don't even want to think about what happened. I poured energy into your systems. You're going to need time to recover, and you're probably going to need to feed, the same as Motre. But I don't have time for that right now. This is a stopgap measure. Try to get up, walk around, see if you're stable enough to be moved. I can't carry you all."

Then dreading this moment, she walked over to stand above her brother. Actually, both brothers. David appeared to be in similar shape as the Councilmen.

The fact that he, Motre, and the two others were all here meant the switch had happened when the two had gone to find the Councilmen.

But it was a scary thought to think that the enemy had the technology that could bring clones in this fast and be so accurate that she had no idea a switch had been made. Had these clones been building and growing slowly over weeks, months, and when the time was right, the enemy made the switch? It seemed so preposterous.

And yet again to have the clones be so accurate that she hadn't known…mind boggling.

She hated that she'd had no idea. She felt like such a failure. She was supposed to protect these people. She, who could see all, had seen nothing. She snorted. There was no way she was qualified to be Hortran's replacement.

Hortran's voice whispered through her mind. *You didn't know what to look for. You will not make that mistake again.*

And do I know what to look for now? she asked sarcastically. *No. If that was the case, I would've seen it already in the Council room.*

In a way you did. But you didn't know what you were looking at. Their energy is different. Close, but not quite the same.

And how do I tell the difference in a different case?

I think now that you've seen it once, you'll see it easier the next time, particularly when you see the two energies side by side. You'll be able to train yourself to see that difference much clearer. And faster.

Is this what the world has become? she cried in anguish. *I have to separate who's the real brother from the fake brother?*

Until you get to the end of this, then yes.

How many more are there? she asked. *There could be hundreds more. I'll never be able to find them all.*

Not very many. Adamson was right there, Hortran whispered, his voice fading. *But selectively chosen subjects.*

She started. *Adamson? Can we believe anything he said?*

Turn around, Tessa. You're missing something.

Tessa spun, realizing that there was yet another man she hadn't been able to see originally as he was propped behind the door. She'd been so focused on coming to Motre's rescue that she hadn't taken a good look around. "Dear God. Jameson!"

She didn't understand how any of this happened or even what to do about the result. She only knew she had to get all of these people back to the room. And fast. *Cody, is everyone still locked up?*

Yes. But I have to say, they are pissed. So I can't hold them for long.

You don't need to. We'll be there in a few moments.

She pulsed energy into Jameson's system, but he was weaker than the others. She worried about Seth, who she hadn't worked on yet. "Motre, can you drag Jameson over to Seth so that I can work on both at the same time, please?"

Motre moved the two men together. He was still weak himself but looked to be gaining strength by the minute. She tossed a glance at the others as she poured energy into the two unconscious men.

David asked, his voice weak. "What the hell happened?"

She smiled at him. "Oh, nothing, except that someone thought you were so great they decided to clone you."

His eyes opened wide and he bolted to his feet. "Jesus, really?"

Swaying in place, the men slowly worked the kinks out of their systems as she brought Jameson back to life. He'd been in hibernation, likely a long time. She didn't know if he was going to make it.

To that end, she didn't know if Seth was going to either.

"We need to get back," she said as she rocked back on her heels. "The Council meeting is going on right now with all your duplicates taking your place."

The men started swearing. She turned to Motre and David. "Can you two pick up these men and carry them back with us?"

Motre nodded and grabbed up Jameson. "He doesn't look very good."

"No, he's in bad shape," she admitted. "There's only so much I can do at this point. I think he's been here for a long time."

"How long?" Motre asked.

"Possibly since this mess began, but definitely since before we met Victor," she whispered.

David picked up Seth, struggling with the weight.

With everyone on their feet and using anger to drive

themselves forward, she said, "Let's go."

Outside the room, she walked back to the second door and called Beast over. "I need you to guard this room, this hallway until I get back. No one goes in or out."

Beast promptly dropped his butt and growled.

She hoped that meant yes. She turned and led the way back to the Council meeting.

CODY STARED IMPASSIVELY at the group of angry and getting angrier-by-the-minute vamps.

Once they realized they were prisoners and he was the one preventing them from leaving, their fury had shown no bounds – except so far, no one had attacked physically.

That was next. Then his father stepped up and stood at his side.

Supporting his decision to follow Tessa's orders – even if they chafed.

"Settle down. I had good reason for trusting Tessa before, and I'm not going to ignore that she needs us to stay inside now. For that matter, you're all getting mighty irate over something so simple as this, so maybe she has a reason," he roared over the din.

Instantly, the room quieted.

"Thanks," Cody muttered.

"No problem. I needed to let off a little steam. That little girl sure knows how to stir up a storm though, doesn't she?" He grinned. "Love it."

Cody laughed. "All the damn time."

"Still, she needs to hurry. It's going to be an all-out war soon."

"She's on her way."

His father turned to look at him. "You sure about that?"

Cody turned to face the door, hearing her cry in his mind. *Open up, Cody. Stay focused, and do not let anyone out. Once we're all inside, lock the door. Do you hear me? No one goes outside as we come in.*

We?

Don't ask. It's too damn complicated. Can you hear our footsteps in the hallway?

Yes.

Good, open in five. Four. Three. Two.

Open the doors, Cody.

He turned and opened the doors wide as the group roared through the doorway. And stopped.

His heart slammed against his chest.

Dear God.

Yeah, like I said, it's complicated.

CHAPTER 18

TESSA WATCHED THE shock and anger – confusion – on everyone's faces as she raced inside. *Cody, make sure the doors are locked behind us.*

She heard them slam and lock behind her. She turned to face the crowd of shocked and confused faces. In a hard, cold voice, she said, "I've decided that Hortran was right. I *am* the gatekeeper because if there ever was a clan in need of a watchdog, this one is it."

"What is the meaning of this?" Morris protested. "What the devil are you doing? Who are these people?" His shock and panic was evident in his voice.

But he wasn't alone. The room rippled with ongoing cries of shock and horror.

Tessa glanced at the group she'd brought with her. Motre was looking a little weak. David was worse. She motioned both men to lay the other two unconscious vamps on the floor in the corner behind her. She needed to give them both more energy. But the other men were desperately in need of sustenance. She snagged Cody's arm. *We need blood, these men have been starving for days.*

Back in a couple minutes.

She watched Cody slip from the room, thankful that once again he didn't ask any questions. She then turned her gaze on Goran and the fury in his eyes as he stared at the new arrivals. He'd stood guard at the door for her.

The men were still weak and shivering as they tried to stand upright. She quickly gathered chairs and set them in a circle to let the men sit down.

Her father called out. "Tessa?"

She nodded. "I'll speak as soon as there is silence."

Ignoring the din around her, she went about making sure that the group she'd brought with her were all now safely sitting. As she passed by, she gave each an additional shot of energy.

"Thanks," Motre responded. "That sure helps."

Soon, the silence she requested fell upon the room. She was just about to speak when she heard Cody's return.

The door opened and he slipped inside, a case of blood in his arms. He immediately gave one to each of the people that she had brought in with her. She walked over to study her brother, her mother now at Seth's side. Jameson had a gray cast to his skin. She crouched down beside them and pulsed more energy through their systems. They were alive, but they weren't capable of drinking yet. Still, she saw some sign of improvement, and that was encouraging.

She turned her attention back to the room, noting her group was busy and greedily drinking blood, their bodies instantly accepting and hungry for the nourishment. Then she turned to address the room at large. "As you can see, we have a problem."

Then she caught sight of Adamson lounging lazily at the table, a small smile playing at the corner of his lips. "Adamson obviously knows more than he's telling." All eyes turned to the Councilman whose attitude bordered on insolent at this moment.

"What's there to say? You found them. Good on you,"

he retorted.

"Not too many, you said, maybe a dozen?"

He shrugged. "You probably didn't find more than that, did you?"

"But now having found these, how can I be sure there aren't many more out there?"

"You'll have to use your superspy skills to figure it out," he mocked.

"You're enjoying this, aren't you?" Now she understood so much of what had bugged her about his attitude. Well, hopefully he'd get his own comeuppance.

"Not really." He slumped back into his seat and stared coldly up at the ceiling and ignored them.

She turned to the rest of the room and explained what she found. Or rather, she explained *most* of what she'd found.

Motre shook his head and bounced to his feet. "That's outrageous. *He's* the clone, not me."

Triton stood up and walked closer, his gaze locked on his own double. "This is just too eerie," he said. "Where did you find these clones?"

Tessa's Triton bounced to his feet. "New clone? I'm not a clone, I'm the original. You are the clone," he roared.

Just then, there was an odd sound behind her. Tessa turned to see Jameson struggling to move.

She raced over to his side and pulsed more energy into his system. As long as his body was willing to accept it, she could feed it. "Take it easy. I don't how long you've been down, but your system is very weak."

As if understanding her words, he lay back, relaxing slightly, then opened his eyes. That black gaze landed on her face and he relaxed a little more. "Thank you," he whispered.

She nodded cheerfully. "No problem."

Cody walked over to her side and held a bag of blood for her. She opened a small corner and dripped some blood into Jameson's mouth. He drank greedily. She kept it up until he took a deep breath and gasped, "That's enough for the moment."

The bag was empty. She placed it down beside him and helped him to sit up. His gaze wandered the crowd beside her, his eyes widening as he caught sight of the two Tritons and the two Morrises. And then his gaze landed on his double. And hardened.

"They were making a clone for every Council member," he announced bitterly, his voice weak but with a thread of steel running through it. "In some cases, it didn't work. Like Sian. They couldn't make her pregnant."

"Well, thank God for that," Sian cried. "It's a horrible thought to think there could be another me running around."

Jameson added, "There was also no way to clone Tessa. But they tried many times. There's something in her DNA that's off. No, let me correct that – that's different. But they also couldn't get a pure sample."

"Good." Tessa didn't want to contemplate duplicates running around the place. "Where are the others?"

Jameson shrugged. "I don't know." He shifted positions and lunged to his feet. "I was imprisoned in the room the whole time. I heard a lot of moving around me, but the only time the door opened was to bring in more prisoners."

"And were any prisoners removed?" she asked.

"Yes, but just one."

"Do you know what they did with the prisoner?" Tessa asked. "What kind of shape was he in?"

"Bad, like seriously bad." Jameson shook his head. "I never saw him again."

"Up until you entered this room?"

Jameson nodded.

"Please tell everyone in this room exactly who you saw being removed from your prison cell."

"Adamson."

SERUS STOOD UP to stand between Jameson and Adamson, his gaze travelling from one to the other then back again. And then slid past the clone Jameson. He had to believe that Tessa had returned the original Jameson to this room. But without her, they'd not have known there were two or how to differentiate between them. "Does that mean this Adamson is a clone or the real Adamson?" he asked in a harsh voice. "And how can we be sure?"

Jameson shook his head. "Adamson was in really ugly shape. He was there when I arrived, and I suffered as they brought everyone else in. Nobody ever checked on him. When they came, they just picked him up and tossed him outside." He turned to face the Adamson in the room. "You, sir, are a fake."

"That I'm not," Adamson said with a smirk. "And you'll have a hard time proving otherwise."

Serus turned around to look at Tessa. "Can you tell who's who?"

She looked around and studied the pairs. There were different definite differences. She nodded. "The Triton, Morris, Jameson, Motre, and David that I brought into this room are the original. These five…" and she pointed to the five men in the room individually, "…are clones."

The clones jumped to their feet in shock and started yelling and crying out in denial.

"Jesus, what a mess," Cody said. "They don't even know."

"How could they?" Tessa said. "They were raised to be as real as they can be. It worked, didn't it?"

Serus studied his daughter. "And there's one you haven't mentioned."

She nodded, her face edging into grim lines. "Adamson is a whole different case."

"See, I told you so." Adamson said cheerfully. "She's good."

"In what way?" Serus asked. "And what the hell do we do about this mess?"

Tessa shook her head, holding her hands out. "One problem at a time. There is another room completely full of more clones. They are still being given sustenance at this point in time and not free from the machines. But they are in the room beside where I found these men. There is one there for almost all of us in this room. And many more besides. We would slowly one by one disappear as these men replaced us. But Adamson is a class all of his own."

The clones stood stiff with anger, disbelieving of the truth.

The originals sat fuming in anger at the duplicity brought in their world.

Serus sympathized until he understood his daughter's words. "Is there a clone of me?" he asked incredulously. "Really?"

His daughter nodded. "Yes, but younger. And of Goran and Rhia and Cody. And more besides. But I think Rhia and you were a problem because of the mindspeak, and you and

Goran can also mindspeak, and that is not a DNA issue but an emotional bond. So they can't duplicate that. Sian is of course pregnant and I'm not really clonable. But there are a good dozen in that room waiting to step in and replace us." She turned to look at Cody. "Including you. All the enemy needed to do was to isolate us so that they could make the switch like they did Morris and Triton, then Motre and David at a different time." She smiled. "They don't know about our mindspeak and likely hoped I wouldn't notice the switch." Cody's eyebrows shot up at that. "Like hell," he said forcefully. "I'm not that easily replaced."

"We need to protect that room," Motre cried out. "Stop anyone else from entering and letting those clones free."

"No one will be getting in there," Tessa said. "I left Beast on guard duty."

"Forget about the other clones. What is going on with Adamson?" Goran stepped up beside Serus. "And how many other people are like him?"

Tessa stared at the man she knew but didn't know. The man that had been beside them all this time was not the man in front of her – not even a fraction of that same man. "Have you killed him yet?"

Adamson laughed. "That old geezer, he's on his last legs. For all I know, he's dead now."

"What did you do – just throw him away like a sack of garbage?"

"He was of no value anymore. We had all we needed."

Tessa smiled, making Serus suspicious yet again. "Why are you not upset?" he asked of his daughter.

"Because Adamson's laughing," Tessa said. "But in fact, he doesn't understand that he's already being replaced."

Silence.

"What?" roared Goran. "What are you talking about?"

Serus locked his gaze on Adamson, who was looking a little worried. And then he got it. "You found another clone, didn't you, Tessa? You found another Adamson clone?"

Adamson bolted to his feet in shock. "No, that can't be."

"Oh, I'm happy to say it is true. In fact, there were several of you in progress. Because of course, as Victor's line, it was too important that you stay alive and on their side regardless of how willing or unwilling you might be. At least in this way, they can keep practicing and working on their cloning techniques and if one failed to function properly, all they had to do was to transfer your new improved memories and programming into the new guy."

"No," he screamed. "You're lying. I'm too valuable to replace." And in a move no one had seen coming, Adamson jumped across the desk, his fingers full of some kind of shiny spikes, and stabbed Tessa in the side.

The attack was so fast, so sudden, his movements at such high intensity, no one was prepared for it.

Tessa went down, her cry of pain filling the air.

Adamson roared once as Cody speared him with silver, and then he blew into a cloud of smoke and spread ash all over Tessa as she lay dying on the floor.

❧ ❧

CODY DROPPED TO Tessa's side. He could hear her scream in his mind, and still the sound reverberated outside in the room. His panic became tenfold as he pressed his fingers over the multiple holes in her side as blood spilled over his skin to pour all over the floor.

"Jesus, Tessa, please fire up your genes or whatever it is that you do and please…heal."

She opened her eyes and stared at him, pain fogging her gaze. "Cody, make sure you terminate the ones still growing."

"I will," he promised. "I will, but only if you're there with me," he pleaded, his heart breaking as he kept trying to stop the bleeding. He'd never felt so helpless.

She slid her bloody hand up his arm and shoulder to cup his cheek and whispered in such a low voice he had to bend down to hear, "I don't know if I've said this before, but I love you."

Her hand fell to the ground and her head tilted to the side. Tessa slipped into unconsciousness.

"No, Tessa, wake up. *Please wake up.*"

"Cody, do something," Serus pleaded. "Can you help her?"

"I don't know how," Cody cried. "This is Tessa."

Motre crouched down at his side. "Yes, this is Tessa, but remember what she did for you? Contact Hortran. Maybe he can help. If anybody is invested in her staying alive, he is."

Cody placed both hands on the wounds and closed his eyes. *Hortran, can you hear me, please? Tessa is severely injured. We need your help,* he whispered.

He waited, and he thought he could feel something but wasn't exactly sure what.

Hortran?

He waited again, and then he could feel the tingle in his fingers. He opened his eyes to see what appeared to be a light blue color emanating around Tessa's body.

Murmurs rose around them as everyone realized something was happening, even if no one was really sure what that was…but there was definitely change going on.

Cody lifted Tessa's shirt to her ribs to show the ugly raw

wounds closing from the inside out, slowly but sure-ly…healing. He sat back and rocked on his feet. "I've never seen anything like Tessa," he whispered in reverence.

"None of us have ever seen anything like Tessa," Motre said.

They all watched as the healing continued until the wounds were fully closed. The color came back to Tessa's face and she opened her eyes. She gave a startled jerk and stared up at everyone as they looked down at her.

Then she smiled. "Adamson got a little pissed, didn't he?"

The others laughed and backed away. She reached up her arms to Cody, and he picked her up to tug her into his lap and held her close. Together, the two of them sat on the floor, arms wrapped around each other, and just hung on.

A private, intimate moment the others respected.

I almost lost you, Cody whispered.

Nah, she said in a low voice. *You can't get rid of me that easily.*

CHAPTER 19

S TILL FEELING A bit weak, she let Cody help her to her feet. She looked around the room and said, "There are now ethical questions that have to be addressed. I'm not sure that they have to be addressed today though. But those clones in that room, they need to be stopped. Those that are still connected to tubes are undeveloped. We need to stop them from maturing. I'd just as soon *not* be involved in shutting them down."

Both Motres stood up. "I'll take care of it," they said in unison.

The original Motre looked over at his clone and snapped, "Like hell you will."

And yet both raced out of the room as if trying to outdo the other.

Tessa laughed. "And that's part of the ethical question that needs to be addressed."

"And there's another question that needs to be addressed," Rhea said quietly. "What about Seth?"

Tessa smiled at her. "It would appear that this is the original Seth. And the one that you rescued may very well be a clone. Which would explain why the implant." She waved her arm toward where her brother was lying ill. "He might still have been involved early on, but he's very sick now. Like Jameson, he's been there a long time." She turned to look at the doorway. "I know you have Seth in with the medical staff, but we need to check on him. And find a way to visibly tell the pairs apart."

"How can you be sure this is our brother Seth?" David asked curiously. "How did you know for sure that I'm the original David?"

She smiled at her brother and mother. "Well, that's easy."

She reached up to stroke David's cheek. "You're my brother and I love you. And no clone will ever be able to duplicate emotion."

David wrapped her up in a tight hug and whispered, "Thanks, sis."

From inside David's embrace, she turned to face her mother. "And yes, Mom, I can tell that this Seth is my real brother. Because in spite of everything that we have been through, I still love him as I love you and I love Dad."

She reached out a hand toward Cody and when he grasped it in hers, she left David's embrace to go to Cody's arms. Snuggled in close, she closed her eyes and rested.

She was so very tired. Tired of life. But more tired of death. She needed a rest. *Did you make plans yet?*

I've considered a few options, Cody said quietly, *but there hasn't been exactly any time to make serious plans.*

She nodded. "I need to rest." She looked around at all the others. "You're all very capable. Please find Adamson even if only his body, so we know his fate for sure. I do understand that we have a hell of cleanup to do, but my body needs downtime. I'm taking off for a few days with Cody. When we come back, we will address anything that still needs to be addressed, and I suggest we move on from there."

She felt Cody's start of surprise.

I did warn you.

We still have to find a place to go.

She shook her head. "If any of you need to speak with us, then you may find us both at Deanna's house. I think I need to check that place out further as it's mine now and I have more than a few nightmares from it." She gave a wry smile. "Doesn't it figure that that happens to be the same house where I found Carstairs Wallace and just missed finding Jared way back at the beginning to all of this."

"I never put that together," Cody said in surprise. "Sian read the address, but I didn't connect it to being where we found the dead man. Are you sure you want to go there?"

Tessa laughed. "I need to go crash. Where does it really matter at this point? Now that I have that house to myself, it sounds like a good place to me. At least until I wake up. Then we can explore and find out all the secrets. I have no idea where Hortran's house is, but if we can grab an address, we'll check out that one too." She turned and walked out of the room, leaving the rest standing there watching her.

❧ ❧

RHIA OPENED HER mouth, only to find Serus laying a finger across her lips.

"No. She needs this. They need this." Rhia shot him a disgruntled look that made him smile. "And she's right again. She's exhausted, we're all exhausted. We can take it from here. She needs to rest. And find some joy in life again. She's seen the worst our species has had to offer, and it's not easy to look in the face of all that ugliness. Not over and over again like she has."

"Is she really all grown up? I'm not prepared," she whispered. "I turned around and she's taking off with Cody."

"And she could have done this a while ago, but she wasn't ready. Now she is."

Rhia smiled mistily up at him. "She's done so well."

"She has indeed." Serus wrapped her up in his arms and added, "We need time to ourselves as well. We'll clean up and then take off too." His gaze warmed. "Maybe it's time to go back to our honeymoon spot."

Her eyes twinkled. "Maybe it is at that."

CODY RACED TO catch up. "Aren't you forgetting something," he asked quietly.

"Nope," she said. "Look." And she pointed ahead.

Beast raced toward them.

Cody laughed. "You sure about this?"

"I've never been more sure of anything in my life."

Pushing through the double doors at the top of the stairs, they walked through Council Hall to the front doors.

"It's all going to change now," she said, turning to the landscape inside and outside of Council Hall.

"And all for the better." Cody squeezed her hand, scooped her up into his arms, and waited until Beast jumped into her arms. "Definitely for the better."

And he jumped off the top stair and flew them to check out Tessa's new home. It was their first chance to be alone since this nightmare started. *I can't wait.*

No waiting required. Didn't Deanna mention something about a love nest? She smirked and reached up to kiss his cheek. *Can't you get us there any faster?*

He laughed and pulled on his wings harder. They soared into the sky, racing toward their future.

EPILOGUE

Two weeks later…

TESSA STARED AT the house in question from the inside of Cody's truck. She hated that after all she'd done and been through, she was nervous.

He opened the truck door and walked around to open hers. She gave him a tiny smile and tried to slide down elegantly. Instead, she damn near fell. It was only because of Cody's supporting hand she didn't end up on the ground.

"Is there a class on this shit," she muttered.

At a strangled noise, she shot him a look. Good for him in that he managed to keep his face straight, but his strangled voice was something else again. He tried to not laugh as he struggled to get out, "What, a class in attending a party?"

She glared at him. "No, a class on how to wear clothes like this." She straightened and tried to look nonchalant as she smoothed the silky material down the top of her thighs. The trouble was it ended there. Exposing long lines of leg beneath it.

Cody stopped in front of her. "You look gorgeous," he said. "And no matter what happens inside, you are still my Tessa."

A smile peeked out. She reached up and kissed him. A kiss she now knew would drive him nuts. He'd been a great teacher and she an apt pupil.

When she pulled back, his breathing hotter and heavier than before, she murmured, "Or we could go home and just be alone together."

"Oh no you don't," he said in a harsh whisper. "You know how much I want to take you up on that, but you're not getting out of this. I've been wanting to bring you to meet my friends since forever. Besides, this is a date, and you are going to enjoy yourself."

"Damn. Alright." She walked several steps forward and straightened her back. At least she'd figured out how to walk in the stilts on her feet. Cody reached out and tugged her back slightly.

"Relax. We're not going to war."

"Are you sure," she whispered. "That might be easier." A note of vulnerability crept into her voice.

He slipped an arm around her waist and held her close as they walked to the front door.

"What if they don't like me?" she eyed the crowd she could see in the windows.

"Not possible," he said. "They are going to love you."

She wasn't so sure, but she'd been through too much to back down now. "At least I'll know some people here."

"You'll know a lot. Some are already our friends and family like Ian and Wendy and David and Jewel, but also many you helped even though you might not have known who they were at the time."

"Too bad Seth wasn't up to coming," she said. "He's been through a lot. He needs to integrate back into society again."

"We'll coax him out next time."

She reached up and kissed his chin. "You're a good guy."

He laughed. "No trying to get out of tonight. You look

stunning, and everyone is waiting to meet you."

"Yeah, that's what I'm afraid of," she muttered. "Do you think Jared is here?"

"No idea. I wouldn't be surprised. There's not much that kid wouldn't do, and he was invited. He knows all of us already, so why not show up and reconnect? Now that you wrote your finals and will be in university – vamp university – you'll have to work harder to stay in touch."

"Not really. Jared is going to be one of the liaisons for the new Vamp and Human Coalition group, so we'll get to see him a fair bit, and of course I'll be on the vamp side so I'll get to see him more often than you." She brightened up. If Jared could attend tonight, then so could she.

"And I'll be on the Clone committee as we set up new lives for the clones. It was generous of you to let them use Deanna's house in the meantime."

"Not really. They have all had a shock. And they are going to need time to create lives for themselves, and I can help. Besides Deanna's house will always be special because of you, but it's a monster of a house to live in right now. I'm much more comfortable back home."

"You are, but I can't have you with me all the time." He grumbled. "Of course the renovations on Hortran's house aren't going to take too long, so it's temporary."

"I really love that house," Tessa exclaimed. "I can't wait until we can live in it. Besides right now, being at home… it's healing for my family. We need that time," she said seriously. "And everyone knows I'll be moving into Hortran's house with you soon, so it's special. And we're trying to make the most of it."

"Yeah, Dad's not too thrilled to be left alone."

"Did you mention that wing to him?" Tessa asked. "It's

huge, private, and could be all his. He'd be with us but not."

"He's thinking about it, but he's also got a date tonight. That nurse from the hospital." Cody's smile flashed. "She's not likely to let Dad walk all over her."

"Ha. Knowing the teddy bear your dad is, I bet it's the other way around."

They reached the front doors and rang the doorbell.

"Tessa?" Jared's voice reached out from the shadows. "We saw you arrive and decided to wait for you."

Tessa recognized the insecurity in his voice and thought about how hard this must be for him. She spied Clarissa in the shadows and laughed in joy. "Hi, Clarissa, how good to see you looking so healthy."

Jared hugged Tessa. "You look stunning," he said warmly.

Cody's hand slid over her back. She smiled at Jared. "Thank you. You look great too. And I'm delighted to hear the law has given you both your aunt and uncle's houses and all their other assets. They lost their lives being crooks, but at least some restitution was made. Are you living in one of them?"

Jared shook his head. "No, I just sold my aunt's house and am planning to sell my uncle's. Then buy one that is free and clear of all those memories." He glanced at Clarissa, who snuggled closer. "Then Clarissa and I will move in together while we both go to university." He grinned. "I got into engineering school."

"Wow, that's great."

"And Clarissa got into nursing school."

"Yay," she beamed at them both. "Life is turning out to be awesome after all."

She could hear movement on the other side of the door.

She reached out a hand and with one hand hooked through Jared's arm and one through Cody's, she took a deep breath and waited as the double doors opened.

A cry rose from inside.

"They are here!"

And she walked inside.

Feeling so very blessed with her life after all.

Author's Note

Thank you for reading Vampire in Charge! If you enjoyed my book, I'd appreciate it if you'd leave a review.

Dear reader,

I love to hear from readers, and you can contact me at my website: www.dalemayer.com or at my Facebook author page. To be informed of new releases and special offers, sign up for my newsletter or follow me on BookBub. And if you are interested in joining Dale Mayer's Reader Group, here is the Facebook sign up page.
http://geni.us/DaleMayerFBGroup

Cheers,
Dale Mayer

Family Blood Ties Series

Vampire in Denial

Vampire in Distress

Vampire in Design

Vampire in Deceit

Vampire in Defiance

Vampire in Conflict

Vampire in Chaos

Vampire in Crisis

Vampire in Control

Vampire in Charge

Family Blood Ties Set 1–3

Family Blood Ties Set 1–5

Family Blood Ties Set 4–6

Family Blood Ties Set 7–9

Sian's Solution, A Family Blood Ties Series
Prequel Novelette

COMPLIMENTARY DOWNLOAD

DOWNLOAD a **_complimentary_** copy of TUESDAY'S CHILD? Just tell me where to send it!

http://dalemayer.com/starterlibrarytc/

Dangerous Designs

Drawing is her world…but when her new pencil comes alive, it's his world too.

Her…Storey Dalton is seventeen and now boyfriendless after being dumped via Facebook. Drawing is her escape. It's like as soon as she gets down one image, a dozen more are pressing in on her. Then she realizes her pictures are almost drawing themselves…or is it that her new pencil is alive?

Him…Eric Jordan is a new Ranger and the only son of the Councilman to his world. He's crossed the veil between dimensions to retrieve a lost stylus. But Storey is already experimenting with her new pencil and what her drawings can do – like open portals.

It …The stylus is a soul-bound intelligence from Eric's dimension on Earth and uses Storey's unsuspecting mind to seek its way home, giving her an unbelievable power. She unwittingly opens a third dimension, one that held a dangerous predatory species banished from Eric's world centuries ago, releasing these animals into both dimensions.

Them…Once in Eric's homeland, Storey is blamed for the calamity and sentenced to death. When she escapes, Eric is ordered to bring her back or face that same death penalty. With nothing to lose, can they work together across dimensions to save both their worlds?

Design series

Dangerous Designs
Deadly Designs
Darkest Designs
Design Series Trilogy

Gem Stone (a Gemma Stone Mystery)

A juvie kid trying to stay on the right path stumbles into trouble...

Gemma takes her camera everywhere. From juvie hall to a halfway home, the new hobby gives her a focus she'd never had before and... hope in a future. Until she takes pictures of something that could get her killed.

And not just her...after she and another juvie girl are chased by a stranger to the halfway home that same night, the other girl goes missing and Gemma knows she needs help. But who can she trust?

Not the authorities that's for sure. Trusting them is impossible for a girl with her damaged history, and besides, who cares about a troubled kid...especially when trouble just naturally seems to find her.

In Cassie's Corner

Faith and loyalty are tested as a young girl learns what it is to believe – in herself, in her friends, and in life after death.

Cassie's best friend, bad boy Todd, is gone. Gone as in dead. Gone as in he's now a ghost.

But she doesn't realize that when he wakes her in her bedroom and begs her not to believe what they say about him. It's not until the next day when her parents tell her about the accident that she learns the truth…

The police believe Todd was living up to the family name, drinking and driving and coming to a predictable end. It's up to her to find out the truth and clear his name.

Todd is shocked at his sudden change in circumstances…and angry. He struggles with his new ghostly reality, realizing all he's lost as he watches his brother build a relationship with Cassie as the two pair up to find out what really happened to him.

The truth isn't always pretty, and Cassie has to be stronger than ever before. Especially when the whole world seems to be against her.

About the Author

Dale Mayer is a *USA Today* best-selling author, best known for her SEALs military romances, her Psychic Visions series, and her Lovely Lethal Garden cozy series. Her contemporary romances are raw and full of passion and emotion (Broken But … Mending, Hathaway House series). Her thrillers will keep you guessing (Kate Morgan, By Death series), and her romantic comedies will keep you giggling (*It's a Dog's Life*, a stand-alone novella; and the Broken Protocols series, starring Charming Marvin, the cat).

Dale honors the stories that come to her—and some of them are crazy, break all the rules and cross multiple genres!

To go with her fiction, she also writes nonfiction in many different fields, with books available on résumé writing, companion gardening, and the US mortgage system. All her books are available in print and ebook format.

Connect with Dale Mayer Online

Dale's Website – www.dalemayer.com
Twitter – @DaleMayer
Facebook Page – geni.us/DaleMayerFBFanPage
Facebook Group – geni.us/DaleMayerFBGroup
BookBub – geni.us/DaleMayerBookbub
Instagram – geni.us/DaleMayerInstagram
Goodreads – geni.us/DaleMayerGoodreads
Newsletter – geni.us/DaleNews

Also by Dale Mayer

Published Adult Books:

Psychic Vision Series

Tuesday's Child

Hide'n Go Seek

Maddy's Floor

Garden of Sorrow

Knock, Knock…

Rare Find

Eyes to the Soul

Now You See Her

Shattered

Into the Abyss

Psychic Visions Books 1–3

Psychic Visions Books 4–6

Psychic Visions Books 7–9

By Death Series

Touched by Death – Part 1

Touched by Death – Part 2

Touched by Death – Parts 1&2

Haunted by Death

Chilled by Death

By Death Books 1–3

Second Chances…at Love Series

Second Chances – Part 1

Second Chances – Part 2

Second Chances – complete book (Parts 1 & 2)

Charmin Marvin Romantic Comedy Series

Broken Protocols

Broken Protocols 2

Broken Protocols 3

Broken Protocols 3.5

Broken Protocols 1-3

Broken and… Mending

Skin

Scars

Scales (of Justice)

Broken but… Mending 1-3

Glory

Genesis

Tori

Celeste

Glory Trilogy

Biker Blues

Biker Blues: Morgan, Part 1

Biker Blues: Morgan, Part 2

Biker Blues: Morgan, Part 3

Biker Baby Blues: Morgan, Part 4

Biker Blues: Morgan, Full Set

Biker Blues: Salvation, Part 1

Biker Blues: Salvation, Part 2

Biker Blues: Salvation, Part 3

Biker Blues: Salvation, Full Set

SEALs of Honor

Mason: SEALs of Honor, Book 1

Hawk: SEALs of Honor, Book 2

Dane: SEALs of Honor, Book 3

Swede: SEALs of Honor, Book 4

Shadow: SEALs of Honor, Book 5

Cooper: SEALs of Honor, Book 6

Markus: SEALs of Honor, Book 7

Mason's Wish: SEALs of Honor, Book 8

Evan: SEALs of Honor, Book 9

SEALs of Honor, Books 1–3

SEALs of Honor, Books 4–6

Collections

Dare to Be You…

Dare to Love…

Dare to be Strong…

RomanceX3

Standalone Novellas

It's a Dog's Life

Riana's Revenge

Published Young Adult Books:

Family Blood Ties Series

Vampire in Denial

Vampire in Distress

Vampire in Design

Vampire in Deceit

Vampire in Defiance

Vampire in Conflict

Vampire in Chaos

Vampire in Crisis

Vampire in Control

Vampire in Charge

Family Blood Ties Set 1–3

Family Blood Ties Set 1–5

Family Blood Ties Set 4–6

Family Blood Ties Set 7–9

Sian's Solution – A Family Blood Ties Short Story

Design series

Dangerous Designs

Deadly Designs

Darkest Designs

Design Series Trilogy

Standalone

In Cassie's Corner

Gem Stone (a Gemma Stone Mystery)

Time Thieves

Published Non-Fiction Books:

Career Essentials

Career Essentials: The Résumé

Career Essentials: The Cover Letter

Career Essentials: The Interview

Career Essentials: 3 in 1

www.ingramcontent.com/pod-product-compliance
Lightning Source LLC
Chambersburg PA
CBHW071736190726
48292CB00003B/774